AVIGAIL GRAETZ

A RABBI'S DAUGHTER

Avigail Graetz was born in Israel in 1975 and grew up in Omer, a small town near Beersheba. She has a B.A in film from Tel Aviv University and a M.F.A from Ben-Gurion University in creative writing. She teaches about "Israeli Society as seen through Film" for the Overseas Program at Ben-Gurion University and "Mindfulness" at the University of the Interdisciplinary Center (IDC) Herziliya. Graetz wrote four plays that were shown on stage. Her play *Ona'at Devarim*- "Verbal Wrongs" was featured at the Akko festival and "In Case I'm Not Around," which she directed as well, was featured at the Israeli festival. She was awarded the *PARDES* Fellowship at the National Library of Israel and the Jewish National Fund-Hebrew Literature Prize (2012), both for her debut novel, *A Rabbi's Daughter*. She has published several short stories, as well as poetry, and had a weekly column that integrated the "Portion of the Week" with Buddhist philosophy.

A RABBI'S DAUGHTER

AVIGAIL GRAETZ

Hebrew Translation
Shira Atik

First & second editions in Hebrew, *Bat Shel Rav,*
Printed in 2012 and 2013
Published by *Even Hoshen*

English translation of *Bat Shel Rav* by Shira Atik

Published in Israel

ISBN 978-965-572-284-0

1. Mother-Daughter Relationships – Fiction. 2. Mental Illness – Fiction. 3. Conservative Judaism in Israel – Fiction. 4. Cancer Victims – Fiction. 5. Death and Mourning – Fiction. 6. Youth Culture – Fiction. 7. Small Town – Fiction. 8. Grandparents – Fiction. 9. Southern Israel – Fiction.

Printed and bound in the State of Israel
Cover Drawing by Lore Herman Pintus
Cover design by Eitan Herman
Cordoba Printing and Binding, Holon

This book is dedicated to the memory of

My Grandparents

Edward (Yehezkel) Lebovics
Charlotte Lebovics
Marion Graetz
Marjorie Graetz

From whom I learned so much about love and life and about the unimaginable possibilities of Jewish geography.

And to the memory of Lore Herman Pintus, my partner's grandmother, the artist who drew the cover many years ago.

May all beings learn to love and accept themselves as they are.

A RABBI'S DAUGHTER

4.5.18

Dear Jordan
I really hope you
will enjoy this book
and maybe find
parts or moments that
will resonate.
Continue the good
work of 25 years
Avigail

One

"What you want and what you get are two different stories." Grandma's motto. That's what went through my mind when a call from Abba stopped me on my way to the university, just as my dilemma between two ideas for a screenplay – one that can expose my Jewish identity that was perpetually smothering me from birth, the other about my burning desire for a boyfriend – was starting to clarify in my mind.

The last time I heard him say "Come home" in such a brusque tone was in 1995, when Rabin was assassinated. Four years ago. And now, again, in a trembling and lonely voice, an uncharacteristic voice, he is asking me to come home because it looks like Grandma is truly approaching the end. He's taking her to the hospital. Death, it seems, can bring people together, but it can also drive them apart. It may be hard to believe, but that's exactly the premise, the framework, of one of my scripts. Perhaps both.

I'm glad I reconciled with Grandma the day before yesterday. She was complaining, again, about my absence, about Ida, her caretaker, about her heart that was betraying her, about how we had agreed that if I got the car while Ima was away, a period of several months, I'd be able to visit her from Tel Aviv more frequently, and, of course, about how I hadn't held up my side of the bargain. With Grandma, every day was a new opportunity to disappoint her again. She was always looking for ways to fill up her little black notebook of complaints. She had asked me countless times to document her memories, her stories, her ironic insights. She had asked me to film her. She was convinced that anyone who studied film turned into Fellini. I refuse to accept that I've missed my chance with her, and I make a U-turn towards the south, towards home. As if this small pivot has the ability to stop time, to effect it.

"Come home." A pair of words that everyone wants to hear. First from their parents, then from someone they love. For me, that someone is so overdue, it's beyond frustrating. And no mouth has ever uttered the precious words I longed to hear. Grandma – who always wanted me to visit, who, ever since I was a child, on her visits would squish over on her gold armchair to make room for me with a children's book in her hands – is dying. Now, what am I to do?

I always thought that some indomitable force inside my grandmother had turned her into an old woman against her will. A woman who was always comparing herself to the biblical Joseph who, in her opinion, suffered all his life just to please his family. What kept me from documenting her? My conviction that she would live forever? My fear that I would uncover more of her weaknesses? Grandma always manages to take up space when Ima's away. Just like she did "back then."

If I were strong enough, maybe "back then" would be the subject of the script that would get me into the screenwriting program. What I do know is that I don't need a third option. We always think we're trying to decide between only two options, and we're not conscious of the fact that there is a third option, the option to waver, to not decide. That's the option that I almost always choose, the option of wavering, without realizing that I'm stuck there. Just like my mother was stuck in the bathroom of the university library when she was nine months pregnant with me. There came a point when she no longer had the strength to scream and push the door, so she just sat down and started reading one of her books. Luckily for her, and for me, the custodian came by and smashed the broken lock. Nonetheless, I have always been angry at her for her intransigence, her lack of effort, which continued to surface after I came into the world. I was angry until what was revealed was revealed. "Back then."

I stop to buy coffee and Bisli snacks, grill-flavored, and to call my beloved sister, who is to give birth imminently. A girl this time. She and my adored nephew, Evyatar are already driving south. Evidently, this really is the end for Grandma.

How things have changed since then.

I traveled the world and became a doting aunt, I changed childhood friends and mostly I started to understand the meaning of death. Yes, I'll stick to the script I've already started. About a first, much-anticipated date that gets cancelled because of a Saturday night phone call from Binyamin, with news of a death. This time Binyamin will play the role of a really best friend. I don't know how I'll bring to life all the confusion I felt. Still feel?

I'm glad I'm heading down to Ayalon South - the long stretches of driving will give me time to think. But just as I'm contemplating my favorite Woody Allen technique - the heroine's voice-over - I notice a woman standing at the junction, looking out of place. That's another thing that's changed since high school and the army. I no longer pick up hitchhikers. Nonetheless, with the instinct of someone who grew up in a small town, an instinct that's hard to shake, I slow down. Perhaps I am subconsciously searching for another story. Suddenly, something in her gaze scares me, and I stammer an apology and drive on, quickly, afraid, trying not to let my conscience torment me. The look on her face obliterates all my thoughts about the film, and despite my best efforts, the "then" joins me on my journey.

The "then," which is a little like a curse, I remember in great detail. "Then" began, when one afternoon, a few days before the holiday of Shavuot, we heard a thundering knock at the door. It must have been thundering, because Abba was in the middle of making popcorn in that air popper that he loved, and I was sitting in the hall upstairs contemplating my toenails and wondering how people used to trim them in biblical times. Abba turned off the machine and looked up at me from the stairwell, asking me if I was expecting anyone. I shook my head. I had no idea. Nobody knew better than he that when my friends came to pick me up, they honked for me, even on Friday nights, in spite of the fact that I'd been asked again and again to make sure it didn't happen. I guess my friends were mirroring my confusion regarding the rules of a conservative's Rabbi's household.

The "then" was during the last days before Shavuot, during the counting of the Omer, but I was counting the matriculation exams (in Hebrew called *bagruyot,* literally *maturity*) that I had to pass before being crowned a full-fledged graduate, mature enough for my age, and thus set free. I remember that my curiosity wasn't strong enough to lure me down the seventeen steps from the second floor, but I did stand up and peer down. Who would be coming at this hour? I must have been hoping that, just like the story of Rapunzel locked in her tower, Eren Shonsky would come to rescue me from my awful label, the awkward daughter-of-the-rabbi, whose chances of staying a virgin, at least until the age of thirty, were increasing every day. My aunt used to say that this was the problem with self-definitions. Unlike dictionary definitions, which are designed to simplify life, self-definitions don't fully encapsulate anything. On the contrary, they are bogged down with a complicated story, like a muddy swamp.

My wish wasn't granted, for there in the doorway stood a pretty woman, white as an almond blossom, her hair brown and disheveled like mine. Her clothes reminded me of Grandma's clothes. They tried their best to look elegant, but even from the top of the stairs I could see the stains that had taken up residence in the material and embroidered themselves into the cloth. Around her neck glimmered a chain that gave her a kind of aura. Behind her we could hear the rumbling of a taxi's diesel engine.

"Rabbi Levy?" she asked with a gleaming smile and an American accent. Abba nodded. The woman shook his hand politely and announced that she was Amy, the wife of a colleague, Rabbi Abe Solomon from Minneapolis. She was sorry she hadn't called ahead, and could she come in and explain everything?

Abba, despite having grown up an only child, was gracious by nature. He opened the door wide and went outside with her to send off the taxi driver. Chivalrously, he carried in one of the suitcases belonging to Amy Solomon, the rabbi's wife.

These kinds of visits weren't unusual in our house. Lots of American rabbis and their wives or their children who were spending a year in Israel to strengthen their Jewish identity came over for Shabbat, but these visits were usually scheduled in advance, and they were always contingent on Ima's being home. It's not that she was a stellar housekeeper, but there was something about her openness, her candor, the pleasure she took in talking about herself to anyone who happened to be present, that created the illusion of empathic, respectable hospitality, even if the food left something to be desired.

Abba turned on the light in the dim living room and invited her to sit down. I decided to use this opportunity to take a break from my schoolbooks, with the excuse that I had to be the perfect hostess and rushed downstairs and introduced myself as the youngest daughter who still lived at home. I asked her politely if she would like some water or coffee, and I told Abba I would turn on the machine and make fresh popcorn.

There was never any cake around for us to offer, not on an ordinary weekday, because any sweets or pastries that we bought for Shabbat were always gone by the end of Shabbat. I was the only one in the family with even the slightest amount of self-control. In fact, when I was little, whenever Grandma came on one of her semi-annual trips, she would put me, and only me, in charge of the colorful M&M's, that she would hide out of sight. Every evening, like young Joseph distributing food to his brothers in Egypt, I would dole out a carefully-counted number of candies to my older sister and brother. And sometimes to my parents when they craved a taste of their homeland.

"Elisheva." She rolled the word out of her mouth in her foreign tongue, with the same soft intonation as my mother, but then she lifted her hands and said, in an ethereal and surprising voice, "Elisheva, wife of Aaron the Priest, sister of Nachshon son of Aminadav, do you have the same great spiritual strength as your biblical namesake?"

Abba and I looked at each other.

Amy, too, paused for a minute. Then, without waiting for a response to her peculiar question with its references to ancient ancestries, winked and said, "Water would be great, Eli."

"Elisheva," my father corrected her, with faint traces of the accent that he struggled with in his sermons. "Elisheva likes her full name."

"Actually, I think your Eli is kind of cute." I smiled at Amy, who was perched stiffly at the edge of the old chair, and at Abba, who was sitting comfortably on the couch, and went into the kitchen.

Seconds after I turned on the popper, Abba ran and banged the kitchen door shut behind him, smiling sheepishly. It was odd, because nobody in our house ever closed the kitchen door.

When the noise was over, Abba rushed back to the kitchen to open the door, eager to explain. "The noise from the popper was bothering her."

From my spot in the kitchen, I could hear Amy explaining that actually, she and her husband were going through divorce proceedings, and I wondered if this was one of those cases where people turned to Abba as they would to a priest.

Tentatively, I approached with the snack - I knew Abba wouldn't have any qualms about telling me they needed some privacy - but Amy turned to me, oblivious to Abba's request, and said, "Come, Eli, sit with us for a bit. I was just telling your Abba about this wonderful position I've been offered." She took a small tin candy box out of her bag and fished out two capsules which she swallowed. I noticed that, like my only aunt, Ora, her face occasionally twitched.

Amy said that the only reason this trip was possible was that she'd gotten an incredible offer at the last minute, which was why she and her husband hadn't had a chance to call ahead of time and ask if she could stay with us for a few days.

Her interview at the hospital had been under discussion for months, conducted via fax - she winked, and said she didn't have to tell us about the ins and outs of working in Israel - and then suddenly, out of the blue, they announced that her fantastic proposal would, in fact, suit them. She winked again and added that some American foundation had suddenly donated money, and she described how she received an urgent fax asking if she could come for an interview within the next few days. And that's why she was here, because of this Israeli off-handedness, which she feared could someday end in disaster.

After voicing this prophecy, she didn't wink, she just paused, seemingly unaware that, as they say in science fiction movies, her spaceship hadn't landed. Jet lag has many side effects, the most common of which is fatigue, but it can also affect one's speech, tossing around words as if they were suitcases in an airplane's baggage compartment. Sometimes language, too, must be carefully opened and repacked.

I didn't have a chance to ask for an explanation because she had gone on to say that the minute her husband heard that the hospital, Soroka, was in Beersheba, the capital of the south, he immediately mentioned the renowned Rabbi Levy, who lives in a small town just outside the city. Her husband told her that Rabbi Levy had miraculously brought the Conservative Movement to Israel in the 1970's, and the way she talked about him - the way many Americans talked about him - made my father sound as important as David Ben-Gurion

I cut her off. Not only because I didn't want to hear, yet again, about how the movement came to Israel and how Ima and Abba moved here after the Six Day War, but also because amidst all her weirdness, I still couldn't figure out what this brilliant idea was, and what kind of doctor she was. The fact that Abba had been quiet for so long indicated that he was as lost as I was.

Amy didn't seem thrown off by the question. She just cleared her throat and said she was a child psychologist, thus confirming my suspicion that she and my psychologist aunt had a lot in common. Maybe in the United States, all therapists are required to have tics so their patients don't feel quite so screwed up.

She also told me that she's a practitioner of integrative therapy, in which the therapist spends time in the child's natural habitat. She asked if we'd heard of the famous article "Ghosts in the Nursery."

I thought it might be a good idea to hear about it. If it was famous, it might show up in the "unseen" section of my English *bagrut*. Abba, as he always did when something "important" was being discussed, put on a knowledgeable, enthusiastic expression. He said that the article would be of interest to me because it was about traumas that parents experienced in childhood, which they then passed down to their children. They were ghosts from the past that intruded and created situations that mimicked the parents' earlier traumas.

That's what was so special about Abba. He really did know everything, except, as it turned out, what concerned his own family members.

Amy's "incredible, wonderful, bizarre" idea was basically nothing more than bringing family therapists to the patient's bedside. She'd thought of it because of the Iraqi attacks, when it had become clear that the hospital staff wasn't equipped to treat families. The war taught us, she said, that when an entire family was in a traumatic situation, under one roof, for an indeterminate length of time, a multitude of ghosts emerged and made things even worse.

"Hey, Ima wasn't home during the Gulf War, either." I don't know why I associated this with Ima, as if she were the weak link in our family, and in an effort to correct myself, to cover up my own testimony, I asked Amy what the connection was between childhood traumas and the Gulf War; after all, not all parents had been threatened by missiles, or by war at all, during their childhood.

Amy made an "Is that a fact?" face and explained that she believed in active therapy. The therapist observed the client in his natural habitat, evaluating the family system in real time and determining what had to be done to improve these relationships. In her opinion, the Gulf War created a particular family dynamic that reawakened all kinds of fears and behaviors that would never have surfaced under normal circumstances.

"Do you think it's possible that your mother's absence wasn't a coincidence?"

I couldn't believe that she had the nerve to speak that way about my mother, to make such outrageous assumptions, and I said I didn't like it when people who lived outside of Israel expressed their opinions about what it was really like to live here, or when they thought they knew how to solve all of Israel's problems. Amy wasn't here during the Gulf War, and the only thing Ima missed by being at a conference in England was that Abba decided to shave off his beard in order to wear the gas mask.

Abba ignored the potential drama and said that later he would show her the photos we took in our sealed room, and that she shouldn't be upset by my belligerence, which was nothing more than teenage rebelliousness. "You know how it is. She belongs to the Scouts, and they can't understand how a person can live outside of Israel and still be a Zionist."

"Abba!" I wanted to tell him that as someone who was the living embodiment of Zionism, he was going overboard in trying to impress her. But before I had a chance to say all this, Amy smiled and gracefully took charge of the conversation.

"It's fine. I have a lot of experience working with all kinds of kids from diverse backgrounds, because Abe is one of those rabbis who moves to a new congregation every three years, with no regard for his children or his wife and what language they do or don't speak. We spent three years in Mexico City. In the beginning it was hard. Mexico City's such a tense and overcrowded place, it was no picnic, but slowly I fell in love with the language and the culture, and when I came back to Gringo-land, I found myself working with Mexican immigrants."

Maybe Mexico served as the icebreaker for us, because again I found the courage to break into her serious, somewhat rambling monologue and ask if she knew the painter Frida Kahlo. And I also said I'd never thought of Mexico as a particularly Jewish place, and asked her if there was any Jewish community there at all.

"There are Jews everywhere," Abba laughed. I had the sense that despite his abundant knowledge, he had never heard of my favorite painter, and it made me happy to think that there were things I could teach him, too.

"People say her father was Jewish," she said, and went on about her experiences, with a look that seemed close and distant at the same time, and every time she said the word "Mexico," I felt a tremor. Amy, too, had something off about her, something I couldn't quite pinpoint. Maybe she had made herself too comfortable too quickly. I thought that perhaps I should listen to her a little more carefully. But she must have been reading my thoughts, because she stopped, and smiled a heart-melting smile that wiped away every trace of doubt.

"Anyway, if you don't mind my staying here, I have all sorts of meetings tomorrow, and my big interview is on Sunday."

Even though Abba was always happy to perform the *mitzvah* of hospitality to strangers, for a minute it looked like he was going to use my mother's absence, and the fact that he had to prepare for Shavuot and for the all-night study session by himself, as excuses to turn down her request. So I quickly said, "We can give her Avigail's room. Avigail's my older sister. She's getting married this summer."

I interrupted Abba, who was telling her about the upcoming wedding and how it made it difficult for us to host people right now. I suggested, or more accurately dared to ask, that Amy stay and help me, because I was studying so intensively for my *bagruyot,* and in the next few days I had exams in both Bible and English.

Amy closed her eyes and laughed a chirping, slightly frightening laugh. Weren't these, she asked, my strongest subjects? Her tone was unclear. Was she angry that she wouldn't be able to help me and that I was exposing my ridiculous effort to make her stay?

When the last traces of her laughter died down, she gave me a piercing look and answered her own question, "No. You remind me of my daughter. You're not the first rabbi's daughter, and certainly not the last, who hates Bible, or, more precisely, feels the need to prove that she's not genetically inclined towards Bible."

I was surprised that she was allowing herself to speak so openly, and I was eager to decipher more of what she said, but clearly Abba didn't like where this conversation was going. From his vantage point, she was pressing my teenage buttons, and because it affected him, too, he suggested we go upstairs to show her "the rabbi's children's kingdom," where Amy would be staying. To his credit, Abba was always able to use humor when relating to issues he didn't want to discuss.

Two

I ran up ahead of them and tried to tidy up the uncontrollable mess that I always left everywhere, but Amy, who, it seemed, didn't miss a thing, picked up my nail clipper and told me, with great solemnity, that you can't leave something like that just lying around; that it was an accident waiting to happen, like Odysseus trying to navigate his way between Scylla the sea monster and Charybdis the whirlpool. Abba smiled at her creative analogy, and I silently thanked my literature teacher Leah who insisted that we learn chapters of Odysseus even though they weren't on the *bagrut.*

Standing at the door of the room that had been designated for Amy, we heard a beep that made our guest cover her ears and stare at us in anger and shock. Abba ran downstairs while I tried to reassure her, telling her not to be afraid, it was just my father's alarm clock reminding him to count the Omer. Despite her attempt to smile, I could see a trace of fear in her eyes, like someone who has come upon a run-over cat at the side of the road and was trying to look away, but couldn't stop staring, fascinated by this life cut short.

"I'm still very sensitive to noise," she said. She picked up her bags and went into my sister's room. "I'll rest here for a while," she said, "in my new room." And with exaggerated confidence, perhaps in an attempt to cover up the extreme distress she'd exhibited moments before, Amy went in the room and closed the door with surprising force.

Doesn't Amy care about counting the Omer? I wondered. And what did "still" mean? Had I missed something? Had she told Abba about something besides the divorce? And as if she heard my thoughts, she came out of the room and, although she looked exhausted, she said, with forced lightheartedness, "All that racket and we're not going to count?"

Now that she had taken off her soiled jacket, I could see the shimmering pendant that dangled from a chain around her neck, a green seahorse. She noticed me looking, and said, "This is the only piece of jewelry I own. This and my wedding ring, which I have never taken off. It's called a hippocampus. Do you know what that is?" The gentle way she looked at me and spoke to me, with a kind of intimacy, as if we were the only two people in the world, felt good. For a minute she reminded me of Ima, who also didn't wear make-up, didn't put on airs, and yet the difference between the two of them was as big as the difference between the seahorse she wore around her neck and the ugly name she had called it in Latin or whatever language - hippocampus.

"In Hebrew we call it a *sus-yam* - a seahorse," I told her, and she responded earnestly that hippocampus was Greek and what was interesting about it was its symbolism.

"Always look for the symbolism of words, of things," she said, as if rebuking me for my shallow preoccupation with the way things looked or sounded.

"It will help you with your *bagruyot,* too," she added; clearly, she had no idea how shallow and concrete these tests actually were. She went on to observe that every human has two hippocampi, one on each side of the brain. The hippocampus plays an important role in the creation of memories and in our navigational ability. "Interesting, isn't it? As if in order for us to navigate our way through life, we have to store up memories. It's basically the journey of Jewish life.

Time is structured around special days where traditions have piled up."

"And counting the Omer," I interrupted her so she would know that I also had nice ideas like hers, "is a very special time because it allows us to think about the nature of time itself, like in Buddhism."

I didn't know if I was referring correctly to the article we had read in preparation for the "unseen" section of the English test, but I couldn't stop. "We read that the meditative life is a life of reflecting on time. And only the person who contemplates about 'what is happening right now' is a person that's really living that moment"

"Come, your father is humming," she said, ignoring what I had said, and indeed Abba had started humming the tune of "Here I am, ready and prepared...," and so I followed her downstairs without telling her the truth.

The truth is that I had never participated in the counting of the Omer, and when it came to anything relating to Jewish law and commandments, I was generally considered the black sheep of the family. They say that from the day I was born I didn't like going to synagogue.

As we walked downstairs, matching our strides, she said something which confirmed that she had, in fact, heard what I said, and it made me happy in a way I couldn't explain. She said, "Counting the Omer is the golden hour for self-reflection."

We joined Abba, and recited the blessing in unison, "Today is four and forty days, which is six weeks and two days of the Omer." It seemed to me that even the ancient chairs and tables took notice of the sense of belonging I was feeling. A feeling that, until then, I'd only experienced during our Scouts assemblies. Not that they're comparable.

When we were finished, Amy dove into the depths of psychology and explained that the kabbalists saw the days of the Omer as an opportunity for spiritual work and self-improvement. Each day of the Omer expressed a particular aspect of the soul. I wasn't sure I understood but I didn't say anything. Especially since there was no chance that a subject like Kabbalah would show up in the English exam or in the next day's Bible exam. All I could do was surrender to Amy's quiet, raspy voice as she explained that every day of the Omer we had to improve ourselves by one letter.

"Today was the letter *taf*, and we counted the goodness of kingship, which is the counting of abundance and love that are constantly erupting all around us. Like the goodness you have shown me by welcoming me into your home." She must have sensed that I was getting lost, and she tried to explain further, which only made things more incoherent.

"Our sages identify the counting of goodness with our patriarch Abraham, who was famous for his hospitality. By the way, Sarah our matriarch was also hospitable, but she is nonetheless portrayed as a woman who is stingy with her love. It doesn't matter what women do; they will always be judged more harshly."

At that moment she sounded like Ima, who studied and wrote about feminist *midrash*. It was probably the similarity between them that made Abba break away and immerse himself into the world of his *siddur*, until he said, surprised, "Wait a minute, it says here that the letter *nun* is the courage of kingship."

Amy opened her *siddur*– I could see that she had scribbled comments in a whole spectrum of colors – and said, "Shit," which is what Ima says when things aren't working out for her. "I got mixed up. Courage is Isaac, that's a whole different story. Here I am, subconsciously ignoring Isaac, tied and bound for sacrifice, the person whose life was dictated by fear. At least I was right about this week being a sign of kingship. In feminist commentary, it is Queen Esther who symbolizes royalty, and she also didn't...." Amy shivered again and covered her ears, and then - it seemed like a few seconds later - Abba and I heard the phone ring. I ran to Ima's study to pick up the cordless phone.

It was Binyamin, wanting to know if I needed a ride to the *bagrut*. I reminded him that my mother was in the States and I had her car all month, until after Shavuot. He wanted to talk more but I told him I had to fulfill the "Honor Your Parents" commandment in a practical way.

"But you said your mother's away, and besides, your scatter-brained father has to respect you, too, and to help you prepare for tomorrow." And before I had a chance to respond, he continued, "Yeah, yeah, I know what you always say, about how even though the apple doesn't fall far from the tree, the taller the tree, the more the apple turns into sauce. Anyway, you have to admit, it's ironic that the rabbi's daughter has to struggle so much to get a decent grade in the Bible exam."

I hated it when he called me "the rabbi's daughter," and the name he and his friends had come up with was even worse: "the blind rabbi's daughter." It was an amalgam of the titles of two stories by Yaakov Steinberg which we had learned for the literature b*agrut,* "The Blind Girl" and "The Rabbi's Daughter."

"Yes, Beni, apparently this is how I rebel," I said without conviction. I was more interested in what was going on in the living room.

He asked if I wanted to go to Scouts with him. Binyamin was the coordinator of our Scouts troop, and I was in charge of the ninth graders, the two most important positions. He and I had both "drunk the Kool-Aid."

I turned down his offer and told him that Saturday wouldn't work, either, because some relative had shown up and we had to host her. It felt good calling Amy a relative. Then I told him I had to get going because I was facing another all-nighter to learn all the material I had neglected, and we hung up.

Binyamin and I could have talked on the phone for hours, unless his friends would show up and he'd shake me off in lightning speed. We were both red-heads. He more than I. I had freckles all over my body and a hot temper, but he was a genuine red-head, the kind that makes women say, "That's exactly the color I want." We were also the only ones who had never been in a romantic relationship, maybe because we put all our time into the youth movement; at least that's what Avigail said. She had a serious boyfriend by the time she was seventeen. He was a secular guy from *our town,* and despite the seven good years they enjoyed together, in the end she chose Effi, who was modern Orthodox, and whom she'd known for at most a year.

I carried the phone into the living room and told Abba that we should probably turn down the volume of the ringer because of Amy's sensitivity. This made Amy happy. I was hoping she would explain her "allergy" to noise, but all she said was that I was very sweet and that I really reminded her of her daughter.

"So where did you grow up?" Amy asked my father in a way that made me even more certain that any time she mentioned her daughter, she would change the subject immediately.

"I grew up in the corn capital of Nebraska."

Whenever anyone hears Abba say Nebraska, you can see them conjuring up a map of the United States, then smiling in bewilderment as they wondered about his Jewish identity. The look on Amy's face didn't let us down, but she didn't ask him about his upbringing. All she said was, "So you ran away as fast as you could."

Rude as her comment may have been, it wasn't far from the truth. Grandma Edith, my father's mother, always told us how she took a train to New York with her only son, who was only eighteen, and he never came back. I, on the other hand, thought of Nebraska as a wonderful place, and didn't understand why people thought it's "the middle of nowhere."

Abba was also quick to defend his roots. "Actually, there was a lot of goodness in Nebraska. You can't really grasp what it means to preserve your Jewish identity until you've lived in a place where kosher meat is shipped in once a month in a delivery freezer truck."

"I bet there was some big rabbi there who influenced you, right?"

I was disappointed by the banality of Amy's question. It must have been a classic question for psychologists.

"Actually, not there. One of my uncles is a real Torah scholar, a Conservative rabbi. Maybe you've heard of him? Rabbi Harry Heller! He's the one who influenced me."

"And me," I cut in. "Uncle Harry is known as a brilliant speaker, and you know what he said at my bat mitzvah? He said that I was always asking, 'When will I be possible?' "

I was so happy that Amy – unlike my father – didn't laugh. And even though it wasn't necessary, I explained, "Because all my life I'd been told that I was impossible. The truth is, I don't really remember ever asking that."

"Yes," Abba said, moving the imaginary microphone back to himself, as if we were competing for Amy's attention, the way we kids used to fight for the guests' attention. "The truth is that after I got my bachelor's degree in New York, I was debating between the rabbinate and, believe it or not, psychology."

I'd never heard this before. All my life I'd wished that Abba had remained a photographer, like he was when they were living in Jerusalem, but a psychologist? That was hard to imagine. Binyamin would have said that even if my father had been a psychologist, I would be just as complicated as I am now, because being the child of a psychologist is also hard. But at least it would have freed me from that semi-official irritating title, "the rabbi's daughter" that I carried with me everywhere.

"I did well on the admission exams. The problem wasn't my analytic skills; it was my personal interview. I talked a little about my infancy, and at the end of the meeting they told me I sounded cut off from myself, from who I used to be, and that while I was clearly very sensitive to my community and to everything around me, I wasn't sensitive enough to myself."

I couldn't believe Abba was admitting this so openly, putting himself at a disadvantage, as if Amy's hippocampus had hypnotized him and changed him into someone else.

"The truth is, I'm glad they spared me all the pain that goes with studying psychology. Once they gave me the seal of approval affirming that I was sensitive to other people, I enrolled in rabbinical school."

"What did you say in the interview?"

I was glad Amy was pressing him for more information.

"It's been thirty years; you think I remember?" Abba tried to make a joke out of it, but Amy's penetrating look made him elaborate. In the earliest years of his life, he said, he'd basically grown up without his father, who was a soldier in World War II.

I had never heard about this, either. I mean, I knew that Grandpa was an officer in the American army, and we all loved the pasta he'd learned to cook from the Italian prisoners of war - you actually rolled out the dough, hung it up to dry, and cut it up into strips of spaghetti - but I'd never thought about the fact that my father had spent the first years of his life alone with his mother.

That was the first time I really understood the extent to which war could shape our personal lives. I knew that our victory in the Six Day War was what had brought my parents here. Whenever I complained to my mother that they should have just stayed in America, she would tell me, cruelly, "You should be thanking us. If we had stayed there, I would have had only two children and you wouldn't even exist." And it was because of the Yom Kippur War that Abba lost his photography shop and was reminded that he had come here to find spiritual fulfillment, and that's why they moved to the south. Ima always says that Abba, who served in the *Chevra Kadisha* in Sinai, preparing dead bodies for burial, came home shell-shocked and told her they had to have more kids. And she replied that wasn't a reason to bring kids into this world, children weren't ammunition. Still, two years after the war, I was born.

"It wasn't just that my father was in Europe, it was also that we lived on an army base, and for two years we were cut off from my mother's enormous family in Lincoln. But how can you complain about a little isolation in the face of all the suffering and turmoil of the European Jews?"

"And Grandpa lost an eye in the war," I stuck in. For some reason, I felt compelled to hide the fact that I had never heard my father talk about his past.

"No, that wasn't in the war, that was after he came back. He was in a car accident. He'd been driving behind a trailer full of horses, and one of the doors got loose and a horse galloped right into his car and made him lose control. He spent a few months in the hospital and was fortunate to get out with nothing worse than a glass eye."

I felt like I was listening to a story from the *Tales of the Arabian Nights* about a family I'd never met. Luckily my father said, "Enough of this, let's get back to what's really important, dinner!" Now I recognized my father once again, for the primary way our family connected was through food. "Let's order pizza." He had gone back to being the father I knew, who would leave us money to buy falafel downtown whenever he was responsible for feeding us.

Amy said pizza would be great. She didn't seem to think our lifestyle was disorganized. She told us she was going upstairs to rest for a bit and we should call her when the pizza came. I watched as she took the stairs with ease, and I was glad she felt so at home, even if I was a little disappointed that she didn't stay downstairs to trade more stories with Abba.

When she reached the top of the staircase, she called down, "If Dr. Silber calls, tell him I arrived safely." She didn't explain who Dr. Silber was, and she disappeared in a way that left Abba and me flustered. I went back to my loathsome textbooks, lost in thought about this strange encounter with my father whom I hadn't really known until now. I had to process Abba's history that had sentenced me to be "the rabbi's daughter." Binyamin claimed I was obsessed with this title, but I showed him that a lot of writers and poets were interested in the concept of "the rabbi's daughter," and that it wasn't just me.

I had memorized the opening lines of Steinberg's "The Rabbi's Daughter."

"When Sarah, the rabbi's daughter, reached her twenty-third birthday, she was already exhausted from meeting so many prospective husbands. From the corner of her mouth, she would chuckle bitterly, the kind of laugh you might hear from someone who had been clenching his teeth for a long time." I felt bad for Sarah, and every time I clenched my teeth, I thought that once again I was suffering from "The Rabbi's Daughter" Syndrome.

Now, I looked around my messy car and chuckled. The uncertainty I felt at the beginning of my drive returned. Should I reveal the truth about Binyamin and his betrayal in my trust or should I pour out my guts and blame my upbringing? Is writing meant to heal one's soul or to work out unfinished business?

Maybe it is only in my own experience and in outdated literature that rabbis' daughters rebel, because my brother is studying to be a Conservative rabbi in Israel. On the other hand, there are virtually no rabbis' daughters in movies, and maybe it would be a stroke of genius to adapt the story into a modern film about a rabbi's daughter from the old country who is overcome by lust and finds herself in an unwanted pregnancy. That kind of adaptation could be the perfect choice.

Three

The tension between adaptation and documentation is with me whenever I write, like the folk tale about the two angels who accompany us home from synagogue on Friday night. I blame this on my excellent memory.

I'm not surprised that I remember how Abba called up to us when the pizza came, and how I had been eagerly waiting for Amy to emerge from Avigail's room refreshed and smiling, but the door remained shut and not a sound could be heard. I decided to knock gently, but just as I got there, the door swung open and there she was, filling up the doorway in a way that prevented me from seeing past her, as if she was using her body to guard her new space.

"The pizza must be ready," she said, and I could smell her breath, the first thing about Amy that repelled me and made me realize that she hadn't asked about a towel or how the showers worked. I didn't say anything, not even when she closed the door hard, as if marking her territory. She'd had a long day. We went downstairs and I saw that Abba had cleared everything off the Shabbat table.

As a rule, the old table remained untouched all week, like a loaded diaper that nobody bothered to change. It was always piled high with bills, scholarly articles, and electric converters for all the appliances that Abba collected like a little boy, never taking the Israeli voltage into account. It wasn't until Friday afternoon that someone would tidy it up, which consisted of taking everything off the table and putting it in another room. On Saturday night, after Havdalah, the piles would reappear as naturally as stars following their charted paths. In honor of Amy, though, Abba went to the trouble of clearing the table ahead of schedule so we wouldn't have to eat in the living room like we usually did.

As soon as we came downstairs, Amy went to the bathroom. I pointed out that there was another bathroom right outside her room, but she replied, in complete seriousness, that she didn't like using bathrooms where the pipes weren't attached to the ground. In contrast to the vigorous conversation we'd been having earlier, Amy was quiet during the meal, but it was a pleasant silence, not at all oppressive or resentful. Apart from her silence, Amy behaved like a member of the family, gobbling down three slices just like me and Abba. Her table manners were surprisingly poor, and I wondered anxiously what Grandma would think of her at our Friday night dinner.

"Which *bagrut* do you have tomorrow?" Abba tried to start a casual conversation, as if we were like other families, who ate lunch and dinner at the table.

"Bible. And it's so boring, even your sermons are more interesting."

Abba and Amy chuckled, and Amy said, affectionately, "Classic rabbi's daughter."

By then, nobody was forcing me to go to synagogue, but the truth is that until ninth grade, when I still had to go, deep in my heart I loved Abba's sermons. Despite my scornful, disinterested demeanor, everything he said resonated with me and stuck to me from the inside, especially during Shabbat dinner, when we always spent a good amount of time talking about the weekly Torah portion, the never-ending story of the Jewish people.

"I actually have some excellent techniques for learning Bible. I even use Bible stories with my clients. For example, we might talk about jealousy through the story of Joseph and his brothers, or about loneliness through…."

I cut her off, even though I was happy to hear Amy's voice again. "There's nothing psychological about the way we study the Bible, it is just memorization! Explain it to her, Abba."

"Well." This time my father didn't say that this was a case of teenage belligerence; he nodded, and started listing all the problems with how Bible was taught in Israel, and how instead of bringing children closer to their identity, it pushed them away.

Amy had to chime in, too, and she told us more about her approach, using Bibliodrama, which was based on acting out different scenarios inspired by the Bible. "That's how ancient words come to life and become relevant in the here and now."

I stood my ground and argued that no drama could salvage a subject like *shmita,* the laws of the seven-year agricultural cycle. Something in my rebellious tone must have made Amy angry, because she stood up and declared, "You of all people, Elisheva, should be able to hear the voice calling out to us from inside the text."

I tried to penetrate her thoughts, and where this "you of all people" came from, as if she knew me inside-out, but Abba, who was never comfortable when things turned tense, said, in an effort to get her to sit back down, something about Buber's dialogical principle, but that just made her angrier.

"Forget philosophy! I'm talking about *feeling*!" Amy's harsh tone reminded me of the dance teacher from the TV show *Fame,* goading her students towards success. Still standing, she said, with compelling fervor and in surprisingly precise Hebrew, "I'm talking about a technique that allows the reader to meet living creatures in the Bible. They hurt just like we do. I step inside the story and become the Biblical character. I speak in her voice; I tell her story."

Amy swallowed hard and closed her eyes. Abba looked at me with an expression I'd never seen before, a somewhat fearful look, and Amy cleared her throat and opened her eyes wide.

"Father? Maybe you're the man? You always knew this day of blame will come, and so did I, only I wasn't sure exactly how." My terror at Amy's transfiguration shifted into an understanding that Amy was taking on another persona, a persona we were supposed to read and decode in real time.

"Enough. I want to say it in simple terms, but it still flusters me. I'll leave my door open so I can hear the sounds of your harp." If I had thought she was hinting at something having to do with my father and me, the reference to the harp helped me understand that she was talking about King David.

"I scrub my lower openings too, which have already forgotten the pain. My mouth. Someone is shouting, rivers of tears stream from my eyes, and then, out of nowhere, you. Floating, whirling around, in endless filth. It seems I should have said to *you*, where will I carry my shame? He who seduces an Israelite virgin pays damages for her shame. And if he rapes her, he pays for the additional sorrow."

Amy swallowed again, and I could feel how the word "sorrow" was coming straight from her gut, floating in the air like a ball nobody wanted to catch, and I mentally scrolled through all the incidences of rape in the Bible. Dinah, the concubine of Gibeah, and Tamar. Surely this was Tamar, King David's daughter.

"The seducer paid with his life, and what about you? You're the one who sent me to him, you have to suffer, to shout to the heart of the heavens. Such a thing should never happen in Israel. And such a thing happened, in the house you were supposed to be responsible for. What happened to your power to intervene on my behalf? I am sitting in your house, desolate! And the rest of the family continues to go about its business. You could have married us, my God, you're the king, you could, at any time, have cured my eternal loneliness. There will come a day when parents will give our names, Amnon and Tamar, to pairs of twins, to flowers, to vacation cabins for lovers!! Will there ever be a sister who will protest in my name?"

I vigorously applauded, and Abba joined in moments later. He must have realized before I did that we were watching Tamar, whose brother, Amnon, had raped her, and she was pointing an accusatory finger at their father, David. There was no question that Amy had won over both of us. Like in the end of the famous fake-orgasm scene in "When Harry Met Sally," she sat back down, satisfied, and reached for another slice of pizza.

The logical thing to do would have been to start a conversation about Amy's interpretation, about the excerpts she had selected and about why she had chosen to identify with a rape scene. But Abba and I didn't have the nerve to ask, and Amy seemed so nonchalant about her performance that we felt we could let it be. I went upstairs to get my review books for the test, and Abba cleared the table and brought out a few beers, which nobody besides him seemed to appreciate.

We sat there in silence until Abba exclaimed, "It's perfect! Amy, you must stay with us awhile longer, we'll use it on Shavuot, in our all-night-learning program, we'll do some Bibliodrama for the Book of Ruth. What do you think?"

To me, this sounded lovely, like a marriage proposal, and in fact, Amy smiled like a bride.

Abba commented on the late hour, and I had to remind him of our obligation to our guest. I could never understand how, on Shabbat afternoons, he could go and take a nap while the guests were still sitting at the table, with the childish excuse that he was the only one who had to work so hard on Shabbat. The guests would always graciously forgive him, because Abba's magic worked every time. The cards he played were his child-like candor, and the fact that he lived his life according to his principles. And of course his enthusiasm, which was so powerful it made you feel, at least momentarily, that the world was a wonderful place and that he, in the starring role as the world's manager, only had eyes for you.

I asked him if he wanted me to take Amy to Soroka, and I asked her when her meetings were. I had to call my friend Liat before it got too late, to tell her what time I was picking her up. Abba put me in charge of making all the necessary arrangements and went to sleep, and Amy told me I had a wonderful accent when I spoke English, it sounded totally American. I told her it was because I had gone to the States with the Scouts Delegation.

It should have been a very meaningful summer, because the delegation sent emissaries to all the pluralistic Jewish summer camps, and I was finally going to reap the benefits of my father's rabbinic connections. Given that I was born into an American, Conservative Jewish family, it would only be natural for me to be placed in such a camp. But when we got our assignments, shortly before our departure I was informed that I had been placed at a Girl Scouts Camp, an American camp with no connection to Jewish culture. My world collapsed. I would go there in the capacity of an Israeli scouting expert, with everything that it entailed. I couldn't admit that I didn't understand the point of building towers out of logs if there weren't any boys around.

My mother, who wanted to help me, called the Scouts office and tried to figure out how this could have happened; after all, I was the daughter of a Conservative rabbi, and pluralistic Judaism was our way of life. They said they'd had no idea, and that on the forms I'd filled out, my response to the question about whether or not I wanted to keep kosher and observe Shabbat was "No preference." There wasn't much left to say. My private rebellion had exploded right in my face. Now I had to decide if I wanted to pull out of this prestigious delegation, or to act like a "big girl," despite the fact that things hadn't turned out like I wanted them to. A summer without boys was definitely not what I had in mind. After a lot of thought and a lot of tears, during which my parents kept repeating that it was my choice, I decided to go with the delegation. Not going was really not an option. Unfortunately, more than anything else, I was concerned about what would people say.

I continued to tell Amy "My point is, one time I called home, and my mother answered the phone and she didn't recognize my voice because I'd been speaking English all summer and I had such a strong American accent."

"I'm glad to hear she's still alive." Then she added, in an apologetic tone, "Don't misunderstand me. It's my fault, for not asking where she was. You and your father have this kind of intimacy that made me think the two of you lived alone in this special house." I wasn't sure what she meant by "special." I wasn't brave enough to look her in the eye, because I was afraid she was fantasizing about how she could take my mother's place, but I did tell her all about my mother. OK, maybe not everything, but definitely more than she had asked.

"My mother's name is Ruth, and she's very strict about being called Ruth and not, God forbid, Ruthie. She's originally from New York City and she has just one sibling, an older sister, Ora. And their amazing mother, my grandmother Sylvia, has been living here for the last few years. My grandfather died a year before I was born, and it's a good thing I was a girl, because otherwise they would have named me Ephraim after him. No, my mother wasn't born on Shavuot, actually she was born the day they bombed Hiroshima. Anyway, she's in the United States now because her book just got published by a top publishing house. It's called *Silence is Deadly: Judaism Confronts Wife beating*.

When I finished my unusual monologue, Amy said, "Hiroshima means 'Wide Island.' Is that what she studies professionally?" I had no idea what she meant.

Something about listening to Amy reminded me of reading a text with footnotes, so I chose the simple interpretation and said no, not at all, she teaches English at the university, it's a course requirement for all the students, but she's always been a writer, at least since I was born.

"So how did she end up studying abused women?"

I never really thought about how she'd chosen that particular topic, which she'd been studying for the past ten years, but even so, I answered for her. "Maybe because it makes her angry that some interpretations of Jewish law make it permissible."

Amy didn't respond to my superficial summary of my mother's research; instead she said, "You're very lucky, you know that? Jung says there is nothing more psychologically detrimental to children than the lives their parents never lived."

"You mean I'm lucky they didn't hit me? Or her?" I didn't really understand what I was asking or what Amy was trying to tell me, but she smiled.

"Nice. I hadn't thought about that. Maybe. What I meant was you're lucky that your mother's not a frustrated artist."

"I want to be a writer, too." I managed to sneak this comment in, which surprised me, since I always told people I wanted to be a lawyer.

"And it's precisely because of what I said that you'll be able to do so on your own free will, and not because you're trying to compensate for your mother's failure."

"The truth is," I told her, quietly, as if I were betraying my mother, "I'm not sure she's that talented, and it has nothing to do with being a frustrated artist. She only writes in English, so she has no audience here. After I was born, she tried to be a singer, too. In English, obviously."

I went to get a photo album to show Amy a picture of my mother, and she asked me if I missed her. I was ashamed to note that I had never associated "mother" with "miss." As if someone had removed that possibility from inside me.

"I'm used to it by now. Once she took a six-month sabbatical." I was glad I had found the right answer, but Amy kept harping on the issue and said, in a critical voice, "You're allowed to take your family with you on a sabbatical. How old were you?"

I thought Amy was being a little hypocritical, because earlier she had complained about how her husband had dragged her to Mexico, and now here she was criticizing my mother, but I answered her anyway. I was ten, I told her, Hanoch, my brother was fifteen, and my sister was seventeen.

"And did you miss her?" I figured Amy kept going on about this because she missed her own daughter, but I didn't feel comfortable challenging her or telling her that there was something unpleasant about her interrogation, and about her judging my absent mother, so I simply said I didn't remember.

"She must have traveled when you were even younger," Amy speculated, and I had to admit that maybe, every now and then, she would go away for a month, but Abba also traveled from time to time. With the confusion of someone bad-mouthing someone else, I opened the album to a photo from my black-and-white period.

I had never thought of that phase as some kind of cry for help, as if I were asking the world to present me with certainty. Growing up in a Conservative home - where on the one hand, you're continuing to carry on Jewish tradition, but on the other hand, everything is open to change, depending on the context of time and learning - can feel threatening to children. Maybe I thought that if I wore either black or white, my life would become clear. They say that clothes make the man, but maybe clothes make us into the people we want to be.

Amy joined me in flipping through the pages, and looked towards the shelf I had taken it from. In a voice full of wonder, possibly mingled with envy, she said, "You have so many albums!" I told her that Abba had once been a professional photographer. I yawned, and took advantage of the break in conversation to tell her I had to get back to studying.

"Talking about a person's origins can be more important than learning. OK, let's go, choose a topic. I'm a night owl."

I didn't tell her that I was not a night owl at all, and I even let her choose which topic we should start with. Amy chose Proverbs, one of the Books of Wisdom.

We started with the famous poem "A Woman of Valor" in Proverbs 31.

"I bet your mother didn't approve of this poem." I felt like Amy was trying to score points, but I disappointed her when I told her she was mistaken. Ima would even point to herself jokingly when we got to the line "You have risen above all others."

"Really? But listen to the kind of woman they're describing - a female automaton. A beautiful, holy creature, and the Hebrew language, every letter from Alef to Taf, serves as a prison for her femininity. The song is an olive branch; it's throwing a bone to the woman who worked so hard to prepare Shabbat dinner."

I didn't say anything because I had to organize my thoughts in the face of this feminist manifesto, but Amy, as I had come to expect, had already moved on to the next thing.

"It reminds me of an argument between my son and my daughter. While they were in the middle of playing, she told him that she would make a brother for him. He said, 'You can't, only boys can make people, like God,' and even though he was very influential in her life, maybe catastrophically so, she thought about it and answered, very cleverly, 'What are you talking about, everyone knows that babies are born through the stomach, and it is girls who give birth.'

"And my son said, with all the venom he could muster, 'That's because you don't have a brain.' "

This was the perfect opportunity to ask how many children she had, even though what I really wanted to ask was why people always saw the mother as the life source when the father also played a role in the creation of the fetus. However, this was something I didn't talk about, because I was afraid it would show her that I didn't understand the first thing about the male sex organ, which always reminded me of some kind of perverted creature peeking out a window.

"I have a beautiful twenty-one-year-old daughter, and my son - *meine tsuris* - is twenty. It's not wise to bring children into this world so close together, but apparently the same thing happened to your mother, the second one was an accident. Now let's start studying or your father will accuse me of standing in the way of your learning."

She put a closed expression on her face, so I couldn't tell her I was horrified. Horrified by her speculative and irresponsible observation about my mother, and also by the way she spoke about her son. The Yiddish word *tsuris* - sorrow - has a trace of affection in it, but if I were him, I would have been insulted. Hanoch was annoying, and he used to tell me that I'd been found in the black garbage can outside our house, and when I refused to go to synagogue he would tell me that it was because I was a Bedouin and I had been switched at birth. Also, if one of us really was an accident, it was more likely that it was me, not him, and that's a terrible thing to know or to feel, and on the back of my hand I wrote a reminder to ask my sister about it.

I tried to still my dizzying thoughts and I looked over at Amy, who was reading one of my books. It looked like she was frozen in that position, like I didn't even exist. Even though I wasn't hungry, I went upstairs to get the snacks I had squirreled away for my night of studying. This would be the first time in my life that I studied at the table and not lounging in the armchair or on my bed. When I went back down I saw that she had turned the page, but she continued to sit perfectly still, like a stone. Only when I opened the Bamba, the peanut butter puffs that are ubiquitous in Israel, did she budge in repulsion. It stank, she told me.

How can Americans, who spread peanut butter on their sandwiches every day, hate Bamba? Inversely, Israelis, for whom Bamba is often the first word they ever say, detest the spread that is generally paired with jelly. Maybe for the Americans, this was their unspoken expression of a latent hatred they felt towards Zionism, which threatened to invent something new, something of its own, without needing the support of American Jews.

I took the Bamba into the kitchen but Amy said she could still smell it, so I went back upstairs and stuck it back in my closet. When I opened the Bissli chips - which everyone knows smell much worse - Amy stuck her hand into the bag, and it was truly not out of stinginess that I asked her if she might want to go to sleep, since she was having all kinds of meetings and interviews the next day, and it was getting quite late.

Amy said that learning Torah outweighed all the other commandments, and thanks to her stubbornness, I ended up learning a lot more of the material. Learning with her was a peculiar experience, because not only did she keep going off on tangents, but she also talked non-stop, and approached many of the Bible's verses and characters with an amusing intimacy. I also noticed that unlike me, she barely yawned.

At about four, shortly after the snacks were gone and we had learned all the different aspects of the *shmita* year - I announced that if we were to go to bed now, we'd get five hours of sleep. I told Amy she could brush her teeth first, and she said that if I didn't mind, she'd prefer to brush downstairs. I realized it must have had something to do with the pipes.

Then she said, "My husband says that when God wants to look at Himself, He looks at us, at His reflection, since after all, He created us in his image. If God were to look at me to see His reflection, He would think He was having a particularly bad day."

I didn't know how, or if, I was supposed to react.

I dragged myself up the stairs. To be honest, I was hoping she would hug and kiss me good night, but asking would have been too embarrassing, and in a way that was not typical of me, I felt quite certain that one night, it would happen.

"Good night, Eli" Her calm voice floated up to me. "And thanks."

"Thank *you*," I replied, and I even decided not to keep studying in bed, eating the leftover Bamba, but to go straight to sleep. I fell asleep, suffused by a peculiar comforting quality that Amy had brought into the house.

The house. I had reached the Beit Kama junction on my drive, where an aura of home always permeated the car, and it was as if the vehicle was being carried along, knowing the route with its eyes closed, as if it could feel the front door instead of the engine.

At this time of year, the fields were their usual yellow, but they were somehow different, too. Like the school assemblies on Holocaust Memorial Day, it was the same subject every year, the same sense of sadness, but different nonetheless.

It's strange to think of the Holocaust Memorial Day in Israel as a measure of maturity. Just as some houses have that legendary wall on which people chart their children's growth over the years, the Memorial Day for the Shoah is like a point in time that the child spirals towards every year, and sees the mental and emotional changes that she has undergone.

For now, the house to which I am speeding, the house I essentially ran away from, is the only house I consider home. This, despite the apartment in Tel Aviv and the trips around the world and the commune, not to mention Ora's house, where I felt closest to home. Maybe it's unfortunate that everyone is tied to a single house and is always looking to build that one perfect home. Like in the children's song where the first verse talks about how a house is simply a box in which you live, a box and nothing more. Then, in the second verse, the narrator observes that even though a house is just a box, it is a box that nobody wants to give up on. Time and again we return to that house, hoping to find sanctuary, to feel that we have a place in the world. What would happen to my home if Grandma wasn't there? How nice it must be for a stork, who makes its home in the cypress trees and is not bound to any particular plot of land. Regardless of this barren landscape that I am crossing, I finally understand, more than ever, what people mean when they say that a home is something that lives in you.

Four

In certain ways, that first afternoon - when we took Amy into our home and allowed her to insinuate herself into our lives- wasn't so different from my new life in Tel Aviv. That afternoon, a whole array of keys was spread across the table, keys that would go in search of the right holes, or that would create new holes for what would eventually be revealed as openings. It was like the introductory courses I am taking at the university, and the wide spectrum of people I meet every day. I never know where they're going to lead me. I remember that on her second day with us, I woke up before the alarm clock, and on my way to the bathroom, an odor wafted over me, the odor I was hoping Amy wouldn't notice and complain about, the odor of Abba's friends. Despite the fact that they'd been gone for hours, a trace of their smell lingered in both stories of our house.

Back then - and to this day - the four runners would gather in our house at around six in the morning: Jerry the Canadian psychologist, Avraham the Australian philosophy lecturer, and Moshe the divorced Israeli linguist. And of course Abba, "The Running Rabbi." Grandma was the only one who ever mentioned the pungent smell of sweat that the four of them emitted throughout the house, as they did their warm-up stretches, before and after their jog through the nearby hills.

In spite of the sharp smell that mingled with the aroma of the fresh coffee that Abba would prepare for his friends, Grandma - although she would never admit to it - enjoyed their quirky arguments and the ideas they exchanged in their various English accents. We knew this because she frequently scheduled her visits for December, just in time for the

International Tiberius Marathon. Every year, we'd rent a mini-van and drive from the outskirts of the arid south to the glittering Plaza Hotel on the banks of the Sea of Galilee.

After getting stuck in the mud during a fierce thunderstorm, Ima decided that she would no longer watch the popular race. The trips to Tiberius - even in the winter- were among our family's most memorable experiences; they gave me a taste of the secular, upscale lifestyle that my friends enjoyed all year long and that I was denied because of the kind of work Abba did, and its correspondingly low salary.

When I went downstairs, I wasn't surprised to see Abba and Amy eating a full breakfast, again on the Shabbat table, this time on a dairy tablecloth that Abba had found in one of the drawers. He had gone to the grocery store, apparently, and bought orange juice and fresh rolls; he'd even bought chocolate milk for me. Generosity wasn't a problem for Abba. On the contrary, his largesse was a sticking point between him and Ima. Ima earned almost twice as much as he did, but had followed in her mother's footsteps and was horrified by wastefulness.

Grandma used to say, under the guise of a joke, that if Ima and Abba ever got a divorce, it would be because of money. She loved to tell people about how when Hanoch was born in Jerusalem, Ima didn't have a single shekel to pay for her hospitalization. Just as she was about to hand over her engagement ring to the bewildered receptionist, Grandma came straight from the airport and saved them from shame. This would have been the perfect opportunity to needle Hanoch by telling him it was a pity our parents hadn't left him in the hospital until they could raise the money to redeem him, but we had silently agreed that when Grandma was around, we would declare a truce.

"So, what happened on Thursday? The fifth day of creation?" Amy asked brightly, as if this were a morning warm-up, and compelled me - having already told her that I was an expert on the creation - to come up with the right answer, that on the fifth day, God created the animals, and, if I wasn't mistaken, it was also the day I was born.

Wearing the same clothing she'd been wearing last night, Amy's face suddenly yellowed, and she covered her ears with her hands, as though she were in the middle of a bombardment. The alarm on Abba's watch that reminded him to take his blood pressure medicine began to chirp, and I found myself thinking that Amy's presence was forcing us to pay attention to sounds that we no longer noticed.

After the crisis was over and Amy recovered from her state of shock, she looked at Abba swallowing his pills, raised her eyebrows a few times like a cartoon character, and impishly informed us that in honor of Thursday - the fifth day - she was going to misbehave and skip her pills. Abba and I laughed because we understood that that's what she was expecting us to do.

"Did you have the pleasure of meeting the young athletes?" I asked Amy, and she replied, "Yes indeed, I have had the good fortune to do so," and she rolled the "r" in a way that made me suspect that she had access to some kind of telescope that allowed her to see the hidden secrets of the soul, and that she was somehow alluding to the habit I had back then, in elementary school, of rifling through the runners' backpacks, perhaps out of boredom, perhaps out of some inexplicable desire to cause mischief. Occasionally, I would even take a bill or some change, but only from Jerry, who had a bigger fortune than the rest of them.

Abba, all set to go, decided we had to take Amy for a hike in Tel Beersheba.
"You can't come to this region without visiting one of the most important sites in the country. There have been archeological digs going on here since the seventies. It was a significant factor in our decision to move to the South."

This was another fact I'd never heard. Abba's Zionism was impressive and well-known, but the idea that this rubble heap was an integral part of his decision to build a new house sounded a little far-fetched, if not irresponsible.

We decided that later that afternoon - in other words, after Abba's sacred afternoon nap - the three of us would go to see the Tel. I was glad, although I had been there before, I liked to hear Abba's lively commentary. I loved these kinds of excursions - the marathon was another example - that made me feel like our family had a special closeness, free of strife.

The morning-of-the-*bagrut* atmosphere began to wane when Abba left for his office at the synagogue, and I went into the shower. After I put on my lucky yellow underpants and shook my wet hair out in every direct ion, a gesture my mother hates, I called out that I was ready, but the walls were silent. I knocked on Amy's door with pointed politeness, but there was no response. The shower, which she still hadn't used, was empty. Hanoch's small room, which was full of books that might have diverted Amy's attention, was ajar and foreboding as usual. I went downstairs, I even went out into both the front and the back yards, but Amy was nowhere to be found. I couldn't find her anywhere in the entire house, until - just like in "Goldilocks and the Three Bears" - I spotted her resting on my parents' bed. There was no question that she had chosen the best, most relaxing option. I also loved to lie there, especially in the winter, when Ima would wake up from her afternoon nap and remain burrowed under her blanket, with just her head sticking out, watching television, curled up in a fetal position as if she had just come into the world. I stood there, trying to decide whether or not to wake her, tempted to jump into bed and curl up next to her, something Ima wouldn't allow.

I cleared my throat, and Amy woke up and laughed a big, rollicking laugh. "Hello, Bible Professor, how was it?"

I was confused, and I wondered if this was what people meant when they said that there was no difference between dreams and reality.

She got up quickly, not mentioning the fact that she had been sleeping in someone else's bed, walked up to me, touched my wet hair, and started prattling on about the advantages of morning showers, which her daughter also preferred. She must have said this to cover up her embarrassment. When she was standing right next to me, so close I could see the black circles under her eyes, she said, abruptly, "Speaking of my daughter" - she caressed my chin and cupped it firmly - "I will take my pills after all." Then she let go and strolled out of the room.

She left me in the grip of bewilderment. What were these pills that she was joking about, now for the second time? What was she looking for in my parents' bed? Something about her behavior suggested a lack of orientation with the world, as if she were a baby. Maybe that was why we'd opened our house to her. At the same time, there was something frightening and off about her.

To my relief, she came back only a few minutes later, wearing a different, although equally dirty, jacket, and breezily announced that she was ready to go. Her eyes pleaded with me to ignore my reservations about her. She resumed her regular speech, which was clever and, as a result, slightly overwhelming. She told me she had spent the entire night reading through my study materials, and I remembered that in spite of the last incident, I liked her shimmering, fluid speech that seemed to invite moments of surreal exaltation.

Amy took a small, tattered pocketbook off the couch, along with Abba's camera, which he had given her, she said, to document the process. I didn't ask what there was to document in a hospital in Beersheba, because the way she was holding the camera reminded me of myself, in my desperate attempts to make an impression.

When we finally picked up Liat, I made a brief introduction, and Liat, despite being ousted from her usual spot in the front seat, was thrilled to have someone to chat with about verses from the Prophets and its ethical teachings. Liat and I differed in so many ways, including our approach to school, that it was hard to believe that we had been close friends since first grade. At least, I consoled myself as she put on her Chapstick, she hadn't started using make-up or wearing skirts and dresses.

I enjoyed listening to them, and to the familiar pressure of Liat emerging, as if it were being pumped through a tube that wound through her golden curls, out her thin and always bitten lips, and back into her percolating brain. I looked at my beloved yellow landscape that reminded me of a pile of peanut butter crystals, and I wanted to carve a giant heart right through the slice of scenery reflected in the window, like I once saw in an American commercial.

"That's the Monument to the Negev Brigade," I cut in, remembering my role as tour guide. "It looks like regular cement, but that's exactly what makes it so impressive, it's in memory of the soldiers who captured the Negev, and it's a blast to play there. The acoustics there are really unusual, full of all kinds of metallic sounds." I knew my description was dry and didn't do justice to the site, but that's how it is with places you love, those are the hardest to put into words.

We got to the hospital. Liat, who never lost her practical perspective, thanked Amy and told her it was too bad they hadn't had the conversation in English, so she would have gotten extra practice for that test, too. Amy smiled warmly and told Liat she was more than welcome to practice her English over Shabbat by coming over to read psychology articles with us.

Without objecting to her deciding when and how I'd study, I pointed to the hospital's main entrance and asked Amy what time she wanted me to pick her up. Amy focused her gaze on the hospital, and Liat, who had moved up to the front seat, looked at me with anxious expectation and suggested that we get moving so we'd have a few extra minutes before the exam. Amy decided it was too complicated to set a time, since she didn't know how long it would take, and added, as an afterthought, that she might be having lunch with Moshe the linguist from the university. I agreed that it would probably be better if she took a taxi home, and I thought how strange it was that she took advantage of every opportunity, every interaction, to forge a new friendship.

As soon as Amy slammed the car door behind her, Liat and I looked at each other and started cracking up.

"She reminds me of your mother, only more…." Liat searched for the perfect word. "Pleasant?" I asked in a decisive tone, and Liat, biting her lips, frowned dismissively and kept thinking.

"More liberated!" she said triumphantly. "And a little more attentive."

Liat had normal, very Israeli, parents. Her father had a Ph.D. in history, and her mother was a social worker, but the kind that was always at home when we came back from school.

In ninth grade, the teacher described us as "a tube of epoxy glue." I used to think the metaphor was a compliment, because epoxy was a powerful glue that was sold in two separate tubes, neither of which had any sticking power until it was mixed with the other. Once they were combined, the glue they made was incredibly strong. Now I know that the metaphor of the glue was not a good recipe for friendship, or for any partnership at all. Every tube has to be strong enough to work on its own.

The summer between eleventh and twelfth grades, everything fell apart. First of all, when I was selected for the Scouts delegation, it was very awkward, because Liat hadn't even made it through the first round. But that wasn't what clouded our relationship. It wasn't just that I had wasted an entire summer at that stupid all-girls Scouts camp; I had also missed out on the school's summer project that took place in a Kibbutz up north where many of our age group finally paired up. As if that weren't bad enough, my Liati (whom I could no longer call by that name) had struck gold - the gold I had chosen for myself - and reeled in Elad whom I was secretly in love with.

When I got back to Israel adorned with an extra ten pounds, I was also greeted with the "wonderful" news that Liat was no longer a virgin. And just like in Beverly Hills 90210, that dumb American TV show we watched religiously every week, it changed our relationship. Not so much on the surface, perhaps, but underneath, everything was stormy and obstructed from the intensity of the change. It was like one of us had become mute. I couldn't even escape into my fantasy life without an image of darling, mischievous Liat appearing before me.

When we got to school, we saw that Amy had forgotten Abba's camera. I was glad she hadn't taken it with her; if she had, who knows where she might have left it? I was afraid the mounting heat might damage the camera, so I took it with me, prepared for the possibility that Binyamin would laugh at me for bringing a camera to the *bagrut.*

Even with Amy's help, the Bible test was torture for my mind and body. Chances are I would have done even worse if we hadn't reviewed the material the night before, but even so, when the daughter of a rabbi gets a 78 on her Bible test, it doesn't look good, not for the daughter, not for the father, and certainly not for the educational system.

Since Bible isn't a particularly sexy subject, the group of us sitting on the grass didn't have much to discuss or compare. The holiday of Shavuot was around the corner, and there was a feeling of an unexpected vacation looming before us. As a result, everyone was talking about the graduation party and the yearbook. Binyamin was overseeing the whole hullabaloo, and once again I saw what a natural leader he was.

The theme that had been agreed upon was Peter Pan. Binyamin was trying to recruit more actors for the supporting roles. I didn't see Liat anywhere, and I decided to take advantage of the fact that I had my father's camera, and announced that anyone who hadn't brought in a photo yet could come with me and I would photograph them.

I could tell that Binyamin was surprised. We had been urging people to bring in their own yearbook pictures so there wouldn't be one uniform "look." Still, I knew that a lot of photographs were still missing, and that if we wanted to finish the book by graduation, we'd have to hurry.

There's something very powerful about looking through a lens, like God, who put more thought into creating humans than into any other creature. There's something compelling about the human face. A secret code of sorts, like when you're starting to sculpt with a fresh hunk of modeling clay. A secret that reminds us that we were all born in the same way, but we will all die differently. It was interesting, which aspects of his "photographic essence" my father had retained. Did he employ his own kind of focus, different from everyone else's, or was it the illusion of closeness that the lens provided that made him keep his distance?

While I was taking photographs, someone suggested that at the end of the yearbook, we add an invitation for a class reunion that would take place in 2003, and someone else tossed out the idea of adding, at the bottom of the invitation, "P.S. Children are welcome." I smiled, even though I could feel something inside me objecting. Objecting to the expected path that we were supposed to automatically pursue after high school. An objection I still have today.

I remember wondering how everyone, even the fat and unpopular kids, could be so certain that this was the road they would take; that this was the natural course of things, getting married and bringing their future children to a reunion that will take place in ten years.

Now, six years later, the world still hasn't implanted that inner certainty in me. It's as if either you're born with it or you're not. When I went back to my friends, I told them about the idea and declared that I would definitely not have any kids by the age of twenty-eight, in fact, I might never have kids at all. Liat actually thought it was a terrific idea, and Binyamin said to me, scornfully, that I had no idea what my life would be like. Although I took offense at his remark, I was a little pleased that he saw me as a regular person, or more accurately, as the kind of woman who was meant to be a mother.

He wouldn't be surprised, he said, if I ended up marrying someone who was very religious, like my sister was going to, and that I'd arrive at the reunion with three or four kids in tow. Liat asked if that meant I would be defined as a "*Baalat Teshuva,*" one who finds religion again, and Binyamin responded, with surprising conviction, no. It wasn't just that I was born the daughter of a rabbi, he explained, it was also a matter of personality. It didn't help when I shouted, "What do you mean personality?" and reminded him of my innate rebelliousness towards anything having to do with Jewish rituals or commandments.

"It's just your nature. Even your rebellions are the byproducts of your zeal. Did you girls know that the Greek word for "enthusiasm" is *entheos,* which translates as 'full of God.' So whichever way you're pulling your wagon, it's always going to be full of something."

There was nothing I could add. Binyamin's erudition, as always, made us feel like he had the last word in the matter. That ability of his must have been why, four years ago, on that Saturday night, he was able to convince me to do what we did.

I shake my head, like I'm trying to rid myself of these painful memories. Now, driving home from Tel Aviv, alone in my car, the knowledge that I was going to say my goodbyes to Grandma was starting to penetrate, and, after all this time, I could truly feel Ima's absence.

That day, when I was driving home alone from school, I thought about all the people I had photographed. I thought about Nirit, who had been diagnosed with cancer at the beginning of the year, and who was yet to be photographed. I wondered if she would choose an old photo with long hair, or if she would want a new one, bald from the chemotherapy. This trivial speculation led me to step into Nirit's life. When I returned home I climbed to my room and took a snooze.

Now, too, with the sun heating up both my windshield and the whole yellow city of Beersheba, all I wish for is to retreat, to have a nice nap, but the sign directing me to Soroka Hospital signals to me that I'm not a teenager anymore and this time it wouldn't be so simple.

Five

Nothing in life is simple. Up until Amy's visit - and sometimes even now - I had chosen to communicate to the world that my family was healthy and normal, and that our only Ahilles' heel, the only thing that kept us from being simple, was that my father is a Conservative rabbi. And that we're all fat.

One of the "simplest" images that was ruined for me was Grandma's presence in our lives. From a warm hearted classic nourishing loving grandma she became a threat, a black footnote in my mother's past. How little attention we give to characters. Behind every Grandma who knits in her rocking chair, there is a whole world of dissipated energy. And even though I remember Grandma's active days from when I was a kid, I will never see her as a mother to her young daughters, a mother who did everything she could to give them a high-quality, Jewish, Hebrew-speaking education in the expensive United States.

What I'll remember most, is this past decade when she was living in Israel. During the day she would work in her little garden, or decorate plates with pictures of the Zionist heroes that she cut out of the Hadassah calendar. At night she would sit in her recliner, opened to a regal, indulgent position, and manage her life. She would watch television, write letters, record her memories, while dipping a piece of matzah in her coffee; occasionally, she would sleep, or bless her god - with whom she also had a complicated relationship - with a deep sigh. Sometimes she invited friends from the senior home where she lived for a game of bridge or a conversation in Hungarian. And always, always, no matter what time of day, she would wait for the tiniest bit of attention from her three Israeli grandchildren and her two daughters.

Not that that stopped her from dreaming about New York, from missing it almost every day. Years ago, she wrote a poem about how she'd rather be a cockroach in a New York apartment than be stuck here in her charming little village. The truth is, though, that she never took advantage of her many opportunities to go back for a visit; instead, she satisfied herself with carrying around the "I NYC" keychain that I'd brought back for her. It was as if missing the city, gave her an identity.

That afternoon, after my nap I could hear from upstairs the soothing conversation of Abba and Amy, the complete antithesis of the screaming matches I used to hear from my parents. Ima would be sitting in the living room, Abba would be in the kitchen, complaining loudly that he couldn't find an item in the fridge, or asking her which pot was *fleishig* –meat, or *milchig* - dairy, and why the hell didn't she just label the pots once and for all.

I went down to the living room to find a scene that was, at first glance, very simple. Abba and Amy were sitting there listening to an opera on the record player and drinking coffee from gigantic beer mugs, as was the custom in our house. They smiled at me with what seemed, to my dreamy eyes, an expression of family harmony. Amy was giving a play-by-play account of the "phenomenal" Bat Mitzvah she'd made for her daughter, and told me about the theme that they had chosen together which was Madame Butterfly.

"We didn't dwell on the tragic story, but on the Japanese elements, which decorated the hall. We bought her a dress in Chinatown; you've never seen anything like it. And of course the theme song, the one praising the beautiful day." Amy continued speaking in sentence fragments.

She jumped up frantically and walked over to the record player. "You've got to hear this," she said, "It's Maria Callas. There's an unmitigated love expressed in Puccini's melodies."

Amy stopped the record with a screech, and, as if she were standing on an imaginary stage, asked how it was possible that all of Puccini's main heroines die. Abba got up - he didn't have the energy for drama - and directed her away from the record player with a dance-like movement. He turned off the stereo and announced that we were leaving. Amy looked at me with glassy eyes. Maybe she was hoping we would clarify Abba's criteria for deciding which issues were deserving of exploration and which weren't. She kept standing there, even as I ran upstairs to put on my shoes. She kept standing there, as if she were expecting Abba to "dance" her again, but he had also disappeared, and it was only when he came back carrying a basket with snacks rustling inside that she turned her head and stepped out of her frozen pose.

"More than most of the archeological sites we're familiar with" - Abba began while we were still in the car - "Tel Beersheba allows us to see what it was like to live in a small town in Biblical times. Time froze the remains, and the site gives us a window through which we can peek into the past."

Amy wasn't really paying attention. The only thing that ignited her interest was a billboard for a multi-purpose reception hall in Tel Beersheba. Maybe it had something to do with the story of her daughter's fancy Bat Mitzvah, which had been cut short earlier. I didn't want to embarrass Abba by telling Amy that even though Abba had come here several times to officiate at weddings that were not sanctioned by the state, he couldn't afford to celebrate his own children's Bar and Bat Mitzvahs in the Tel's elegant tent-like pavilion. Abba seemed to be disappointed that Amy wasn't captivated by his words or even by our desert landscape.

When we parked, Abba went on explaining that the ruins suggested that the village was built in the second half of the twelfth century BCE. Abba and I climbed out of the car, but Amy just kept sitting there. She looked at us as if we were strangers. Abba was standing there stretching, not looking the slightest bit upset by the situation.

After a while, I opened her door and waited. Amy got out of the car and marched over to us, but the expression on her face showed utter indifference, as if it was safeguarding some secret which, if exposed, could be dangerous.

Abba raised his voice, as if he were trying to ignite her Biblical imagination. "There are strata," he said, "that show that the village that once existed here thrived, and that it never experienced any kind of violent destruction. As a result, this is what they found...." Abba stopped next to a gigantic stone cube.

When he saw that Amy was ignoring the cube too, he grabbed her arm. Her first reaction was to recoil, but her second was to open her eyes widely. Abba took advantage of her new heedfulness and continued, in his tour-guide voice, "It's a reconstructed horned altar. Parts of it were discovered buried and covered up at the site."

Now that Amy was listening to Abba, we were able to go see the deep well outside the village walls. Abba explained, "Once the well was 130 feet deep; it went all the way down to the groundwater." I threw some pebbles in, and we immediately heard them crashing into the ground.

"So this is Abraham's well?" Amy asked, with the enthusiasm that Abba had been waiting for. They started discussing how Beersheba served as a central settlement area in the stories of our forefathers, and during the times of the Judges and the Kings.

When we passed through the gate of the restored city, Abba expounded upon the important role of the gate. "Here's the interior gate, where you can still see remnants of the benches where the city elders used to sit...."

"We forgot Hagar." Amy cut off his lively description and called out, in an offended tone, "Hagar, who was chased out of Abraham's tent and wandered - as it is written - through the Beersheba desert."

I suddenly realized that Amy's associative imagination resembled Talmudic discourse, which was unfettered dialogue, made possible by the fact that all the participants knew the entire Torah by heart and were able to create a collaborative culture that allowed them to interpret the words as they wished.

I felt a stab of envy for their freedom to express their thoughts and feelings, and, even more, to enter the minds of other people and express their thoughts, too. Amy made me pay attention to all the sounds around me, but she also extracted the voices inside me.

Abba smiled, a crooked smile that resembled the letter N on his Nebraska baseball cap. At that moment, I loved him even more, perhaps because on trips like this, he looked more like a classic American tourist and less like a religious Jew with the mark of Cain on his head.

Abba informed us, in the tone of someone soliciting donations, that underneath us was a giant water tunnel that the Department of Antiquities couldn't afford to excavate. Finally, we climbed the metal tower in the middle of the Tel and took in the breathtaking view.

We looked at the towers all around us. First, the minaret from which we heard the *muezzin*, Sheikh Nasser, praising his god every Friday. Then, a row of terrifying electric towers that looked like miniature Eiffel Towers, and of course the water tower, which was the symbol of our town. Across from us, the round tower of the Negev memorial stood erect. Last of all, sparkling in the distance, was a glass building of the new Beersheba mall.

"And one day, my child, all this will be yours…." Abba made us laugh, interrupting the first moment of silence since we'd left that afternoon.

We sat down on a wooden bench to eat our snacks. "There are a lot of places here for someone to commit suicide," Amy said, chewing loudly.

"There are more buildings in the city." I took her seriously, and added that the urban lifestyle can doom a person to solitude. I likened the misery of city-dwellers who live in cubes to people who use the same piece of dental floss over and over.

Amy disagreed. "There's a Mexican expression, 'a small village is a large hell.' It's true, there's a lot to be afraid of in the city, but every person is a potential gift, everyone can teach you something." And Abba, cutting her off like a child trying to pierce a balloon, said, "Basically, when you're older you'll understand the advantages of city life."

And he turned out to be right. Outside my apartment house there is a small convenience store. In the evening, if I run out of milk, or even if I'm just bored, I'm more than happy that it's there. Not only does it give me a reprieve from the boredom, but it also allows me to expose myself to the never-ending wonder of urban life.

He stood up straight, waved his hand in the direction of the effulgent scenery and said, "If we had a torch, we could signal that tomorrow is *Rosh Hodesh,* the first day of the new month, just like they used to in ancient times. People leave behind them piles of rocks, tradition and seeds of words."

Abba's words seemed to influence the scenery, which began to shine in the presence of the setting sun. This was one of his unique affects, to provide moments of spiritual elevation, moments that emanated from an intelligence that belonged to him but trickled down to you as well. He was always telling us about the book *Ulysses,* which he had studied in college and was considered the classical creative work of all time. I couldn't even make it through the first page, but because of Abba I felt a certain familiarity, a closeness with it, like I did with Judaism, which on the one hand was a burden, and on the other hand was a constant presence in my life. Back then I wasn't sure what exactly happened on *Rosh Hodesh.* I remembered Ima saying that on that day, women were exempt from doing housework.

Abba picked up his backpack and headed down the steps; we took the hint and followed, with Amy saying, in a sympathetic yet all-knowing tone, "It's a mitzvah to eat a large festive meal on *Rosh Hodesh.*"

Abba nodded and decided that we would eat at the city's famous *Beit Ha-Ful,* and I asked if we could have dessert at Beersheba's famous ice cream shop, *Glidat Beersheva.*

After eating the enormous meal that had been placed before us at the restaurant, nobody was hungry. But since in our family dessert had nothing whatsoever to do with hunger, we went to the ice cream parlor, where Amy and Abba continued to talk about Ulysses, which takes place in Dublin. I took a break from their conversation and gazed at the people standing next to the chest of colorful ice cream bins, hesitating, searching for their true love. Or maybe just a temporary love. I remember feeling, at that moment, that I would have settled for a casual, ephemeral love.

When we got home, loaded up with carbohydrates and glucose, seven phone messages were waiting for us: Three baffled messages from Ima, one from Grandma saying that Ima was looking for us and what kind of adventure were we having without her, two from Binyamin, the second one saying that since there wasn't much to study for Sunday's English exam, he wanted to see how the yearbook was coming, and one from Hanoch, who wanted Abba to get back to him with some ideas for the all-night learning session on Shavuot.

Aside from Grandma's tone of rebuke, which managed to pluck at my heartstrings, I felt that the rest of the messages were trying to destroy the alternate world that the three of us had created for ourselves, even as we stood there, listening to the voices erupting from the machine as if it were the 29th of November, and we were following the results of the United Nations vote on the Partition Plan.

Amy's mouth emitted a loud burp, which made us laugh hysterically. I wanted to keep the laughter going, but Abba's insistence on picking up the phone to call Ima put an end to that. Amy pointed out, as if her life depended on it, that we still hadn't counted the Omer, and maybe we should recite the evening prayers because it was *Rosh Hodesh*. Abba glanced at the big clock in the kitchen, the clock that always kept track of how late I was to synagogue.

Abba calculated, "It's three in the afternoon there; the call can wait. Are you ready?"

And once again, we chanted, "Today is five and forty days, which is six weeks and three days of the Omer."

This time, when Abba and Amy began their cryptic Kabbalistic discussion, I had already run out of patience for all things mystical, and went to call Grandma.

It was already ten at night, but I wasn't afraid of waking Grandma, who rarely slept.

"Hello!" Grandma answered in the Hungarian-American accent that vaguely reminded me of Dracula. She said she was glad to hear that we were all healthy and that she wasn't angry because she knew I was in the middle of *Bagruyot.* "Learning is the most important thing," she said. She told me this regularly, perhaps because she herself stopped going to school when she was a young immigrant working to support her family in Brooklyn.

"What's that singing in the background?" she asked. I told her about our colorful house guest.

"Tomorrow," I assured her, "you'll get to meet her." I could feel her loneliness through the silence.

Until she was twelve years old, Grandma had a happy, full childhood in Hungary. She was given a private education, and her family had servants who cooked and cleaned. When the plight of the Jews began to worsen, her parents were able to leave for the States. That was the first time she saw her mother wearing an apron, holding a cleaning product, ashamed to invite friends into their small apartment. For better or for worse, Grandma educated herself.

"Tomorrow they're opening the outside pool," I said, trying to lift her spirits.

"I can't swim the length of that pool, sweetheart. I'm doomed to stay in the indoors pool for the rest of my life."

"Maybe Abba will grill us some steaks tomorrow, to fortify us for the meat-free holiday of Shavuot." I refused to give up.

"Yes, but even my false teeth are getting weaker."

"Let's hang out in a café tomorrow." This was my trump card. "You always wanted to go to a café on a Friday, just like you did when you were a little girl in Hungary."

"We used to go on Saturdays, don't you remember? We'd pay for the cake and coffee in advance, then we'd go there in our best blouses, get pampered like princesses, and leave like queens."

There was nothing I could say to this embittered declaration, which resonated with the thundering echoes of a lost childhood. Grandma must have realized that I wasn't responsible for her stolen childhood, because she broke the silence and said reluctantly, as if waving a white flag, "Fine." But at the last minute, she couldn't restrain herself, and added, "Even though I know that you're doing it more for this guest of yours." I settled for this temporary conciliation and we said goodbye.

There was something frustrating about Grandma's approach to life, which could be summarized in the sentence she was constantly repeating to us, "What you want and what you get are two different stories." Maybe when you're the youngest of nine, and your life begins in the idyllic period before the two world wars, and then your childhood is destroyed by the first one and your life is complicated and convoluted by the second, it's understandable that this expression of discontent would be your own personal motto.

After I hung up, I continued to spin around in Ima's desk chair. Not only was I proud of my resourcefulness, but I also knew that it would be good to get out of the house, since the cleaner was coming and she didn't like it when people were underfoot. I listened to the two of them in the living room softly singing different arrangements of *Ya'ale Veyavo,* the prayer recited at the beginning of a new month. While I was debating between calling Binyamin or simply popping over for a visit, Amy beckoned me enticingly, "Eli, oh Eli… I call out to thee from the depths…," and with that, I set aside my secular life and joined them in sanctifying the new month.

All of a sudden, Abba closed the *siddur*. "I really have to call Ima." Amy and I exchanged looks, as if we were trying to guess what would happen and how this day would end.

"Let's go look through your mountains of photo albums." Amy cut off my thread of thoughts and wove it into a satisfactory response. While she was piling up the albums, I went to the bathroom. Abba put Ima on speaker-phone so we could all listen to her talk about how she bought Avigail a wedding dress in a second-hand store, but I didn't get to find out if she had found the sandals I'd asked for, because it was at that particular moment that Abba remembered Amy's sensitivity to noise and turned off the speaker.

While I was using the bathroom, I heard the faint sound of a car honking twice. I knew Binyamin was looking for me, but I didn't rush out as I normally would have. Then I heard someone softly knocking at the door, twice, and the sound of a key turning, which was surprising because we didn't usually lock the door when we were home. Then came the most surprising thing of all, a shriek, followed by the slamming of the front door, a key turning quickly, hurried footsteps upstairs, then, more softly, the sound of another door, further away, being slammed. When I heard all this, I quickly wiped, flushed, and ran to open the front door, where Binyamin was standing confused, even more ruddy than usual. Abba appeared, telephone in hand, to see what was happening, but there was nothing to see. I pointed upstairs to indicate that Amy had gone to her room, and he shrugged his shoulders, perplexed. This time, for a change, he seemed engrossed in his conversation with Ima, and he went back to continue their phone call.

"Who was that?" Binyamin asked, a terrified look on his face.

The last time I had seen him like this was when he almost drowned on our Shavuot trip up north, a trip that went down in our group's history because we hadn't gotten permission from the police, which, as I said, almost caused Binyamin to drown in the Jordan River.

I told him, excitedly, about Amy, but all he could think about was why she had slammed the door in his face when he said hello. He asserted that we should watch out, because these days, you could never be sure. "Look at David Koresh's cult, all the neighbors thought they were a bunch of friendly hippies, nobody had any idea that they were having orgies and stockpiling weapons to fight the FBI and to top that, they had a plan to kill themselves like the Jews at Masada."

Even though I didn't have any answers, and I, too, was dying to solve this mystery, I mobilized all my energy to defend Amy's honor and mentioned the conspiracy angle. He didn't seem particularly impressed when I told him that according to Avraham our philosopher friend, the cult was just an unusual group of peculiar families that didn't pose a threat to anyone, and that they didn't commit suicide, they were burned alive.

It was only after I reminded him that sometimes people do things that are unexpected - like the time he tied me to a shopping cart and locked me in the scout's storage room - that he agreed to let it go. He smiled sadly and, out of habit, rubbed his hairy, freckled hand. We smiled at each other self-consciously. If this had been a Hollywood movie, that would have been the moment for a passionate, stolen kiss, as if to affirm that despite the unexpected turn of events, despite our uncertainty about the simplest things, we were alive, because we could kiss.

I stood up to shake off the awkwardness, but it seemed to have rooted itself inside me, stamped itself on my body and my conscience. This feeling was, without a doubt, accompanied by a sense of missing out, like when you hear a piece of music but you don't get to find out who composed it.

That moment on the stairs left its imprint on Binyamin, too. I know that, because in the days that followed, when the opportunity arrived, he did demonstrate normative (and, in retrospect, unnecessary) masculinity.

Abba had already gone to sleep, so I couldn't tell him about the Binyamin and Amy episode. Maybe he reminded her of someone from her past - her son, perhaps. The moment I tiptoed up to her room, in an attempt to hear voices from within, Amy opened the door as if she were guarding a treasure. She smiled like a statue and said, as if she were trying to word a telegram to an illiterate patient, "It's been a long day, sweetie. We'll look at the pictures tomorrow, sweetie. Good night, sweetie."

Binyamin would surely have said that her words were artificial and untrustworthy, but me? That was exactly the sweetness I wanted to hear.

I fell asleep while trying to calm my breathing. Out of nowhere, I started to think about Ima. She would never have behaved the way Amy did. Yes, she hardly remembers my friends' names, but she always enjoys talking to them. They think she's funny, and I don't explain to them that humor is a skill that is easy to develop. Humor isn't personal, it's public, and what I yearned for was something private. I went to bed hungry from all my deliberations on the abundance that life was offering me. A fictitious abundance, because even the possibility of kissing Binyamin was a passing thought, a hollow image, and anyway, wasn't I in love with Eren Shonsky and with Liat's Elad? Because they all seemed like possibilities, I couldn't assuage my hunger.

It makes me sad that even now days, before I go to sleep, I scroll through all the guys I bumped into over the course of the day and wonder how it could be that I didn't have a romantic encounter with a single one of them. And now, again, at the outskirts of Beersheba, I feel a chill, and my tear ducts are threatening to burst. I can opt to pull myself together; after all, in the end, Binyamin did want me, and today, I get to choose for myself how much I want to observe Shabbat. But it's useless. Something unnamable is gnawing at me. I pull over for a minute by the grey apartment buildings full of people. I yearn again for a simple, uncomplicated life. Why is it so hard, in this life of ours, to find someone to love us?

Six

Just as I was consoling myself with the knowledge that despite everything, I was actually redefining myself, my sister called.

"Come straight to the hospital," she said. In the background I could hear the cassette playing the lively children's songs that my nephew, Evyatar, so dearly loved.

"We may have to say goodbye to Grandma today." Even though I understood why I had come all the way to Beersheba, my first thought was that I wasn't sure I could tolerate any more of these telephone-induced dramas. Even though four years had passed, I often found myself reenacting the phone conversation I had that Saturday night. Binyamin called; he asked if I was sitting down, then told me that Nirit had died. Now I had that same feeling. It wasn't that the phone was broken, but that the information it was conveying couldn't be true. Maybe it's this same cryptic feeling that keeps me from writing a screenplay about that evening, perhaps in an effort to fix something broken. But this time it's just a prologue, I assure myself. Just like that Friday morning, Amy's second day in our house, when the sound of the telephone was a kind of warning signal.

Even though we had turned down the volume on the ringer, I could hear the phone ringing. It felt like neither day nor night. According to the glowing numbers on the clock, it was seven in the morning. Amy, still in yesterday's clothes, was sitting with the phone - she had reached it first - wide awake and speaking in English.

"Oh, looks like your granddaughter is awake. What a lovely girl...."

I indicated to her that I was going to the bathroom for my morning pee, and I could hear her continuing to sing my praises. When I came out, she was saying, "That's how it is with adolescents, they do what they please." Grandma must have complained about how I always slept late, or how I didn't keep my promises.

Amy listened carefully; occasionally, she laughed. When I heard her confirming that we would pick up Grandma in half an hour, I realized that I wasn't going to get a turn on the phone, and with mixed feelings about the role that Amy was assuming in our house, I went into the shower.

I washed my face as if I were abashedly trying to scrub away my recurring dream, in which I am living with, and cavorting with, a faceless man. There is nothing, just emptiness, that's what this constant dream kept telling me. It worried me that I couldn't give my beloved a face, that his face was as amorphous as the desert sands.

Once we went on a school trip to a Hasidic home in Rehovot, and the lecturer, a newly religious woman, suggested to us that if we wanted to get rid of recurring nightmares, we should recite the special Shema prayer before going to sleep. Even my fear of the faceless lover couldn't persuade me to pray. What troubled me most was the fact that even in my imagination, I couldn't patch together something normal, like what Liat and Elad had.

I looked at my face, which I always thought had been sculpted in an offhanded way, with a kind of divine carelessness that had been passed down from God to my parents. I tried to smile in a sexy way, to bite my thick lips the way Liat, with natural grace, bit her thin ones, but I only looked more awkward and ungainly. At least I made myself laugh.

Downstairs, I was horrified to see Amy sitting there just like Ima, on Grandma's armchair, reading and eating cornflakes. The "show" we had been performing until now, of dining at the Shabbat table, was over, and Amy understood that in our house, everyone ate whenever it was convenient, wherever they wanted, and alone.

I was reminded of what happened with Binyamin but realized that, just like Abba, I hated conflict. My fear of conflict led me to drink my water in the kitchen, where I found a note that Abba had left me. He had cancelled our plans to have Friday night dinner with Baila - Ima had arranged for us to eat our Shabbat meals there when she was away - and that instead, he would cook dinner himself. He also reminded me that Ronit, our housekeeper, was coming.

When the guard at the entrance to Grandma's gated retirement community smiled at me and raised the barrier to let us in, Amy expressed surprise at this "village within a village." It's true that the houses were on the small side. But for someone like Grandma, who had first moved to Israel right before the Yom Kippur War and who, when her husband died unexpectedly of lung cancer six months later, decided to move out and leave all her furniture behind, the house was just the right size. Of course Grandma blamed Israel for her husband's death, ignoring the fact that he had been a heavy smoker ever since he was a young man studying at the Sorbonne.

"You look so much alike," Amy chirped the moment Grandma opened the door. Over the years, a lot of people had commented on the resemblance between us, but as Grandma's skin grew darker and more lined over time, this became less and less of a compliment. Her wizened eyes, remarkably alert, expressed both a distant ache and a fundamental joyfulness. Her high forehead emanated courage, and her lips were thick and always pursed. Because of Chernichovsky's story about the Cossacks who raped the rabbi's daughter, I always attributed her small, flattened nose and her bushy eyebrows to the Tatar genes that had been passed down to her over the generations, and which - as everyone will tell you - were passed down to me.

Nothing whatsoever escapes the slightly slanted eyes of Grandma, who reached out, unhesitatingly, and touched Amy's necklace. "What an unusual hippocampus," she remarked.

Grandma had mastered many disciplines. The hodge-podge of bizarre facts that she carried was concocted from all kinds of material, most of which she had read in *Reader's Digest*, to which she subscribed. "You know, that's also the name of the part of the brain that stores all the information we collect." She wanted to demonstrate that she, like her favorite magazine, was good at digesting everything she read and regurgitating it, usually when appropriate.

Amy, always the perfect hostess, nodded, and complimented Grandma's furniture.

"When I left Israel, after they killed my poor Fraime'le and Elisheva was born, do you know how ridiculous it was? My daughter Ruth and Elisheva's abba, Jesse, were poor and downtrodden, like in the stories of Sholem Aleichem, but their house was furnished with my regal furniture. Precious antiques that Fraime'le had collected in New York, and I just didn't have the strength to send them back. The new house, that the Rasco building company built and that I helped pay for, looked like a castle inside and out, but the people who lived in it were destitute."

In the car, Grandma sat next to me, clutching her plastic shopping basket.

"See how inconsiderate they are?" Grandma pointed out the window. "They decided to build the new cemetery right next door, as if not to disturb the family's routine. One day they're here visiting their old relatives, eating cake and drinking coffee, and the next they're laying flowers and stones on top of them, right there on the other side of the gate."

Once we were on our way, grandma started interrogating Amy and that's how I found out that Amy was forty-five, had grown up in California, and had been raised as a Conservative Jew. She had studied psychology and spent one year studying in Tel Aviv. No, she didn't meet her husband here, she met her husband, Abe, in Los Angeles, where he was studying for the rabbinate. It couldn't have worked out better for them, because she was doing her thesis on Oedipal relationships in the Bible. No, he hadn't been the rabbi in just one place, they had moved from one congregation to another, but Grandma didn't have to worry, wherever Amy went she was able to find work in a children's clinic. Of course she had children of her own. When she was twenty-three she had her oldest daughter, the joy of her life, then unintentionally, and against all the advice in the psychology books, had her son Daniel only one year later. Debbie, Deborah, had just started college, and was planning to be a psychiatrist.

"You should have seen the extraordinary Bat Mitzvah we made for her. The theme was Madame Butterfly." Once again, Amy described the Bat Mitzvah in great detail. Grandma seemed to be out of questions, or perhaps she just wanted to float, like Amy, inside that breathtaking Bat Mitzvah, and she started to sing, with her thick voice, English words mingled with Hungarian. Amy joined in. All I could decipher from the off-key duet was the word "love."

On the way to the café we saw one of the local beggars, and I told the others that when I was a little girl, the first time I saw a beggar lying on the ground with his hand extended, I asked what he was giving out. Amy responded surprisingly harshly. "It's not the least bit funny. It turns out that many of the homeless people living out on the streets suffer from mental illnesses that are actually pretty straightforward, and if they could only be admitted to the proper institutions, the doctors could give them the appropriate medication and cure them."

I was lucky to have Grandma there. She put her hand on Amy's arm and told her not to take life so seriously, and Amy, uncharacteristically, stopped pulling words out of the air like a magician.

When we sat down and ordered toasted bagels and blintzes and all kinds of other delicacies, wrapped in napkins decorated with flowers, Grandma said that the café smelled just like her hometown, Dej, which had been a beautiful place until the Eastern European Jews arrived.

Amy asked, "Why? Did you think you were better than them?" And Grandma answered, "We didn't think so, we were."

I smiled at Grandma, who thought of herself as a woman of the world, and Amy extracted six pills from her candy box. I realized that once again I had forgotten about what happened with Binyamin, and I thought that maybe I should look for what is known in literature as "subtext."

Amy confessed that she didn't actually know Grandma's name. "You didn't introduce us properly," she scolded gently.

Grandma cleared her throat and wiped her mouth and her faint mustache with her napkin.

"Sylvia Sidonia Sara Gittel Jaray Lefkowitz." She recited her full name as if she were a countess, the name which is practically the only remnant of her upbringing - at least for the first ten years of her life - as the daughter of aristocrats. Grandma spoke about her parents, who decided to leave their Hungarian town on a fancy express train to Italy, where they sold her mother's jewelry and bought tickets to America. Four of her siblings, all married and settled, stayed behind. Everyone else traveled in the boat for almost a month, until finally, one foggy night, they saw the Statue of Liberty. But just as Moses was only allowed to glimpse at the promised land, their ship was sent back to Europe, where it had come from.

"Had my parents been passive, lazy, or unambitious, traits which I loathe, they would have stayed in Dej indefinitely, until the city was invaded by the Germans, at which point my whole family would have gone on one last, long journey - to Auschwitz. But my parents, of blessed memory, were as stubborn as mules, and after a year of asking their neighbors for money, once again they requested permission to leave, once again they begged the older brothers and sisters to go to Italy with them, this time on run-down carriages, and once again boarded the ship without them. This time, the voyage was successful. Lady Liberty welcomed us into her burnished arms, stationed us in a transit camp on Ellis Island, and ultimately allowed us to enter the real promised land, and even to settle in Brooklyn. "

Even though I had heard this story many times, I suddenly looked at Grandma from a new perspective. I saw a woman who had been robbed of her idyllic childhood and was still angry at the world for leaving her abandoned and alone at every turn.

I could count on Amy to revive the gloom that had descended upon the kitschy café. "My Hebrew name is Sarah, too. Supposedly a fine and honorable name, but the truth is, Sarah suffered quite a bit during her lifetime. She left her homeland because of Abraham, and it's not always okay to move people from one place to another as if they were trees."

Grandma liked the comparison. "My Ephraim was such a Zionist, always dreaming about living in Israel, by the sea. He'd seen too many emissaries with oranges over the years. After Ruth moved to Israel, we visited every year, and we paid their living expenses as if we were the Rothschild's. Then, when we finally moved here before the Yom Kippur War, he knelt down and kissed the land, like a Yemenite. And then what happened? The land cruelly repaid him by filling his lungs with cancer. Can you imagine if Sarah and the rest of the family had come all the way to Canaan and Abraham had died from neglect? That would be the end of the story, right?"

Grandma wasn't a bitter woman when I was a child, or at least I don't remember her that way. She was a smiling woman with a bright, high voice, and her hands always smelled like oranges and garlic.

After she fell on her hip in New York, and decided to buy a house here - or perhaps it was after the Gulf War, when it became clear to her that she was having trouble breathing - something changed. It was as if she could no longer live her life with the same freedom. The truth was, she'd never really been all that free, because she was so influenced by how her daughters treated her. She was constantly shuttling back and forth between the two countries. When she was with us, she was like a queen coming to the rescue of her people, and when she was there, she volunteered in Mount Sinai Hospital and the UJA and lived the life of the Big Apple.

If Grandma had looked at me in the café and asked me if I believed it was her, the same Grandma who had taught me to read English, who bandaged my knees, who cooked stuffed cabbage and went gallivanting through the streets of New York, I would have had to say no. It was hard to believe back then, and it's even harder now. Her false teeth were bigger than her mouth, and when she was very tired, she would remove them and look so old and powerless that I wanted to cry.

"And why did they choose to name you Elisheva?"

I told her that even though the long name (which didn't fit on the sticker beneath my cubby in pre-school) had Biblical roots, my sister Avigail was the one to blame. She had chosen it. "In 1975, when I was born, an album of Miriam Yellin-Stekelis's children's songs had just come out. Have you heard of her? Anyway, she had a song about Elisheva the doll, which Avigail loved, and she imagined that I would be some kind of girl-doll that she could play with."

"The amazing thing," - Grandma, like Amy, liked to analyze the connection between reality and literature - "is that when Avigail was little, she loved to play with Barbie's that I would bring her from New York. She would talk to them in a soft, maternal voice but sometimes she would take their legs off, just like in Yellin-Stekelis's song about the handicapped doll."

I thought Amy would analyze Avigail's behavior, but she kept talking about the biblical Elisheva. The story of the doll, she said, actually complemented the Midrashic interpretations of the original Elisheva. Even if she was only mentioned once in the Torah, the Midrash teaches us that no man or woman ever merited more joy and happiness than Elisheva, who was privileged to live to see her family members reach positions of power. "But despite all her success," Amy added, giving further proof to the parallel, "Elisheva also heard the knock on the door, and all her joy turned to grief when her two sons, Nadav and Avihu, were consumed by divine fire. As if her two legs were cut off with no warning."

Grandma, who had been listening closely, was pleased, "See, great minds like ours think alike. Just like I always say, 'What you want and what you get are two different stories,' and Amy, as if she were on an American game show, finished the line, " 'But just don't forget what you really need.' "

Grandma and I stared at her with an astonishment that Amy couldn't understand. "What?" she asked. "Isn't that the second part of the sentence?" I couldn't believe there was more to Grandma's favorite sentence, and I asked Amy to repeat it.

In retrospect, I likened that moment to the prisoner in Plato's cave who discovers that there is an entire world outside the tiny alcove that he thought was the entire universe. I'm starting to forgive her, because now I understand that deep down, she thought she could outsmart the sentence's conclusion, against all odds. After life had beaten her down, time after time, after all the wandering, the Holocaust, tuberculosis, poverty, and most of all the premature death of Grandpa, she felt resentful. Life had disappointed her, and that's what made her keep the second half of the sentence to herself.

After Amy repeated the sentence, Grandma waved her hands as if trying to drive away my thoughts, like they were nothing more than a pesky fly. She continued to insist that the meaning of the sentence hadn't changed at all. Her immutable smile made it clear to me that even she knew this wasn't true. She was entrenched in her position despite herself and this only made me more upset. To her credit, she picked up on my frustration, and, in her second-rate Hebrew, called for the check.

Amy, like Abba and Ima, related to the Biblical sources as if they were candies that you might toss out to appease the children. "And look," she said, "right here in this week's Torah portion, we have the death of your sons, that is, of Elisheva's sons, Nadav and Avihu."

Evidently, Grandma couldn't tolerate the tension between us, which only intensified in the face of Amy's non-stop chatter, because she stood up and headed towards the bathroom without a word. Amy may not have grasped the severity of the friction between us, but she must have detected something in my loneliness, or in herself, because she put her hand on my shoulder, and presaged, "She's not so young anymore, your grandmother, and you, well, you're a big girl, and forgiveness is a skill that you have to hone every time you use it, especially when it comes to forgiving the person who brought you into this world."

"But it bothers me that Grandma's motto leaves you feeling helpless against reality, even though the rest of the sentence puts the ball back in your court."

"You know, Rashbam says that you can't force the heart to love what it doesn't love, and that's why the Ten Commandments tell you to honor your father and your mother, not to love them. The ball is always in your court."

Of all Amy's comments, this one satisfied me the most, because I loved Grandma with all my heart; yes, I loved her dearly. When she returned from the bathroom, I stood up as a sign of respect. I wrapped her neck with the black velvet scarf that she had left on her chair, and thanked her, warmly and sincerely, for the wonderful meal.

"There was something to it." She joked. Grandma didn't like spending money. She also wanted to show that she, too, had erased the earlier episode from her mind. "I'm glad I can still spoil someone, and be spoiled, too," she said, linking her arm through Amy's. Seeing this gesture made me realize, beyond any doubt, that Grandma had never touched Ima like that. Ora, yes, and of course us, but Ima? Never.

Now I was walking across the grass in front of the hospital where I'd been born. The last time I had been here was when they amputated Nirit's foot. When we visited, we were completely tongue-tied, and in the end, she was the one lifting our spirits, reminding us that she was sacrificing her foot to save her life. A few months later, they found out that the cancer had already spread past the knee, and she was moved to Schneider, a children's hospital in central Israel. An eighteen-year-old girl, who died at the age of twenty.

Rabin was assassinated a few months after she died, and I remember that two weeks later, I wrote in my journal that if he didn't come back, even though he was in such high demand in real life, then most likely, Nirit wouldn't be coming back, either. I thought of this now, as I was climbing the stairs of the Intensive Care unit, and it was so hard, I could feel my insides shuddering. When would I understand how adults manage to live in such close proximity to so much death?

That morning, on the way home from our outing, Grandma fell asleep in the back seat, like a little girl. There was a time when she wouldn't have allowed herself to do that. I was pleased that, at least for the moment, she could stop agonizing over this new stage of life, one which she considered cumbersome and humiliating.

I forgot to drop off Grandma, which reminded me that once again, I had forgotten about what had happened with

Binyamin. I was letting my guard down. Amy, who saw me stealing a glance at Grandma, the furrows of my brow wrinkled with worry, misinterpreted the reason for my disquietude.

"You really have to forgive her. You have no way of knowing what happened before you were born." I couldn't understand why Amy wouldn't stop talking about my family history. And even if there were things I didn't understand, or things that we never talked about, she had a lot of nerve to talk about forgiveness and family secrets after she slammed the door in my best friend's face, but I didn't have the courage to say anything.

Grandma yawned in the back seat and told us how much she loved to nap in the May sunshine, and that she had dreamt about preparing a Hungarian feast. I invited her to come over and cook for us like she used to do, especially when Ima was away.

"I'm glad you reminded me of your mother. Remember how Abba told us about that movie he saw on the way back from New York, the one he loved so much? Well, I saw in today's paper that the movie has come to Israel, to Beersheba. It's called 'Groundhog Day.' "

"What day?" I asked, and Amy explained that according to legend, the groundhog emerges from hibernation on February second. If it sees its shadow when it comes out of its burrow, that means that there will be six more weeks of winter.

I wanted to say that I didn't think Israelis would be interested in a movie about a groundhog, but Grandma wouldn't let it go, and she asked if we could all go see it on Saturday night. Of course she had to add that taking her to the movies was yet another of the many promises I made but never kept. Again I felt pangs of guilt over Grandma's existential loneliness; she was like a little girl who's been taken on an outing, and before it's even over she's already pining for the next one.

We planned for the shul's pick up. As soon as I got my license, Ima and Abba decided that I would serve as the family's "Shabbos Goy," and give Grandma a ride to the services. Grandma didn't keep Shabbat at home, but nonetheless she objected to the plan; she took her role as the rabbi's-mother-in-law very seriously. I pleaded with her, saying that driving her allowed me to use the car for the rest of the evening after I'd taken her home, and that's how I managed to break Shabbat with the rabbi's consent.

In the hospital's hallway, I bumped into my brother playing with Evyatar. I stopped, opened my arms wide, and said, "Who's that coming over to me?" Evyatar, who'd been playing with the wheels of an upside-down car, stood up, looked at me with a charming but bashful smile, looked at my brother, then ran to me without a second thought. How easy it is to touch children, to enfold them in your embrace. My brother gestured that he was going inside, and I could feel his fear of seeing Grandma.

When my sister came out of the room, I went in. My first reaction was, Wow, how did she hang on all these years, then I immediately rebuked myself, she wasn't an object making it through trying circumstances, she was my grandmother, a living, breathing person. On her eighty-fifth birthday, there was a horrible attack on the number five bus in Tel Aviv. At the time, I thought how scary it was that a person could die, could vaporize into the atmosphere and never again live his mortal life, all because of a terrorist attack that erupted out of nowhere, on a day that began like any other day, with a ray of sunshine streaming in to wake up the sleepers. As a soldier, I found it difficult to accept random bursts of violence, and I thought there had to be a reason for every phenomenon. I also thought that every time you said goodbye to someone, it could be your last time. Does that make life easier, remembering that at every parting?

That Friday, after we parted from Grandma I knew which home would welcome me with open arms. I suggested we go to the library to read English books in preparation for the exam. We had no shortage of English books at home, but I wanted to show Amy my beloved library, my second home, which not only offered me shelter, but also guarded my childhood secret. My secret was this: I believed that the road to becoming an author was, quite simply, the physical path from my house to the library. Three hundred and seventy steps from my house.

As usual, Ne'ima, the librarian, greeted me with a slightly sour smile. It wasn't a smile she reserved exclusively for me, but something she had developed over years of meting out books. It was as if she were a kindergarten teacher in charge of thousands of brilliant, mute children who had taught her this crooked smile, which hinted at something beyond the everyday reality.

While I roamed the stacks, Amy appeared with an armful of books. On the top was a book with a shining Buddha on the cover. Apparently she remembered that we'd read about Buddhism in our English class.

Ne'ima appeared behind her, her face like a clock. "So does your mother have another sister we didn't know about?"

The librarian pointed at the books in Amy's arms. "She's just like your mother, and your grandmother, too, back when she was still reading." The three of us smiled uncomfortably.

During my adolescence, I felt a powerful bond with the world of books. In my mind, it was a lot like falling in love. I imagined that if I put a book near my face, I would inhale its special vapors and bring it to life, igniting a white fire that rose between the lines and confirmed that I was fine just as I was.

Grandma gave me that same affirmation. And now here she is, smiling her toothless smile, gesturing for me to remove her oxygen mask from her nose, telling me in a weak voice that she left a big bag of M & M's in her pantry for Evyatar, her first great-grandson. Funny, what people choose to pass on to their descendants. I can't imagine what it's like to be a mother, much less a grandmother. I put the mask back on her face, trembling. As much as our relationship meant to me, as much as it was an integral part of my life, I hadn't taken proper care of it.

And now, these may be our final moments. She's having trouble breathing. This time I know better. There were so many signs that Nirit was going to die, but I wasn't able to see them. She was grunting and coughing, and she seemed to literally shrink. Her last words were reserved for the doctor. She said, in an aggrieved tone, that he didn't believe her when she said she couldn't breathe. It will always remind me that despite the fact that she was twenty years old, and despite all the hardship she had endured over the last three years of her life, she was still just a girl. A girl who understood, that if her respiratory system was refusing to breathe, something was wrong. Not with her, but with the world. Maybe everyone has trouble coming to terms with the fact that they will stop existing. And maybe my ambitions for being a screenwriter emanates from my desire to decipher what happens in those minutes when you know, or feel, that you are going to die. But maybe death wasn't something that had to be polished and filmed; maybe it was a secret that was meant to stay hidden, like a perfectly-wrapped gift waiting for the right moment.

Grandma is growing weaker; the nurse comes in, glances at the monitors, and tells me to leave so she can hook her up to the ventilator. I want to ask Grandma about last words. Not, God forbid, as a statement of fact. I know that in books, last words are important. If I'm going to write a book, at least I know what its closing words will be. For her last words, Grandma will surely choose something similar to what Heinrich Heine said, that God will forgive him because that's his job. Or maybe she'll prefer Karl Marx's last words: "Leave me alone, go away, last words are for fools who haven't said enough!"

Seven

We had just gotten home when the hospital called, telling us to turn around and go back. It was time to say goodbye to Grandma. Even though I had seen her only a while ago, toothless, hooked up to a ventilator that looked so out of place on her, I became hysterical. I couldn't believe that this was happening, that my strong, lucid grandmother, who still kept track of her own medications, was going to leave this world.

Avigail, on the other hand, was eager to return. She, Hanoch and Abba all went back to bid farewell to Grandma, while I stayed behind to look after Evyatar, who had fallen asleep. Avigail was strong enough to say that she wanted to see the body, and to ask where they were taking it and what they were going to do with it, but I didn't have the courage to see Grandma dead.

Three weeks before Grandma died, Ora came for a ten-day visit, to help Grandma who wasn't doing well, to lift her spirits and, in retrospect, to say goodbye. Maybe there's something about older sisters, first-born daughters, that makes them stronger, more accommodating, more mature. During Ora's visit, Grandma kept saying that even though she had promised not to complain, it was hard for her to restrain herself because Ora was such a good listener.

Now Ima and Ora are waiting for us to call them with an update. I wonder if Ima will be angry at herself for not being here for the last four months of her mother's life. Even with all our technology and ideology that leads us to believe that we are in control of our lives, the truth is that we never really know how things are changing, unfolding, and what surprises await us around the corner or even inside our own houses.

When Amy and I returned from the library on Friday, we came home to a spotless, sparkling house filled with the smells of Shabbat that I love so much. Amy went over to the pots, opened them one by one, breathed in their aromas, and shouted out her compliments to the chef. I asked her to keep her voice down, as the chef was sleeping. Then I saw the surprise that was waiting for me, a note that Abba had left for me in Hebrew. My father only used Hebrew when he wanted to be absolutely certain that I understood him, and it was usually accompanied by a disapproving tone because I had done something bad.

The note said, "Elisheva, stay home, I have to talk to you."

What did he have to talk to me about? In an instinctive act of denial, I crumpled up the paper and shoved it into my pocket. Maybe something had happened to Ima, or to another relative in America? I pulled the wrinkled note from my pocket and scoured it for any sign that I was supposed to wake him, but all it said was that he needed to talk to me. I reread the assortment of words that were so simple and yet seemed complicated, like in the "unseen" on the *bagrut,* which contained reading passages we had never seen before, followed by multiple choice questions.

And why did he instruct me to stay home, as if there were some kind of danger lurking outside? He could have said only that he had to talk to me; of course I'd stay home. Was this how our ancient sages created *midrashim,* interpretations of the text - by allowing their imaginations to gambol around whenever the words were stripped of meaning, even if they were as clear as the sun?

I didn't have the strength to speculate on what he wanted to discuss with me; really, the worst thing he could have said was that someone died, and if that was the case, if God forbid someone died, it wasn't an urgent matter and there was no reason to wake anyone. I leaned against the counter for a few minutes, waiting for a sign, but no sign arrived. Amy had disappeared from the horizon, and I had the sense that there was no point in sharing the note with her.

I found her in the living room, sitting in Ima's armchair, eyes closed. If that had been me, I would have offered to do the dishes, like I always did when I was a houseguest. Despite Abba's perplexing note, and despite my belief that Amy and I were going to use the time to practice conversational English for the oral part of the *bagrut,* I was glad to hear a horn honking outside. Forty-eight hours of family togetherness was a little too much. I told Amy I would be outside, and I left.

Outside, Binyamin was waiting for me. He got out of his car, and, in a reference to what happened the previous night, checked to see if the coast was clear.

"What a coward you are," he chided me when he heard that I still had no idea why she had slammed the door in his face. I started to justify myself, the way we do in my house, and to bring up some of his own fears to put the ball back in his court. In the end I admitted that he was right, I really was being a coward. Too bad I hadn't told him about my crush on Elad; he might have encouraged me to do something about it and I wouldn't have lost him to Liat.

"Maybe I'll try to put out some feelers tonight, after Shabbat dinner."

"You'll need a strategy. Sometimes it takes a little pressure to get to what's real. Think of it like an olive press."

"That's not really my style, as you know."

"You have midrashic genes in your blood; you have to take a big detour just to get into your own house."

"OK, I get it. You don't have to be so philosophical about everything. I told you, I'll find out."

"You're not going to one of your 'uncles' tonight?"

Since my parents and their Anglo friends didn't have family in Israel, they were always hosting each other; Binyamin liked to tease me about this strange custom. In my eyes, it made a lot more sense to share your Shabbat table with friends, to recite *Kiddush* together, than to just eat in front of the TV or whatever it was that my friends did on Friday nights. I didn't actually know what they did. Maybe nothing.

"What about you?" I asked. "Did you decide about the year of service before the army? You have to give them an answer in a few days." It was clear to me that Binyamin was going to follow in the footsteps of his sister, who had done a year of service in the Scouts.

"I don't think I'll do it. No, I'm pretty sure I won't. You'll have to represent us," he teased.

"But your draft date is so late. It's not until March, right?" I don't know why I grabbed on to this practical argument in an attempt to change his mind. Maybe because his response, which left me alone with our decision, terrified me.

"I thought I might travel around the United States or something."

"So it's just like the delegation, huh? In the end, I'm going to be the only idiot putting herself out for the greater good, for other people? I've been fighting with my parents and I don't even know why."

"OK, don't get so angry, nobody thinks you're an idiot, you handled the delegation with aplomb. Besides, you know perfectly well that it's not just other people who will benefit, you're going to get a lot out of this, too."

"But really, can you imagine yourself without the Scouts?"

"To be honest, no, not at all. I think it wouldn't even be the same 'self.' But I'm ready to pull back a little."

I wiggled my toes on the sidewalk, and he repeated, "Don't be angry."

"I'm not angry, and I don't know anything. I just am. I have to go back home."

I think this was the first time in my life that I felt like home was the safer place to be.

"To your nutcase?"

"She's not a nutcase!"

I wanted to ask what would he do in America by himself, and why didn't he think that he would also "get a lot out of" doing a year of service, but all I did was remind him that tomorrow, my group was in charge. The Scouts were going to run the activity themselves, and he should keep an eye on them.

When I was already at the gate, Binyamin honked briefly. I was afraid he was going to comment on my excessive need for control over my group, but he opened his mouth without opening his window, like in the final scene of "Breathless," and bashfully mouthed the words "Shabbat Shalom."

When I went back in, Amy was sitting on the sofa eating ice cream. She beckoned me over, and, like a lawyer presenting her evidence to the jury, pointed to a photo she had taken out of one of the albums scattered around her. Without meaning to, I snorted when I saw the picture.

In the photo, I'm in my pajamas, sprawled across my unmade bed, and my face is buried in a big pile of sheets. Near my head, in their usual spot, are three books, I couldn't see what they were, although I could tell from their plastic covers that they had been checked out of the library. My bed takes up most of the picture, because all three of us had big, bouncy American beds that Grandma had hauled over to Israel. If you look closely, you can see the soles of my feet, grimy as usual. Hanoch had capitalized on the opportunity, with a considerable amount of pleasure, and taken a picture of me sobbing.

Amy asked if he ever hit me.

This time my laugh was intentional. "Of course he hit me, and I would go yelling to Avigail to come and save me, and she would come over and smack him. She says that one time, when she laid her hand on him, he grabbed hold of her and shoved her so hard that she knew it was all over. He was stronger than she was. Everyone hits their siblings, right?"

"It depends. Where were your parents?"

"They were always at home," I defended them automatically.

"It can be very confusing. Parenting is complicated, and it can be deceiving. Sometimes we think our parents are very much present, when in fact they're not really there. It's hard to grasp. I've seen it with mothers and daughters."

Maybe because there was some truth to what she was saying, I mustered up the courage to ask why she had slammed the door in my friend's face.

Amy wasn't as brave as me, and she stood up to get herself some more ice cream. Like a good guard on the basketball court, I followed her, but she didn't get flustered as I had hoped. Instead she asked, "Which friend?"

"Binyamin, you know, that red-head, last night."

I sensed that she didn't really have to ask, she knew exactly which friend I was talking about, but still, she was speaking with honesty and warmth, and with weariness, as if she had answered this question before.

She said, "If I were to tell you that I suffer from an illness that is characterized by a faulty understanding of reality - surely you learned about synecdoche in your literature class - well, my 'illness' is that I see synecdoche everywhere, particular details that represent a whole. In other words, I have a tendency to jump to conclusions. Sometimes, seeing a redhead like your friend is all I need to persuade myself that my brother, who lives in Netanya and whom I haven't spoken to for years, is standing in the doorway in all his redheaded glory."

I wasn't sure I understood her correctly. I just smiled empathetically, suddenly realizing that Amy was trying to teach me the new language of sincerity. We carried our enormous bowls of ice cream into the living room. I thought to myself that Binyamin would never have been satisfied with her response, but I wasn't planning on telling him about her "illness."

We delved into Amy's psychology article. I didn't really understand the first paragraph. It asserted that there are ghosts in every children's room, and that they are like uninvited visitors from the parents' suppressed pasts. I tried to hone in on a particular scene or moment that I had experienced as a little girl that had unwittingly been passed down to me by my parents, but nothing came to mind. I was glad that my family didn't have any tragedies that were transmitted from one generation to the next, despite the fact that in the diaries I kept as a child, I described the incidents in which my parents forgot my birthdays as a catastrophe.

On the second page, Amy had underlined the questions "What is it that determines whether the conflicted past of the parent will be repeated with his child? Is morbidity in the parental history the prime determinant? I understood that she was hinting at the death of my grandfather, Grandpa Ephraim, before I was born, but I wasn't willing to discuss it any further, since I had no idea what kind of impact, if any, his death had on my mother.

When the article had become more comprehensible, something unexpected happened when I read about a particular family's experience. "The meaning of separation and loss was buried in memory. Their family style of coping with separation, desertion, or death was, 'Forget about it. You get used to it.' " This was a sentence I identified with so strongly I felt like someone had grabbed me by the throat. And while plenty of books have made me cry, I had never shed a tear over an article, much less one in English, much less in front of other people, but I couldn't hold myself back. I had heard those words – *forget about it* – so many times, and reading that hurtful phrase was a familiar and disheartening experience. Of all the responses I could have given her to explain my sudden outburst, I didn't expect the hodgepodge of words that tumbled out of my mouth.

"I didn't make the TV louder just because he was sleeping, but he thought I did, and he would come out of his room and I'd run into mine and slam the door. I would hide in the space between the bed and the wall, and yell for Ima and Abba. He would beat me up, and say things like, 'Forget it, you're just a Bedouin we brought home with us, something we found in a trash can. Nobody cares about you.' Then we would hear Abba downstairs, shouting up, 'Be quiet already,' and Hanoch would get scared and go back to bed."

Amy was looking at me the way someone might look at a painting in a museum. I wanted to understand if this meant I was an abused child, and if it meant that my parents hit Hanoch. And how could that be, since all in all, I love Hanoch, and anyway, all siblings hit each other, don't they? But Amy put her hand on my shoulder and spoke into the silence, her eyes gazing off into the distance.

"If Freud had based his theories on the book of Genesis instead of on Oedipus and the rest of Greek mythology, maybe he would have discovered that what really influences and shapes a person isn't his relationship with his parents, but his relationship with his siblings, whether they came before him, after him, or alongside him. Cain and Abel, Ishmael and Isaac, Joseph and his brothers and the list goes on...."

I felt like Amy wasn't listening to me, like she herself was arguing with the imaginary ghosts or quoting her own dissertation, but, like the baby in the article, I didn't know how to refocus her attention on me. I looked at the pages in our hands like someone who fluffs the pillows to make a house feel more like a home, and I spoke loudly.

"This has nothing to do with siblings; the mother or the father is supposed to take care of the infant's needs. To pick her up when she's crying, to hear her crying in the first place, to understand that you have to smile at her when you change her diaper, to allow her to make mistakes. It says here that siblings are also children, and they need their own support."

"Nice," Amy said coldly, as if she were playing a role on "L.A. Law." "It's so easy to absolve the siblings of all responsibility, to blame Adam and Eve, or God, for the fact that Cain wanted to kill Abel. We'll have to read on to see which one of us is right, and why you instinctively blame your brother and then immediately shift the blame to the parents. I need some coffee."

I hadn't anticipated this. Amy was becoming aggressive, like kids who didn't know how to lose gracefully. I sat there, cautious, like an embarrassed guest, and all I wanted to do was call my sister and ask her what she had to say about these theories which had unleashed all these memories, and to tell her about Amy in general. "This isn't fair," I thought to myself. I had agreed to ignore the "illness" secret that she had disclosed – that she was so excessively attached to her brother – and in return she was intruding into my life. Confused and a little scared, I decided to sneak upstairs. From the kitchen I could hear Amy singing softly, or possibly talking to herself. When I was halfway up the stairs, I heard Abba opening the door of his room, and I decided that this would be the perfect way for him to cover for me.

I went into my room, amused by the idea that I had to search for the remnants of harmful ghosts the way I searched for leavened bread the night before Pesach. Then, too, it's the parents who hide little pieces of bread throughout the house, and they're the only ones who can put the kids on the right track, with only the faintest light from a candle to guide them.

I wanted to go back down so I could retrieve the article and read it by myself. On my way down I bumped into Abba, on his way to find me. He didn't say a word. We stood there, suspended between heaven and earth, staring at each other, like in a Western. He just stood there opposite me, like he was waiting to ambush someone. The note he had left for me was his pistol.

I had to free myself from the imaginary cables that bound us together, so as I went back downstairs, I told him

Grandma's news, that the movie about the groundhog, which he classified as a philosophical comedy, had come to Israel, and that I promised Grandma we'd go with her.

And then, it seemed, the truth came out, the thing that was really bothering him since we had met on the steps.

"Elisheva," he said, "I need you to come to my office with me before services. Can you come? I just need you for a few minutes."

"What's wrong? Did something happen?"

"No, nothing happened, I just need your help." His face was troubled. He was clearly hiding something. What did that mean, nothing happened? I felt like I was in the fable of the mouse who begs the lion to spare his life and promises that one day he would pay him back, but I wasn't sure who was playing which part. This was awkward; after all, how could I help him? His voice, too, was unusually aggressive. There was something deliberate in his tone, I couldn't put my finger on it, something that made it clear that this wasn't the time to argue or to ask, "But why?" like I always did.

Amy, who didn't pick up on the tension so uncharacteristic of Abba, stopped us and asked what was happening with the movie. She added that she hadn't been to a movie in four and a half years. The precision of Amy's time frame, as well as the confession itself, struck me as odd and in need of further elucidation, but Abba, who was always pushing me to see his favorite movies, even if it meant going the night before an exam, just smiled a peculiar smile and said we'd go tomorrow. This satisfied Amy, and she went back to Ima's armchair.

Abba drove us to the synagogue in silence; he still looked like he was being chased by something imaginary. I wondered if something had happened to someone. Maybe Ima?

But if that were the case, why wouldn't he have said anything in front of Amy? This drive with Abba felt like a coming of age journey. I remembered how in the beginning of twelfth grade they gathered us together to tell us that the doctors had found cancer in Nirit's bones. On our trip to Poland she had complained about pain in her knees, but everyone was griping, and the doctor who examined her told her they were growing pains. Fortunately, her parents insisted on a second opinion. The results came in while she was on school's summer project, the one I'm always complaining about missing out on. Her doctors were astounded that she had sent her parents, by themselves, to get the results of the bone scan. Does everyone have their own "maturity moment?" Can we miss it without even realizing it?

When we went into Abba's office, I remembered that I had once read that you have to think of death as a surprise party. And indeed, there was a pile of gift books in the corner of his office, but it was just a coincidence; there weren't any balloons or candy.

"Abba, what happened?" The suspense was making me crazy.

"You might not understand all of this, but it's not a game. I need you to listen carefully and not argue, this is a matter of life and death and I need your cooperation. Promise?"

I felt like a character from one of those stories about the Palmach, being sworn into the Israeli underground movement.

Overcome with emotion, Abba sat down in the "rabbi's petitioner" chair next to him. I walked around the table and sat in his upholstered desk chair, awaiting his words.

"Something's wrong with Amy, and I have to figure out what it is."

I cut him off with my questions - what did that mean, wrong, and how did he intend to figure it out - which he didn't like. He insisted that I listen until the end, and that I not allow my affection for Amy to confuse me. Ronit, he said, had come to clean the house earlier in the day, and didn't know about our guest, so she went into Avigail's room. Her heart sank, he said. It sank like a ton of bricks.

"You can't begin to imagine the mess that had taken over the room. Your room, even at its worst, even around the time of your Bat Mitzvah, could have won a neatness award compared to Amy's room. Clothes, newspapers, leftover food, cigarette butts. The whole room had been trashed."

"So she's messy, she's going through a rough time with her divorce and everything, but…."

Abba silenced me with a glance and said that nothing could excuse that kind of messiness in a normal woman of her age. He found it deeply troubling, and had asked Steven to come over. From one look at the room he agreed that they were very worrisome signs.

Even though there was no point in saying "But" again, and his tone was quite alarming, I said "But" anyway, which made Abba reiterate his objection.

"It's not a matter of a rough time. Ima looked into it, and it turns out that Amy's been divorced from her husband, Rabbi Solomon, for six years already. We have to understand her situation, it's not something you can just ignore. Ronit was so horrified. You have to help me with this, we have to find a solution as soon as possible."

"But when did Ima find this out? What are you doing, conducting an investigation?"

It seemed to me like they were overreacting. It's true that when Abba told me about the room, I thought about how

Amy would stand at the door, preventing me from even peeking in, and of course about what happened with Binyamin, but on the other hand, couldn't an adult have one or two quirky behaviors? It didn't mean we had to treat her like a fleeing criminal. I considered telling him that she herself had admitted to some kind of illness, but I had a hunch that Abba would use that information against her.

"Ima happened to meet some of her husband's acquaintances before I even realized that something was wrong. And now, of course, she's going to try to find out more about Amy's life."

I didn't respond, although I had no doubt that it wasn't just by chance that Ima had bumped into Amy's husband's rabbinical acquaintances. Grandma's updates must have made her jealous, and so Ima used her connections with the northeast Jewish community, to dig up some dirt about her "usurper."

"So what do you want to do?"

"It's not what I want to do, it's what we have to do. For now, we'll behave normally. We'll be better informed after Steven assesses her. I hope I'm wrong, but if I'm not, we'll have to ask her to leave."

"You want to kick her out? Her messiness isn't contagious. You saw for yourself what a kind, smart person she is." I almost said she was the kind of person you fell in love with, but I had to make sure to keep the conversation rational. The last thing I wanted was to say that I was insulted on Amy's behalf.

"This has nothing to do with her intelligence or her charm; she might be a sick woman who needs help. And it's precisely because she *is* so smart that I don't want her to suspect anything. We should probably go home."

"What kind of sick? Mental illness? And if she does need help, isn't the house of the rabbi a good place for her to get it? And don't you think you're exaggerating a little? That she'll 'suspect something?' She's not here to take over our lives."

Abba took a deep breath. I thought I could detect the slightest twist of a smile on his lips, as if he were thanking me for reminding him to breathe.

"The scary thing about this kind of illness is that you can't really know how the person is doing. Maybe she needs to take medication, or to be hospitalized. We don't have the tools to figure out what she needs, and it's irresponsible for us to try to help her based on what we think. It's a very sensitive situation, and that's why I don't want her to suspect anything. She might hurt herself or her surroundings. I hate to say it, Elisheva, but there are some things in this world that you don't yet understand. Fortunately for you."

Abba was quiet. I tried to figure out if there were any other steps to his plan that he wasn't telling me about, or perhaps events that had already happened that I hadn't seen. There was nothing I could say.

"Believe me, Elisheva, I want this to end well; I'm praying for it. Maybe you're right, maybe she's just a sloppy person. I'm not a psychologist, and I'm certainly not a psychiatrist, so let's wait until we hear what the expert has to say. Until then, I'm asking you to cooperate. I know you like her a lot, she really is a very special woman, but there are things we don't see, things we've misread; maybe we've chosen not to see them. Either way, you have to admit that she's a little strange."

He heaved himself out of his chair, which seemed to have changed him, to have put a mask on him that contorted his face. Just like on Yom Kippur, when he would hold the shofar, wrap himself in his *tallit* and stand in front of the large congregation, and I would be inexplicably terrified. Although it was a violation of Jewish law, there was always someone in the group of worshippers who would take out a stopwatch and measure the length of Abba's *tekiah gedolah,* the long shofar blast that concluded the fast.

"But how is all this going to happen? Can Steven make a diagnosis based on a regular conversation?"

"Of course. Every disease has its own set of symptoms. And don't forget, he's the head of a psychiatric hospital."

Abba was genuinely concerned. I could tell he really needed me, since he normally didn't explain himself or try to win me over to his side. I was anxious about whether or not I could pull off the ruse, and as ridiculous as it sounds, I was counting on Amy to help me.

We came home filled with a cautious sense of excitement at our little mystery, or maybe a sense of embarrassed awkwardness. I forgot to ask him exactly how and when he proposed to set up this diagnostic meeting with Steven. Was it really possible to seal a person's fate simply by shaking hands across the synagogue's *Kiddush* table?

Amy was sitting serenely, sunk deep into Ima's easy chair. She wasn't sleeping; she was reading a book, which on closer observation turned out to be the Bible. Abba suggested we set the table for Shabbat, and Amy, who may have sensed our renewed interest in her, took the opportunity to compliment me on the productive learning we'd had earlier. I had already forgotten about it. It's interesting how quickly things can change, leaving you with an entirely different perspective.

When you're eighteen, you can't imagine where life will take you. Like a horse with blinders, you can't imagine where you're going.

I still can't articulate what I've gained in the last five years, since I left my parents' house. Perhaps I'll never be able to put it into words. Certainly a little modesty. Certainly the understanding that there is *only* new under the sun. And now, the phone that I put on vibrate so as not to wake Evyatar, is also news breaking. It brings the painful news. I'm surprised to learn that the knowledge of Grandma's death isn't causing me the unimaginable grief that I had been dreading.

Grandma could never understand why God made his creatures suffer so much when they were dying. It drove her crazy, the knowledge that her own death might make her suffer, and she even looked into the possibility of medically-assisted suicide. Apparently, despite her intransigent and demanding personality, she must have managed to stir the compassion of heaven, because according to Avigail, her death was smooth and painless. She had no grandiose last words, but died with the peace that she deserved.

Feeling depleted, I collapsed into my chair. Like I needed some kind of ventilator. Like the whole world needed some kind of giant blast of air to wake it up. That was it. Grandma had died. After Nirit died, there were many days when I felt like I was in the Auden poem. "Dismantle the sun, stop all the clocks." The hard part was imagining the world going on as usual. Take now, for instance. I have to pee, and I'm wavering between my desire to sit down and cry, and my physiological needs. And truthfully, I'm also disconcerted by the slumbering Evyatar, who won't necessarily remember his great-grandmother, because after all, one day the stash of M&Ms she gave him will run out. And, as if to ground myself, I check that he's still breathing, and only then do I head towards the bathroom.

And then there are Ima and Ora, across the sea. Right now they're waiting for airplane seats to become available. They still don't know that their mother has died. And while Abba and my siblings are making the final arrangements for Grandma, it's my job to bear the bad tidings and tell them the news. So much sadness. If only someone else would call Ima and tell her. Funny how things have turned around. Now I'm the one who has to say, "Come home." Of course she, too, has always been waiting for this pair of words. But from me? Is that why women like to have daughters, to repair the relationship that they had with their own mothers?

Eight

I've always felt that on Fridays, new air flows through the world, carrying new spirits and promising a life filled with sweetness, love and freedom.

My favorite time was "between the suns," the Hebrew term for twilight. Although it took place every day, it was different on Fridays, grounded in an enigmatic, fantastical sense, with a dab of science fiction mixed in, the way it first appears in the Talmud. It is written in *Pirkei Avot, the Ethics of the Fathers*, that as God was finishing the creation of the world on a Friday, He created ten things at twilight that were unique and miraculous. Miriam's magic well, for instance, and Balaam's donkey, which opened its mouth and words came out. Even the manna that fell in the desert. It's not hard to understand how this timeless time, neither day nor night, ushered in by the twilight backdrop, turned into a time of mystery, with the capacity to call forth mercy and good will. The list names wondrous things that God created at the very last moment. As if He sat and looked at His world and saw what was still missing. The way a painter looks back on his painting.

During this moment of dusk, "between the suns," I missed Grandma. A lot. I could barely feel Friday's cosmic force that I loved so much. I had spent the first part of the day in the park with Evyatar, the middle part posting death announcements, and now it was the time I hated the most: getting ready. The same irritating time as always, when I had to pick out "nice" clothes for synagogue.

That night, when Amy was here, I chose to lie in bed and read. Next to my pillow were the books we'd taken out of the library. One of them was the Buddhist book that Amy had selected, the one with the Buddha who, like me, seemed to have something against getting dressed. I opened it and thought about how Amy's adjustment process, and her reaction to things, was somehow different. I had mentioned Buddhism for one passing second when I was talking about the "unseen" section of the test. Her experience of time seemed to be molded from a different material, as did her use of language, which she would sometimes take apart and then put back together. If that's what was making her sick, I thought to myself, there must be a lot of sick people out there.

I had barely finished the first page when Abba called up, American style, "GIRLS! Lighting time!" This was unusual. He rarely waited around for the candle-lighting ceremony that marked the official beginning of Shabbat, choosing instead to call out a general "Shabbat Shalom" towards the interior of the house, then hurrying off to work. Whenever my friends would complain that I walked too fast, especially in places where the whole point was to stroll around slowly, I would blame it on Abba's large and energetic steps, which were very hard to keep up with; those were the steps that taught me how to walk.

Quickly, I pulled on a pair of black pants and a shirt that Avigail had given me. Amy appeared in my room, looking like she had just pulled a rabbit out of a hat. She was wearing a light-colored shirt that accentuated the hypnotic seahorse pendant, which in turn brought out her olive-green eyes. She had gathered her dry hair into a bun, which could easily have been mistaken for a slightly flawed Japanese hairdo, thanks to her long dangling silver earrings that made her look so sophisticated. She still hadn't changed out of her pants or her stained jacket. I wondered what she could possibly have in her suitcases if she never changed her clothes. When she came downstairs, her whole appearance radiated elegance, and I felt bad for her. All this effort, when the evil decree might fall on her head.

Abba, who had decided to hide his suspicions, had set up the candles in the silver candlesticks that came from Grandma. There was a feeling of presence in the room, of something, we weren't sure what, that was preventing us from lighting, as if entering "Shabbat mode" required special preparation, like entering a palace. Abraham Joshua Heschel, one of the leading thinkers of the Conservative movement, with whom Abba had been fortunate enough to study with, dubbed Shabbat "a temple in time."

Uncharacteristically, none of us bothered with words. Despite the ticking of the clock, which I knew was exacerbating Abba's stress, the three of us stood in front of the candles, just staring at them. Abba, who was apparently horrified at this excessive intimacy, or who suddenly felt, as I did, the absence of the real lady of the house, lit a match and rushed through the blessing. Maybe what really worried Abba about Amy's illness was that we hadn't told anyone she was here, and he might be found guilty on two counts for misreading the signs.

Abba and Amy walked to Shul and I went to pick up Grandma.

The gate of Grandma's nursing home was open, as Friday night was a popular time for visiting. Grandma, too, was wearing black, and seemed to be smiling more than usual. In the car, she continued to smile suspiciously, and I finally asked what was new. Usually I avoided that question, since it would give her an opening for her usual complaints. But this time, Grandma responded mysteriously, "It's been a long time since I've seen your mother worried." I felt better. One way or another, I realized, this had something to do with Amy. I was just surprised that Grandma knew about what was going on, since she's not exactly the queen of discretion.

"She's never called me this often on any of her other trips. She says the cost of calling has gone way down, but if you ask me, it's this guest that's keeping her up at night. Your mother's dug around a little, and it turns out that Amy has a brother in Netanya! An important Orthodox rabbi."

"I know that already, it's not a secret," I quickly replied, even though I still wasn't clear about all the facts. I realized that Grandma hadn't been told all the details. In fact, I could tell from her face that she hadn't expected me to know anything. I wondered if this was like a card game, if she had some trick up her sleeve that she was saving for later. She said, casually and out of the blue, "Can you believe that this Shavuot, they're celebrating their thirtieth anniversary? Thirty years! 'And Joseph was thirty years old.' Think about all the things that happened to Joseph after his brothers threw him into a pit and sold him. Not that I'm comparing your mother to Joseph, but look how much a story can develop over thirty years."

I was surprised. Not by the Biblical analogy - Grandma was an authority on the Joseph stories - but because I didn't think that anything about Abba and Ima's marriage was an issue to be discussed and it seemed to me that between the lines she was referring to pits that I didn't know about. All the questions I asked, like "What prompted Ima to look into Amy's past?" were actually pretexts for what I really wanted to know about, and at the same time didn't want to know about: my parents' marital history. And so they were answered with a venerable and disingenuous nod of the head. And for my part, I wasn't about to tell her about Amy's messy room, which could certainly have alleviated her doubts about Ima and Abba's marriage.

As I parked, I decided that there was no point in bringing Grandma into the Amy mystery. In our family, secrets were always being revealed and transformed into jokes. She'd find out if she had to. I got out quickly and opened the car door for her, the way she likes. In return, I got a typically Jewish sigh, a fusion of contentment and bitterness.

You wouldn't think someone would yearn for the things that had once driven them crazy. Right now, I'd give anything to walk to synagogue with Grandma at my side one more time. It had been like walking with a human suit of armor. Maybe because of all the experience she'd gained jostling her way through the crowded streets of New York, or perhaps it was the feeling that, like a well-made jacket, her very presence brought out the best in me.

In his sermon, Abba talked about the importance of balance in life, alluding to both the midrash and Grandma, whom everyone in the synagogue knew and cherished. He talked about how World War One had destroyed her childhood and cut short her education at the age of thirteen, and how that was the reason she so deeply admired highly educated people, and how she was disappointed that her daughters never completed their doctoral studies. At the same time, she respected people who were hard-working and diligent, like she had been her entire life. Surely, Abba said, many people remembered her tagline, and I waited for her usual slogan, but he surprised me when he said, in English, "Adversity should make you better, not bitter." Not that it didn't suit her, and not that she never said it, but clearly Abba had chosen this phrase out of respect for the newly deceased.

That night, when Amy was with us in shul, Abba surprised me when I heard him proudly calling my name. Every year, the synagogue held a ceremony in which they presented all the graduating high school seniors with books. I suddenly understood why there had been so many gifts in his office that afternoon, and why so many of my classmates were there. The fact that nobody had invited me didn't surprise me. Everyone assumed that Abba would make sure I was there.

I went up on the *bima* to accept the book, "The Culture of Dissent in Israel," from Abba and the synagogue president, Emma. Emma was married to Steven, the psychiatrist, who wasn't there that evening, even though Abba had been expecting him.

I wondered if the day would ever come when I actually chose to be here, and would enter the synagogue like an equal among equals. The rabbi's home is never private. That's why Jewish writers like Yaakov Steinberg, Shaul Tchernichovsky, Devorah Baron and Shalom Aleichem all chose that setting whenever they wanted to say something about the Jewish world at any given moment. I felt a deep affinity for these assorted stories. My father wasn't considered a "real" rabbi in Israel, so I couldn't even enjoy the lusty description of the pious rabbi's daughter who had to be conquered, like in Tchernichovsky's ballads or the movie "Footloose," which portrayed the relationship between a priest's daughter and a city punk.

Six years have passed, and I still haven't freed myself from the burden of this appellation. I've only become more sophisticated about it, and I'm thinking about making it into a movie - camouflaged, of course. "The Rabbi's Daughter." In the end, it turns out that even in Steinberg's short story, the central conflict is with the mother. In that story, the daughter beseeches her mother to help her with her unwanted pregnancy, but there is "nobody to talk to." Who am I fooling? At least in the story, the daughter is brave enough to follow her heart. It's upsetting to think that the words from a short story from the beginning of the nineteenth century sound so familiar, so much like mine. "She didn't understand anything; Ima didn't understand anything." Maybe now, with Grandma's death, I'll finally come to terms with the fact that she wasn't capable of understanding.

And maybe that's what was so painful, that Friday night with Amy. In spite of the wicked suspicions against her, I was finally with someone to whom I wanted to belong, in Abba's court. And just then, of all times, I was asked to doubt. And doubt is a slippery slope, it's never self-contained, instead it's like an avalanche of snow, provoking and eroding all the emotions.

I stood behind Amy's straight back, and I felt like I was finally free from the eyes of the congregation. Just as they had examined my posture, now I could study the short, thin body in front of me, so different from Ima's. Unlike me, Ima took pride in her height. She had all kinds of foolish slogans on this topic, like, "Short people don't have the luxury of putting on weight, because if they do, they look awful, like boxes.

Without taking my eyes off Amy's brilliant white shirt, I felt tears welling up slowly, as if her presence, however silent, however emotionally damaged, was banishing all the ghosts I had collected over the years. As if her very essence created a kind of intensive care room where she could fix my life. And before I could open my mouth to shout out, "Look, Amy - this is where it all began," like the disabled shepherd's boy who didn't know how to pray on Yom Kippur and so whistled instead, I pulled myself together and buried my face in the siddur, skimming through the Mishnaic tractate "Pirkei Avot," crammed in the back of the siddur. I read, "Five years is the age for the study of Scripture, ten for the study of Mishnah, thirteen for observing commandments, fifteen for the study of Talmud, eighteen for the wedding canopy, twenty for pursuing a livelihood, thirty for full strength, forty for understanding, fifty for giving counsel, sixty for old age, seventy for a hoary head, eighty for extra strength, ninety for a bent stature, and a hundred as if dead and gone from the world." I pondered this curious timeline over and over again, thinking about how many years passed between each milestone. Maybe, like the silences that you were supposed to create in literature or music, it was the intervals that would teach me how to live. What was it that went bad between the age of five, when I loved the Torah stories, and the age of ten, when I turned my back on the books of the Mishnah and was crowned the Wild Daughter?

Or maybe nothing went bad. Only now do I dare to think this, now that Grandma has died, between the ages of eighty and ninety. Maybe I really did complete my designated task, and the prescription outlined by our sages is just another of society's vague promises, another way to create a myth. Career, marriage, children, retirement. I don't think life is so linear; it's more like a spiral, with its peaks and valleys. As a child, Ima, too, hated going to synagogue, but the upscale Conservative synagogue in New York had no patience for such nonsense. They instructed Ora, who was responsible for her on *Shabbatot*, to stop bringing her to services. And then here, in Israel, after moving south and after having me, Ima started to appreciate the house of worship and to attend regularly. Shortly thereafter, she was lured into reading the Torah, and has been the principal Torah reader every week since then. On Friday nights, she sits in her armchair and practices reciting the Torah notes in her strange accent, as if she were standing before an imaginary congregation such as the Park Avenue Synagogue, showing off both her new status as rabbi's wife and her independent decision to follow the laws of the Torah which she used to despise.

Before the *Amidah* prayer was finished, I slipped out the back door. I just stood there, feeling frustrated, looking for some way to change my ongoing, perhaps eternal, scream into a story that might be of interest to someone.

A dog walked past me, as if he knew exactly where he was heading. He stayed close to the sanctuary's eastern wall, stopping to sniff the exact spot where the Torah Ark stood. Just as everyone stood up and turned to the ark, asking to be saved, the dog raised its leg and peed, unaware that he was fulfilling my wish to scandalize the holy congregation as it opened its heart to God's Torah. There is no joy more wicked than that caused by someone else's misfortune, but I couldn't help smiling. If Abba had still been a photographer, I would have suggested that he photograph the back of the eastern walls of different synagogues, and try to determine if that is the preferred spot for living creatures, especially rebellious females, to urinate on. I returned to the sanctuary more relaxed, as if I was the one who had relieved herself.

After the *Aleinu* prayer, nobody sat down. We still had to count the *Omer*, which was approaching its end. Singing in unison, the members loudly declared their readiness to "count the sheaves." Again and again, I looked at the ambiguous sentence that appeared in small letters underneath the counting blessing, "Our shouts call out the eternity of kingship." Does the God of the Jews, the one I had quarreled with over my parents' attention, really hear our shouts, like the siddur says?

As she does every week, the president of the congregation, Emma, walked up to the lectern to make the announcements. Emma was a psychologist and a friend of Ima's. She and her husband Steven had come here from England, and therefore were somewhat different than the rest of my parent's American friends. I had the impression that Emma was eying Amy with some suspicion. I wondered if Steven had said something to her, despite the rules of patient-doctor confidentiality. But really, Abba was the client. Maybe in the end it would turn out that the essence of the whole Amy fiasco was the fact that it revealed something disturbing about Abba. Or Ima.

Emma concluded her remarks, instructed the congregants to turn to page twenty-four in their siddurim (the most thumbed-through page in the book), and walked down to the singing of *Adon Olam.* Grandma detained her with a prolonged handshake. She was the only one who really took pride in Abba's profession; it made her feel like she was still in the Diaspora, where the synagogue was the epicenter of Jewish life.

Hanoch, too, was happy with our lifestyle. Now he was the one studying to be a Conservative rabbi. With time, he would no doubt become one of the movement's leaders, thus completing the circle that my father had begun in 1974, when he realized that it was incumbent upon him to leave his job as a photographer and establish a religious movement that was different from anything else that had existed here at the time. The burning urge began after he had served in the IDF's *Hevra Kadisha,* the army's religious burial unit, in the Sinai Desert. There he discovered that Israeli soldiers didn't know how to recite the *Kaddish,* much less understand the Aramaic words that they were saying.

Maybe that's what motivated me to eulogize the dead. The first time I went to synagogue after my class trip to Poland, I instinctively knew that I had to join the mourners. All the talk about how countless victims had nobody to say *kaddish* in their memory made me stand up and recite it for them. Then came

Nirit. Her parents wouldn't enter a synagogue. And now Grandma. She has her daughters to mourn her.

That Friday night, Grandma stayed in her seat, waiting for the mad rush to the *Kiddush* table to die down. She clutched Amy's hand and told her to sit with her; she'd introduce her to the most important doctors in the south, she promised, not one of whom would ever leave the building without shaking her hand. Amy stayed seated, but you could tell from her face that she resented this Jane-Austen-like role that had been thrust upon her - to sit and smile like a little girl while Grandma introduced her to the most elite members of society. This would actually have been a good opportunity for Amy to meet Steven the psychiatrist. I wondered how Abba was planning to orchestrate that meeting.

Amy asked Grandma to excuse her while she went to the bathroom, and disappeared. I saw that when she passed Emma, she merely nodded to her, with uncharacteristic shame. I thought about how it wasn't right of me to assume that the two of them would like each other, so much so that the friendship that developed between them would squeeze out Ima. It was only then that I noticed how similar the names Emma, Amy and Ima were. I remained at Grandma's side, mostly because I didn't want to make idle conversation with my classmates about the two hot topics: The *Bagrut* and the army. I had nothing to add on either of those subjects. Emma approached us again, and Grandma made her usual joke, "You spoke nicely, even though I didn't understand a word." This was also the way she greeted Abba on Shabbat, by giving him a compliment, an incomplete one, of course, on its way to being an insult. I let Emma lead Grandma into the *Kiddush* room, and I kept my eye on Amy. I saw her leaning on the door. Her face looked frightened and pale, as if she were the rabbi's daughter from Tchernichovsky's ballad, moments before her death. I tried to figure out why her heart had grown so sad, and I was afraid that in some kind of symbiotic process I had infected her with my own fears and grudges, until I realized that perhaps someone else in the room had triggered this outbreak of her mysterious "illness." I scanned the room for any red-headed suspects, or maybe just any overconfident man, since she hadn't specified what it was about Binyamin that reminded her of her brother. Or perhaps it was only the acrid smells of Bamba and smoked fish that sent her running.

The way she leaned on the doorframe, as if she were a mezuzah, reminded me of a picture book I had loved as a child. It was one of a series of books that had come packaged together in a colorful cardboard box. All the books were about assorted characters from Jewish folktales. The nicest was the one about Hillel the Elder, who nearly froze to death when he climbed up to the rooftop to hear the voice of God. Of course all the stories were pedantic, but because the illustrations were somewhat surrealistic, they left something to the imagination. Stirring up inside me was the desire to cure Amy of her snow-covered illness and warm her back to health. I decided to show her where I kept the only Hebrew children's books I owned; they actually weren't mine, I shared them with the congregation. I took her by the hand and we went into Abba's office. The same one in which, that very afternoon, a Pandora's box about Amy had opened. Lucky for me, words don't leave traces.

The office was, and still is, jam-packed with books and photos, some of which Abba had taken himself, some of which were of his parents. As Amy noted, he had, in fact, run away as far as he could, but the fact remained that here, in the holy of holies, he was still a child needing his parents. I'm sure that the

Jewish God's "ratings" could have been higher if it would have been allowed to photograph events on Shabbat and Hag.

Amy made herself comfortable in Abba's swivel chair, reminding me of baby Moses reaching for a gold plate in Pharaoh's court and proving that he was fit to be king. She smiled again, illuminating the room like a string of lights, and began to spin around like a child. I left her and headed back to Grandma, who was telling Emma how Abba had stopped smoking and started running. When Abba turned thirty, the doctor told him that if he didn't get in shape, he wouldn't live to see his son become a Bar Mitzvah. She capped it off by saying that it was too bad her Freimele didn't have a doctor to stop him from moving to Israel. She knew I had no patience for her puerile anger at the country, and as soon as she saw me, she changed the subject. "Where's Amy?" she asked. "Did you notice what a beautiful voice she has? How my poor Freimele would have enjoyed her singing."

At the end of that long evening, Abba turned away from all the handshakes and joking, and he, too, asked where Amy was. I told him she was in the office, and he motioned to Emma, awkwardly and with some confusion, that they had to talk. They went off to confer, presumably to arrange her husband Steven's visit. I thought about how similar he and I were, and how rarely we acknowledge it.

When Grandma wasn't looking, Abba updated me. Steven had been called in to the hospital for an emergency, and would only be able to pay us a social visit on Saturday night. "Are you OK?" he asked, not waiting for a reply; maybe the real reason he asked was to assure himself that *he* was OK. With that same abruptness, he asked if I could manage with Grandma and Amy in the car, and got ready for his short walk home. But something stopped him, maybe remembering that as long as he was still within the confines of the synagogue, he was on duty. Perhaps he realized that even if there was something wrong with our guest, she still observed Shabbat, and he invited her to walk with him.

When we visited Nebraska, I used to get very confused when, on Friday nights, after we were all clean and polished, we would pile into Grandpa's car and drive to synagogue. It's too bad nobody bothered to explain the Conservative ruling that allowed people living outside of Israel to drive to synagogue if they lived too far to walk. I was a ten-year-old girl who hadn't seen her mother for four months. I had suddenly discovered a real family of new uncles and aunts who didn't think I was the least bit troublesome, and, moreover, were allowed to drive on Shabbat. And if they had explained it to me, would it have made any difference? Can you explain laws - or the breaking of laws - to children? I think it would be futile, like when you show kids how a card trick is done and they continue to believe in magic and want to see it over and over again.

After Amy and Abba left, I slowly made my way to the car, accompanied by Grandma, my personal bodyguard. I was even happier than usual to leave the synagogue, which I had felt, earlier that evening, was physically strangling me. As I walked, I looked at the dedication in the book I had received. Abba had inscribed the book with the first verse of *The Path of the Just,* by Rabbi Moshe Chaim Luzzatto. "The foundation of saintliness and the root of perfection in the service of God lie in a man's coming to see clearly, and to recognize as a truth, the nature of his duty in the world and the end towards which he should direct his vision and his aspiration in all of his labors all the days of his life."

So much is expected of a person: to know every day where she is trying to go. I never understood why my parents didn't send me to a religious school. Pluralistic education might be a good catchphrase, but for raising children, you need something a little tidier. Of course, as a child I didn't parse it this way, but I certainly resented my parents for raising me in the midst of such complexity. Unlike Don Quixote, who battled with windmills, we couldn't even say what it was that we were fighting against.

Nine

According to tradition, a person is given a second soul on Shabbat. In our case, it looked like what we got was a second mouth. Perhaps food is at the epicenter of every Jewish family; like Alan King said about the Jewish holidays, "They tried to kill us; we won; let's eat."

In our house, our wars were domestic, too. Hanoch would tell everyone that I was eating with my hands, and that this just proved what he'd been claiming all along, that I was a Bedouin who had been abandoned in a garbage can. I had a hard time explaining the urge to put my hands into my food, and the special taste my fingers conferred on whatever it was I was eating, and so I was happy when Amy said that in the Talmud, nobody less than Rav Huna himself extolled the virtues of eating with one's hands.

"He found his father eating porridge with his finger, and he asked, 'Why is my master eating with his hands?' He said to his son, 'Porridge that is eaten with the finger tastes better, how much more so with two fingers, how much more so with three.' "

It's been a long time since all three of us siblings have been under one roof. New players joined the cast. First Effie, then sweet little Evyatar, who was such a long baby that the nurse joked that she hoped the newborn ward had a crib big enough to hold him.

And now the star of the show has been taken from us. It was only for Grandma's sake that, in recent years, we would try to make time in our busy lives to come together for Shabbat. The truth is, it was Grandma who made food into an issue. Specifically, her habit of criticizing everything Ima cooked and comparing it to Abba's savory dishes led to a never-ending discussion of food. She herself used to collect all the leftover bits of food as if she were a Holocaust survivor, as if there wasn't enough to go around. She passed that trait onto her daughters, who would walk out of restaurants with their pockets stuffed with small packets of condiments, hand towels, tiny tubs of jam and butter, and anything else they paid for but didn't use. I know this sounds terrible, but sometimes I thought it was a pity that Grandma wasn't actually a survivor. Then, at least, there would be some scientific or psychological basis for our family's complicated relationship with anything having to do with food.

When Amy was staying with us, Grandma even asked her how she, as a psychologist, explained the fact that so many families had issues with food. At first, Amy didn't play her designated role, and instead looked at Abba, who was dunking his cookie in his mug (he didn't drink tea) and nibbling it hungrily, expertly filtering out anything he didn't want to hear. Maybe he was waiting, like an undercover detective, for Amy to fall into some psychological trap.

Grandma, who could tell that her question wasn't being addressed, decided to divulge everything that was on her mind. "When Ora was little, she wouldn't eat anything unless it was very sweet or very salty. It was hopeless. I'd get so desperate that in the end I'd put her on her tricycle and tell her to ride around the table, and every time she passed me, I'd stick a spoonful of something healthy into her mouth. And Ruth? She ate like a little piglet. And there's no denying it! Look at how Ora's whole family is thin. I don't really understand how genes work."

I looked at Grandma, and I, too, tried to understand the concept of genes; how they traveled through the autostrada of the umbilical cord and dispersed, seemingly randomly. With my thick lips and my keen, narrow eyes, I resembled her the most. She believed that I was the most talented person in the family, and she loved all the silly plays I used to put on in the backyard. In her mind I could do no wrong, and if it weren't for my one crooked tooth, I could have been a model. Too bad I didn't inherit her willpower. She even managed to steer the conversation back to food by telling Amy how, as a child, I would carefully crack open sunflower seeds with my teeth, like a diligent bird. Of course she equated my diligence with her own, describing how I would take each seed out of its shell and immediately hide it from the outstretched hands of my lazy family members as they tried to loot the spoils. Then, after stashing the seeds in dried apricot, I would give them out, with a generosity that reminded her of her daughter Ora.

When Amy finally deigned to reply, all she did was quote the Talmud. "A man must always take pains to provide wheat for his family. There is no strife in a household except for the matter of wheat," and she looked to my father for confirmation that her words were accurate. Abba nodded, adding that in that same discourse there was another aphorism asserting that when the pitcher is empty, strife comes knocking at the door.

I was surprised, since food was part of the human experience, and everybody ate, why did the Talmud have to add that bit about strife? Abba said that was true, but, like everything else that people needed and were responsible for, food could get us into trouble. Take the story of the Garden of Eden. If there weren't a desire for food, there wouldn't have been a story, and we would never have left.

Amy, who until then had resisted answering Grandma's innocent question about why families have such a complex relationship with food, began by saying, "Think about the deeper side of things, the dark side. You're right, it's in our nature; but food is at the core of the human tragedy. We can't just hunt and gather our food, we have to process it in order to make it edible. Yet, the hunger remains."

She went on as though talking to herself, "It really is dark. The story of a family that fights over food. After all, your family feeds you during childhood, then it starts to eat you, and then you have to get up and leave … and to think that that's at the core of family, of every single family…."

"No need to exaggerate." Abba cut off her vilification of the family structure. He didn't stop there, though; he added that in the stories of our forefathers, too, the motif of food played a central role in the family's power dynamic. Like when the Jews went down to Egypt because of the famine, or the twins fought over the lentil stew. Because the Bible stories were fresh in my mind from studying for the *Bagrut,* I mentioned that according to the Torah, Isaac loved Esau because he liked the food that Esau would bring back from his hunt. "Love that's dependent on food," I joked, and I speculated that the reason Isaac loved meat so much was that every piece of meat he ate was a kind of victory that echoed back to the most influential event of his life, the *Akedah,* in which his life was spared and the ram was sacrificed in his place.

Tonight, when we siblings are all gathered here, Ima's chair looks unusually lonely. Never, not once, did anyone sit there in her absence. Maybe Amy had sat in it when she was here, and Grandma had told her to move. I looked at all the other diners sitting around our Shabbat table, about to open their mouths. Mostly, I looked at my sister and brother who hadn't witnessed the whole Amy saga, and what had been revealed in its wake. In a large crater, you can see the different colors in different layers of the earth. People try to collect the sand in glass bottles so they can preserve the sequence of colors, but just as I look at these people and try to figure out who had a greater influence on me, my siblings or my parents, I realize that like looking at a scabbed-over wound, it's hard to know what came from what, or from whom. Besides, in most sibling stories, almost all of the arguments are over parental attention.

Whenever Ima was away and it was the right season, Abba would make chicken with mango, and tonight, despite the mourning, was no exception. Ima had become allergic to mango at a very late age, and the thought that it might happen to me, too, scared me. This late-stage allergy added yet another layer to our complicated relationship with food. Ima felt compelled to eat as many foods as possible, just in case, God forbid, she would have to stay away from them someday. I too never passed up a mango, even if it was starting to rot. Ora had the opposite approach to food. She taught her children not to see themselves as garbage cans, and was always saying, "Don't throw it in, throw it out."

Evyatar calls my sister's stomach "baby sister," and even though Effy thinks it's bad luck, they start nonetheless discussing possible names for the baby. I happen to like the name Sara, Grandma's Hebrew name, even though I can't even begin to picture myself as a mother. Despite the fact that they keep a religious home, Avigail and Effy aren't willing to call her Sara. They think it sounds too old-fashioned.

Deciding on a name, creating something new in the world, still strikes me as impossible. And the truth is, in my screenwriting class, the hardest part is to give my characters a will and autonomy.

And maybe that's why I'm reminded of the whole Amy saga, because that was when I resolved to want something. Her presence, like a sedative before a dental procedure, softened me, encouraged me. I remember the scene very well. It was

Friday night. An awareness of Amy's messy and perhaps pathological room was floating in the air, and it was making Abba tense. Grandma asked if I was planning on going out that night, and I responded that I still didn't know. Abba said he'd prefer it if I didn't go out, and tried to give me an intimidating look so I would understand that his "preference" was actually a forbiddance, and that he meant what he was saying. I could tell from how hard he was trying that it was actually a look of fear, as though he was afraid of staying home alone with Amy, and I said, again, that I didn't know. Abba couldn't forbid me to go out; that was crossing the line. Since he wasn't very good at expressing his thoughts without words, silence prevailed. I decided to use that silence to my advantage, and announced that I had decided to do a year of service.

"Oh lord," Abba blurted out. Amy asked what "a year of service" was.

"Yes, really, what's so important that she has to put her life on hold for a year?" Grandma added, ignoring Amy's question. Perhaps she thought that "putting her life on hold for a year" was enough of an explanation.

"That's exactly what it is. It's postponing the army for a year," I confirmed, choosing my words carefully. "It's a chance to give something back to the community. You spend a year living in an underprivileged neighborhood, working at a recreation center or volunteering for the Scouts, whatever they need most."

Grandma cut me off. "If what you want to do is 'help where they need you,' you can help the elderly. You don't have to postpone the army for that, you could do that with me, which you always seem to forget."

I tilted my head in her direction to see if she was serious. "It's not the same thing," I said. "These people are deprived. They're poor."

"So am I," Grandma persisted, now with a distinct note of humor.

"And they're stuck in the middle of nowhere!" I shouted with authority.

"We're not exactly living on Fifth Avenue ourselves." She was joking, but I was trying to have a serious conversation.

"Having a whole group actually living in the towns is essential. There are six or seven of us, and we serve as a kind of model community. Our relationship with the rest of the town is very casual; we just want to give people another perspective on youth." Listening to my own attempts at persuasion, I was suddenly a little skeptical that a person like me, who dreamed about someone's shoulder just so she could cry on it, could help an entire town. Nonetheless, I continued to rehash every word of what the leaders had told us.

Abba didn't know what to say. He asked, as if he was channeling Ima's spirit, "And who's funding this year of service?"

"I still don't know all the details, but don't worry, the Scouts pay for everything."

"And what if you lose your spot in the army?" Abba, surprising me with his knowledge of the situation, boasted to Amy, "She went through a rigorous selection process and was accepted as an educational instructor." All of a sudden, it felt good to have Abba back in his role as concerned father, as the one who bought me my own Legos, who took me to the Book fair and bought me pink cotton candy that got tangled in my hair.

"How can you possibly object to a year of service? It's the most Jewish thing I can do at my age, or any age, really. What's better than giving something back, repairing the social fabric of this country?"

Of course, this shot from the hip invalidated the core of Abba's argument, but, he said, he still thought this was too big a step and I would regret it, "just like you did on the delegation," invoking what was then the biggest embarrassment of my life.

Abba accepted my secular lifestyle, but he felt that social activism played too large a role within that lifestyle, and that I, like him, would only find true happiness through reading books and studying at the university, or, he added as an afterthought, "even through a career in film." I had to take my oratory talent, he said, and invest it in getting a doctorate or entering academia. I hoped that perhaps Amy would point out how fixated he was on the cerebral, but she and Grandma just listened, as if they were trying to give us some familial privacy.

Confidently, I replied that I wanted him to come hear the lecture about postponing my army service that was going to be given in Beersheba, and although the look on his face attested to his lack of enthusiasm, he agreed and I went to wash the dishes as if it was part of the deal.

Grandma came into the kitchen and saw me washing dishes in my funny way, in which I tried my best to avoid touching the dirt. Ima used to get so angry at how long it took me to soak, scrape, soap, and finally rinse the dishes that she would sometimes take over in the middle, hauling me over the coals for wasting water.

Inspired by Amy, I contemplated the ghosts from Grandma's Hungarian childhood that had turned her into such a hard-headed woman. Never towards us, though, her grandchildren.

At the time, I had no idea what else, other than her love for us, was behind her constant willingness to support Ima and Abba in various ways, even though she was not wealthy. I would give a lot to forget the answer I received, an answer that now, with her death, is likely to rise up from the shadows and hurt other people.

Grandma continued to stand in the kitchen doorway, and it looked like she wanted to say something important, maybe even confidential, but couldn't find the right words. Finally, she said, "Sweetie-pie," in a soft voice - a stark contrast to her rough hands that would carefully stuff rice into peppers - and left.

Now it's Friday night without Grandma. There's nobody I need to drive home. I offer to do the dishes. My sister and Effi go upstairs to put Evyatar to sleep, and Abba and Hanoch discuss a Talmudic tractate. Who would have believed that, as a boy in Nebraska, Abba would sneak away on Shabbat and play football, a ruse that ended when he came home one day with a broken arm? At least my rebellion was out in the open.

As if a bell had rung, we all gathered around the table for dessert and Grace after Meals. Now, in the absence of Grandma, we were all united, or at least that's how it appeared. At around this time she would most likely be repeating one of her favorite sayings, "Nine rabbis don't make a *minyan,* but ten cobblers do!" She was referring to something she loved, arriving at synagogue at the last possible minute to complete a *minyan,* a quorum required for prayer services.

When Amy was here, we got into a discussion of the "*Gomel*" blessing, a blessing of gratitude recited by anyone who has emerged safely from a dangerous situation. This was at a time when our suspicions about Amy hovered above her like a cloud. She asked what time we read the Torah, so she could *"bentch Gomel."* I had never heard of this blessing, and I asked her about it. She clutched her seahorse, closed her eyes, and quoted, "Four kinds of people need to be thankful: those who have crossed the ocean, those who have walked through the desert, those who have been released from prison, and those who were sick and have recovered."

Her answer befuddled me even more, and I looked at Abba. He said, slowly, "It's a blessing that is recited on Shabbat, after Torah reading. Anyone who was sick or in an accident, anyone who falls into one of the categories that Amy just mentioned, stands up in front of the congregation and thanks God for bestowing goodness upon him and rescuing him from his predicament."

I thought it was odd that I had never noticed this blessing before, or at least hadn't known its name. Grandma, who didn't know about Amy's delicate position, didn't hesitate to ask her why she wanted to say the blessing, and Amy replied that she was just so happy to be here, and that she felt like someone who had crossed a vast desert and finally reached an outpost that was not merely a mirage.

I wondered how someone who just got out of prison could stand in front of the congregation and recite a blessing thanking God for His "divine kindness." What if he had to go back to jail? Amy said it was an excellent question, and added that in modern discourse, a similar question was asked regarding mentally ill people who were cured; after all, those kinds of illnesses were apt to come back, and then what? Were we talking about an endless game of ping-pong, going back and forth between gratitude and hospitalization? Abba and I perked up, as if we were finally getting the information we'd been waiting for. I had seen Binyamin's favorite movie, "Birdy," so many times, and from what I could tell, a mentally ill person was something concrete, something defined. I couldn't imagine a mentally ill person entering our synagogue, or for that matter any synagogue, just to recite the *Gomel* blessing. The thought that Amy might do exactly that the next day seemed as far-fetched as the thought of me standing under the marriage canopy one day with my groom.

Abba, who must have been trying to loosen Amy's tongue, continued to think out loud.

"Right. And what about people who attempted suicide and were saved from themselves; do they recite the blessing themselves, or does their family? After all, the family was saved from the death of a loved one."

"That's a nice idea," I said, so that Amy wouldn't have to respond, "that your family can say the blessing instead of you." I was reminded of an old fantasy of mine in which I had a robot that could follow the commandments for me.

It's interesting that it wasn't this discussion that irked me, but what happened at the end of the evening, when Amy swung the door open for Grandma and said, "In Brazil, the custom is to hold the door open only if you want someone to return." Grandma smiled and leaned on her as she went down the outside steps that she detested so much, and I couldn't help thinking that maybe there really was something strange about Amy. On the one hand, she had all her Talmudic quotations; on the other hand, there were her folksy customs and, especially, her desperate and boundless yearning to be unique, yet part of our family. Fortunately for her, my resentment about her conduct was pushed to the back of my mind after the conversation I had with Grandma when I drove her home.

Now, were it not for the knock on the front door that caused the whole family to instinctively look at me, we would surely have finished off all the desserts, forgetting to leave

Evyatar the sweetest ones which he loved so much. The death notices I had hung up had summoned Binyamin and Liat. I didn't even know they were in the country. When I was traveling abroad, they were working together in Tel Aviv. Then one night, according to Liat, they suddenly realized that one was the lid to the other's pot. They moved to New York to study law, far from their shared past, a past which also included me.

Ten

Everyone was thrilled to see Binyamin and Liat, my childhood friends, who were now sitting here wearing the wedding rings they'd purchased in Lower Manhattan, near City Hall. Everyone, that is, except me. I felt like I was witnessing a forbidden romance. Hanoch was particularly pleased. Even though I could feel his heart pinch, he kept repeating how happy he was for them, and how people never know where relationships would lead them. I tried to determine if he was pouring salt on my wounds to help him cope with his own jealousy, but he seemed to be perfectly content relying on some mysterious natural law which dictated that one day, he, too, would be saved from his longtime bachelorhood. Moreover, I reminded myself, he and the rest of my family didn't know about the romance, or more accurately, the unfortunate incident, that had involved a different combination of people in our trio.

Like in the card game "War," I felt that the stack of secrets in my hand was about to explode, and that any minute I would lose control and the cards would scatter in every direction. I wanted to get out of this endless game. If Grandma were here, I would have used her as an excuse and driven her home, like I so often did. While the rest of them were swept up in a conversation about New York, I remembered that while Grandma usually served as a stabilizing anchor for me, on that Friday night with Amy, she was the one who played an unexpected card.

"So you're going out later?" she asked as I started the car.

"Why?" I asked suspiciously. Then I added, "Yes, definitely, I don't know yet."

"Don't go out." Grandma liked to get all emotional on me and tell me how while I was out having fun, she would be all alone with the television, but this time I wasn't sure of her motives. I didn't know if Abba had had a chance to tell her Amy's story, so I asked her if she was worried about the *bagruyot*.

"It's not that." Grandma gave a twisted smile, and continued to embroider her peculiar thread of words, watching me closely the whole time. "Do you know when Abba first went to America?"

"What do you mean, went to America? That's where he's from. He goes back almost every year...."

Grandma cut me off as I was indulging in my habit of answering a question by searching for the right words, which was really just a veiled attempt to understand the question.

"No, I don't mean now. I'm talking about back then, when they moved here in sixty-seven, after the war. It was ten years before they went back."

I had never thought about it. Just like children can't believe that the world existed before they were born. In my mind, Abba and Ima were always going to America, and the only problem was that their trips weren't accompanied by fanfare or big send-offs like my friends' families. It's strange to think that there was a period when they didn't go, and suddenly I remembered Ora's old and renowned anger over the fact that her younger sister, her only sibling, didn't go to her wedding or to the *brit* of her eldest son because the tickets were too expensive.

Grandma continued, "After all, they were so poor, and even though there were relatively cheap tickets available through Iceland - yes, Iceland - look out! You almost ran over a cat - they didn't have enough money for the return trip."

"So? Did you give Abba money for a ticket?" I had finally managed to regain my focus, and I was sure that Grandma was going to talk about how much she contributed to the family's income. Maybe she wanted to tell me about her fear that Amy might run away with the silver.

"No, not at all. I mean, you know that before you were born, before your family moved to the south for your mother's job at the university and your father established our wonderful congregation here, he essentially brought the Conservative movement to Israel."

This series of well-known facts that were part of the biography I loathed so much didn't make things any clearer, and Grandma didn't help matters when she concluded, "So after about two years, they invited him to come to America to give a presentation about the movement in Israel, all expenses paid."

"OK...." I tried to figure out if we were still talking about money.

"And on this trip, after ten years of not leaving the country, he met a woman. Someone very similar to Amy."

"What do you mean, he met?"

"He met. Someone very similar to your mother." My face must have shown that I was trying to understand if she meant Amy or Ima, because the face she made in response seemed to be saying that these two women were similar to each other. She repeated the incomprehensible story, "Similar to your mother. Smart and funny and pretty. But she didn't have kids, she just sat in the seat next to your Abba, drawing pictures of clouds."

"What exactly do you mean by 'met'?" I wasn't trying to raise my voice, but I didn't understand why she was telling me this. And how did she even know about this airborne encounter? And what the hell did she mean by the word 'met'?

Grandma continued to be vague, "I'm not saying that something's going to happen with Amy, I'm just a little concerned. She has a certain softness that your mother will never have. And she speaks wisely, but in moderation."

I didn't understand what she wanted from me, or, for that matter, what any of them wanted. And why was she telling me this? Because she was old and bored?

"Abba had an affair?" There was no other way to phrase what Grandma was saying, even if it sounded like the most outlandish thing in the world. What else didn't I know about my past, which suddenly seemed like a braid of pain, joy and happenstance, entangled and inseparable?

"No, not an affair. Not exactly. Like I said, he met her. She had a very unusual presence. Like Amy, do you see? That's why I was remembering it. And it wasn't good for your mother, because of the awkward circumstances. After a while, your mother, I think it was in the beginning of seventy-seven, also went to America for the first time. To get some air. And it was because of you, because you needed someone to look after you, that I came here and dodged one of the worst blizzards ever to hit the east coast."

There was too much information flowing in my direction, and I didn't know how to sift through it and distill it afresh, a process Ima taught me for deciphering the "unseen passages." Too many questions were pursuing me, and I couldn't focus.

"And what happened?" A child's question.

"Well, actually, something tragic happened. Your mother flew to the States, I think it was for a month, maybe two. And your father went, too, to reconcile or I don't know what, because she was with Ora the whole time. A while after they came back, Rebecca, who was on another visit in Israel, was killed in a car accident."

Grandma smiled at the guard of her miniature village, and just as he lifted the gate, she concluded, "And that was that. You know that big book you have, the white one with all the pictures from the Bible? That's her book, and your father edited it after her death. Her parents had a lot of money."

I stopped next to Grandma's house, which suddenly looked like an enchanted shack. Her stories made me nauseous. I thought that maybe, like Ima, I had developed a mango allergy overnight.

While I got out of the car and escorted Grandma to her door, she continued to tell me, eagerly, about Abba's financial misjudgment. He had to decide if he wanted to receive royalties for editing the book and writing its preface, which he dedicated to Rebecca, or immediately transferring money into his bank account, five hundred dollars' cash, which at the time was a fortune.

"It's too bad he didn't ask for my advice. Clearly, there was something mystical about her pictures, something unique, and of course there was the fact that she was an American Zionist who died in Israel. The book was published in several editions. It's still in print."

"Did she also illustrate children's books?" I was thinking about the series of rabbinic legends that I loved so much.

"You never heard this story?" Grandma was surprised, and at the same time was trying to demonstrate empathy, both because of the information that had been heaped upon me, and because she was afraid she might be blamed for divulging the secret.

"No," I said, my voice full of accusations. Then, trying to tone down my response, I repeated it, this time more gently. I had noticed that we owned several copies of that big white book, but I hadn't known how closely it was connected to us.

We reached Grandma's door, and she told me that tomorrow, she would walk to the synagogue. With feigned indifference, she added that if I had the energy to go out and have fun, I should certainly go.

I knew that in an instant I could shift her whole way of thinking; I could shatter her peace of mind. I could have told her about the mental illness that Abba was ascribing to Amy. I felt like something inside me had cracked, and I had lost the ability to be coherent.

"So did Abba have an affair?"

Grandma had already stepped inside her house, and, without hesitation, said no. Then she said it was more significant than "a simple affair," because it left in its wake a charged emotional atmosphere in the house. I nodded in agreement, as if it were a matter of moving the furniture around.

I waved goodbye to show her that everything was fine, despite the fact that I was burdened with a sense of uncertainty, the same way I'd felt after hearing Liat's vague account of the loss of her virginity with Elad. We never mentioned it again, and I never found out if it still hurt, or how often they did it, or whether they did it in her house, too, or just in Elad's room in the kibbutz where they had all the privacy in the world.

Maybe if she had described her first time, we wouldn't be so far apart, and I would have a better role model. And maybe it's actually because she didn't talk that I had no grounds for comparison, and I could be content with the event that had taken place, which was both casual and significant at the same time.

Now I look at our old trio and think about how time has changed us into a trio of monkeys, with one who didn't speak, one who didn't hear, and one who didn't see. On the surface, it seemed like I was the one who had lost the game; after all, I did leave the trio. At the same time, if Liat didn't know how I lost my virginity, she was one card short. It was hard to believe that as close as we were, we still had tiny seedlings of secrets.

In our youth, she couldn't understand what she thought of as "my obsession" - my attraction to Eren Shonsky. I couldn't explain to her that my fixation was a substitute for her Elad. For three years, I didn't have the nerve to tell anyone, including Liat, how much I loved him. And then, while I was with the delegation, she unknowingly stole him from me, and from the first day of senior year, I had to fill my head with "Eren Shonsky," an alternate "Elad." It's true, maybe I went a little overboard with my constant chattering about him, but even Liat was impressed by how he and I very cautiously reached the point where we had regular and meaningful conversations.

I look at their partnership, the newlyweds, and I'm reminded of all the things Liat said over time about the carrot-head who was now her husband, and of the many things she envied about the intimate, unquestioned friendship he and I shared for so many years.

That evening, after Grandma galvanized my imagination with all her talk about Abba's extramarital affair, I didn't want to go back home. As if it would make the time stretch out, I took the detour past my friends' houses and listened to the classical music that Ima always had on, hoping the sounds would clear my mind. They didn't.

When I reached Binyamin's house, I stopped. I had no idea what I wanted to say. His bedroom light was on, and I honked gently. He peeked out of the porch off his room, and I could see that he wasn't wearing a shirt. I was dying to tell him the disturbing news, as if the fact that we were in pre-school together meant that he would remember if I was particularly troubled in the winter of '78.

He was sweaty; I'd caught him in the middle of his work-out. My confusion made me regret my decision. In spite of everything, his parents still attended my father's Bible class, and despite our close friendship, we had never exchanged embarrassing stories about our parents.

Binyamin stood there and looked at me; instead of spouting words, I seemed to be swallowing them.

"What's up?" he asked leisurely.

"I just dropped off the old lady." I had never called her that, but Binyamin didn't comment. I asked if we were going to go out with Liat and Elad. There was no reason to specify a venue, since the only place we ever went at that time was the pub in Eren Shonsky's kibbutz.

Binyamin said yes, and asked which car I wanted to take, but then immediately decided we should take mine, because he wanted to dance. In order for Binyamin to dance, he had to drink a lot of alcohol to overcome his inhibitions. I couldn't understand how that could be an issue in someone with so much self-confidence. I didn't like him when he was drunk.

He asked if I wanted to hang out with him until it was time to go, but I was scared that the whole truth would come surging out of me, and I said I'd pass the time with Amy.

"Oh, she's still with you?" He tensed up and added, "When is your mother coming back?"

"Why do you ask? She can still be our guest when my mother is here."

"Of course she can. No, it's just that you'll have two mothers at home."

"That's all I need," I responded reflexively, even though I'm not sure that's what I meant. Mostly I was feeling the same despair that Sara the rabbi's daughter must have felt when she asked her mother to help her with her pregnancy.

"Hey, didn't you say you'd find out what all that business with the doorway was about?"

"It wasn't about anything. She has a few quirks, but mostly she's awesome. She has this brother, a rabbi, who lives in Israel; they're not in touch anymore. Maybe you reminded her of him."

"Oh, well, that's a good reason for slamming the door in a person's face." His cheeks turned red, as if they were reliving the experience. His offended expression gave me a glimpse into his vulnerable interior.

"What do you want from me? I don't know how to find out. It feels too sensitive, too embarrassing, to bring it up out of the blue."

Because he was so angry, there was no way I was going to tell him about Abba's concern for Amy's sanity.

"Look for a way to weave it into the conversation. Do what is done in judo. Use your opponent's momentum and energy to flip him upside-down."

"I'll try," I said with a crooked smile, and I turned on the ignition.

Now, I'm trying to decide if it's my imagination, or if he really is looking at me with those same appraising eyes he had back then. Like Grandma, Binyamin also thought I was capable of achieving greatness.

When I got home that evening, the front door was locked, and in light of Grandma's story, all kinds of suspicions leaped to mind. When I stuck my key into the keyhole, I realized that it wasn't pushing through to the other side of the door.

I had no choice but to knock, but before I had a chance to generate any more suspicions, Abba opened the door and explained that Amy, not knowing the house protocol, had locked the door. Inside, nothing looked out of the ordinary. On the dining room table were two beers, a pile of books, and a bowl of popcorn that Abba had prepared before Shabbat - all perfectly normal.

I decided to set aside Grandma's bizarre speculations and go up to my room; she had said, after all, that he hadn't had an affair. Yes, Abba had shown an interest in Amy from the beginning, but not in an overtly romantic way, and definitely not now that this can of worms had been opened.

Abba asked why I was so late, and said he hoped I wasn't planning on going out again. I desperately wanted to fling his betrayal in his face, to wave it like a banner and let the pieces fall where they may, like in a game of pick-up-sticks. I wanted to ask him if the Conservative movement made special allowances for cheating on one' s spouse, if there was a middle-of-the-road way to look at it. The thought of confronting him, of demanding an unambiguous explanation, was so unbearable and so unnatural that I had to retreat to safety, the way a dog would take refuge in his dog house, and respond with a sentence that was rarely spoken in our house, "I don't know."

I explained that I had gone to visit Binyamin, and I was on my way up the stairs when I saw something that sent me right back to the dining room table. Rebecca Klein's art book was sitting there, shimmering in front of me, reminding me, as it always did, of a box of instant vanilla pudding, a food I had loved since childhood.

Amy didn't notice me walking towards the book, transfixed as a zombie. I picked it up gently, as if it might crumble to bits with the slightest touch.

"Your father said he remembers her as having a big heart."

"Did you know her?" I asked immediately.

Amy shook her head to indicate that she didn't and explained. "Your father and I talked about the alien fire that consumed Aaron and Elisheva's sons. Your father took this book out to show me Rebecca's powerful depiction of fire and tell me how special she was."

Amy took the book from me and opened it to the picture of the blue flames. Our gazes sunk into the mesmerizing picture, when suddenly the sound of someone flushing the toilet startled me - and only me - as if I'd been caught looking at pornography. I realized how challenging it must have been for Amy, being so sensitive to noise.

Abba looked at the book that the two of us were holding, as if we were fighting over it, and said to me, "You probably don't remember Rebecca. You were too young. I think Hanoch and Avigail remember. She's the one who gave Avigail the doll's head. Remember that blonde doll's head? You and Avigail used to play with her hair."

"What? When did she give her that doll?" I asked, genuinely curious. I'd always thought that Ora gave it to Avigail so she would feel feminine despite the fact that Ima had cut off all her hair.

"Rebecca Klein, she was a very good friend of mine. Yes, she visited us, several times. We took her hiking in the craters and to the Dead Sea. She loved my desert photographs, and would draw pictures based on the photos. You were little. You must have stayed home with Ima."

"And where is she now?" I asked somewhat cruelly, maybe in an attempt to unearth a trace of shame or excessive affection.

"She died in a car accident. On the old road to Haifa. A truck overturned on her; it was a real tragedy. She was an unusually independent and gifted woman. Fortunately, like Emily Dickinson, she had organized her collection of sketches before she died, as if she knew something might happen to her. She wrote down all her various ideas for books. So her work was almost ready for publication after her death."

I would have interrogated him some more about this woman whom I had never heard of until a few hours earlier, and whose color now flooded the room, but Amy said, somewhat bitterly, "Emily Dickinson did that because she was bored and rarely left her house, other than going to the post office to send out her poems and letters. It's because of her listlessness that we have amazing poems like 'How Happy is the Little Stone.' "

They launched into a discussion of Emily Dickinson, whose poems I didn't really know, and I thought about what would happen if I died tomorrow. It was not the contemplative, what-is-the-meaning-of-life kind of thinking. Rather it was whether or not it would be possible to piece together the story of my life from my journals, and from the various scraps of paper on which I'd scribbled unconnected words. And if it was possible, would it serve a purpose? After all, a word can never represent a table, or the tree from which the table is constructed, and I barely represent myself. Would anyone ever be able to truly read me? I knew Abba wanted me to stay with them, and yet I left them to their literary discourse and went upstairs to call Liat. There was no answer.

I felt like listening to music, but on Shabbat, I followed my family's custom and refrained from using anything electric that wasn't in the spirit of Shabbat. It's true, I could have listened with headphones, but I didn't bother, because honestly, music wasn't one of my passions. So, instead of actually playing the music, I picked up the CD of the *avant garde* rock band Carmela Gross Vagner. I had never really gotten used to their style, and I had to admit to myself that I only bought it because of peer pressure.

I opened the plastic case and removed the cover, which I knew well. The face on the top belonged to the band's guitarist, and resembled the portrait of my heartthrob Eren Shonsky. They had the same thin, cherry-red lips and a commanding expression, like that of Superman; an expression that didn't seem to belong to the real world, a slightly alienated look that accentuated the chiseled cheekbones. A look you might see on a classical Greek statue.

The first time I had an opportunity to chat with him, we talked about film. It started when I asked him why he never danced. "I like to watch," he said, which, in addition to his perfect, mysterious appearance, confirmed that I had made the right choice. "Like watching a movie," we laughed in agreement, and we decided that someday, I would write movies and he would star in them. When I told him about my regular movie dates with my father, he asked what my father did for a living, and for the first time in my life, I lied about it. Knowingly and strategically, I said that he was a professor of film, and that twice a week he taught a class at Sam Spiegel, the new film school that had just opened in Jerusalem.

I took the CD cover that I had studied to death, and lay down on my bed. I felt like a gumdrop had been inserted between my legs, and that it was shifting shape and stretching inside me.

As I studied the picture, I grew embarrassed by the pleasure it was bringing me, so I sat up on the bed and decided to write a story. What I should have done was to write about Amy, make up an exotic story about her life and a mysterious explanation for why she came to us, of all people; maybe a saga of revenge between siblings within the rabbinic world, a story of suspense in the manner of Agatha Christie. But of course, as always, I gave in to temptation and wrote about myself, and about the love that awaited me in the wee hours of the morning at Eren Shonsky's faraway kibbutz.

I scooted closer to the wall so I could lean against it more comfortably, and I noticed that I was sitting on something. If I had been a princess, maybe I would have been lucky enough to find some kind of treasure hidden among the rickety bedsprings that had been broken since the time Liat and Hanoch jumped on it (Hanoch had blamed me). But I wasn't a princess, and there weren't any peas underneath me. What was underneath me, was the shimmering Buddha, his face both smiling and serious, sitting there with mesmerizing tranquility. On the back of the book, it said that the word "Buddha" meant "The awakened one," and that the title was originally given to an Indian named Siddhartha Gautama who had woken up to reality. Something in his smile invited me to browse through the introduction.

About two hundred years after the Buddha's death, Buddhism split into different factions. The Tibetans believe in personal enlightenment, which would help the rest of humanity be redeemed. This sounded a lot more appealing than observing six hundred and thirteen *mitzvot,* commandments, that didn't get you anywhere, so I read on. "In order to reach enlightenment, we must work on our collective consciousness and develop universal mercy and love for all. And in order to do this, we must train our thought and consciousness that all living creatures are our mother." I reread this sentence to see if the author was serious.

It said, in black and white, that because we'd undergone countless reincarnations in the past, we had countless births, and thus we have countless mothers. And, the author asks, where are these mothers now? "All living creatures," he replies, "are our mother." The more I read, the more I understood that this was said in complete earnestness, and that, in language that was Chinese to me, in every sense of the word, the author explained that it would be wrong to think that all the mothers from our previous incarnations stopped being our mothers only because it had been a long time since they had to care for us in a hands-on way. He reasoned that if our mother were to die today, we would still relate to her as our mother, we'd still pray for her happiness wherever she might be. The same was true for mothers from previous lives who were essentially still our mothers, the only difference being that they didn't recognize us because of the physical transformations we'd undergone.

Just like in the summaries before the tests, I recited the material to myself in simple language to make sure I understood. "In every incarnation, I had a mother. If that's true, then where's my mother now?"

The book concluded with the assertion that if we relate to every person, every creature, as our mother, we will treat everyone equally and it will be easier for us to cultivate love and mercy for all.

How could the author be so sure that everyone treated their mothers with this kind of benevolence? Would it really be so good for all those living creatures if I treated them the way I treat my real mother? I didn't know if I believed in this stuff, but I did know that I was confused, and I lost my desire to write.

I looked around at the scenery of my life. I noticed the pile of "absolutely private" diaries, which I hoped would eventually be bound between cardboard covers and transformed into books that would sit on a shelf in the library, and one day a little girl would wander in and read it all in one sitting. I was about to get up and, in a silly gesture of protest against myself, rip the diaries to shreds, when I heard someone knocking softly at the door. Again I felt like I had to hide something, like I had been playing with myself in a forbidden way. Maybe I was just surprised by the nearby knock; usually, people just called for me from downstairs.

The cover of the disc was still on the bed, and Amy, who walked into the room, picked it up right away. She touched the faces of the four musicians, then thrust the disc in my direction and said, "When I was a girl, I used to listen to music all the time. No, really, all the time. To the point where my parents had me tested to see if I had some kind of condition. You wouldn't believe the fights we used to have on Shabbat."

I wanted to tell her that I never listened to music and that it wasn't a big part of my life, but she was swept up in her almost ecstatic talk about classical music, in which she clearly heard the voice of God, and she sat down on my bed.

"Basically, that's what led me to my choice of Debbie's Bat Mitzvah theme. Giacomo Puccini said that the music of *Madame Butterfly* was composed for him by God, and that he was just the vessel that put the music on the paper and presented it to the audience. When she finally paused for breath, I was able to squeeze in a couple of words and tell her that I was going out.

Poor Buddha! Amy had also sat on him. Now she freed him from beneath her, smiled, and said that it was too bad I hadn't studied the weekly portion with them. "You could have impressed all your friends… or maybe one friend in particular…."

I felt comfortable enough with her to shoot her a look informing her that studying Torah wouldn't win the hearts of Israeli boys.

"So what are you going to wear? And where do kids go these days, anyway? To the disco?"

"I was planning on wearing this."

"You should stand out more. I'll help you with your make-up."

This could have been a perfect opportunity for me to feel that Amy, like every other living creature, was also my mother, and to let her touch my face, but I had no patience for make-up other than on Purim.

"No. I don't want to put on make-up."

I was glad I had said No to her. She stood there, reminding me of a turtle, and I began to feel that if I didn't leave, she would stay in my room forever, settling there until it became her extended home. I held her lightly and gently led her out of my room and into the armchair in the hall. She sank down into the chair like a tired child at the end of the day. As I was going downstairs, I was sorry I hadn't taken advantage of her exhaustion to lead her back to her room, where I could have inspected the damage for myself.

As I was turning the key on my way out, Abba grunted and gestured for me to follow him into the kitchen, and from there to the master bedroom.

"I thought you said you weren't going out," he said with a tinge of anger.

How, from all my "I don't knows," did he manage to hear what he wanted to hear? Surprisingly, instead of responding with my own frustration and bringing up the questionable episodes from his past that Grandma had shared with me, I decided that this time, I would simply say no! I would say no in a manner that left no room for doubt, that would show him that this time, his lack of boundaries between himself and the rest of the world - including his inviting Amy into our house, including all his good intentions - was his problem alone. He would have to let me go pursue the love of my youth, no matter how he might tarry.

Eleven

I went out to escort Binyamin and Liat. They told me they weren't going to make it to Grandma's funeral because they were flying back the next day. The nightscape at the entrance to our house gave me chills all over, because it was so similar to the night we found out that Nirit had died.

Binyamin and I had been sitting on these very steps outside, trying to understand the finitude of life, and the longing that went with it.

Now, when I hug and kiss them goodbye, completely naturally, I get a feeling that I am separating from the pair of them for good. I loved them dearly. Each one of them gave me a great deal, and all that was left for me to do was be happy for them, even if they didn't seem particularly happy with each other, or at least not happy enough.

The night Amy was here, it was half past midnight when I stopped at Binyamin's house. He brought cassette tapes to listen to, since he knew that in Ima's car, the only options were classical music or female cantorial music in thick American accents. It was actually nice to drive without having to talk too much. I could spend my time thinking of clever things to say to Eren Shonsky. R.E.M.'s new cassette helped. Binyamin said that this album would end up being the most influential album of the nineties. With a name like "Automatic for the People," it seemed inevitable, and of course, he was right.

Despite the dimness and smokiness of the pub, it was easy to find Liat and Elad because, as always, Elad and his friends were on the left side of the room, dancing in their wild-monkey style, while Liat, standing next to them, was holding a tinted-glass bottle of shandy and swaying back and forth.

I stood next to Liat; in other words, I danced like she did, a kind of gentle swaying, even though I would have preferred to go crazy and dance like the boys. I scanned the people, meaning the tall boys who were at eye level. After a little while, Elad pulled Binyamin aside to organize a basketball game, and the two of them, along with several others, left the dance floor. Liat and I went outside to plan our next move. Suddenly, I saw Eren Shonsky coming from the kibbutz's teen house where he lived. I shook out my pony-tail, then gathered it again, and Liat, who was familiar with this gesture, smiled without looking at him, and something in her approving and all-knowing glance made me ask her if she wanted to help me. She bit her lip, and I persuaded her that we had nothing to lose, Elad was going to play basketball anyway, I had a once-in-a-lifetime idea, and she should trust me.

Meanwhile, I could hear his footsteps, and his chewing, getting closer. Liat whispered her consent ("whatever you say"), laughing boisterously as if I had just said something hilarious. She said, just as Eren Shonsky walked passed us, "You're awesome."

I turned around, trying to mimic Liat's casualness, and smiled with all my heart, so much so that I forgot to hide my crooked tooth. I introduced them to each other, even though I might have done so already, and told him that the pub was packed, and maybe, if he didn't mind, he could give us a tour of the famous pigpen.

Eren Shonsky's kibbutz was known all across the country because it raised pigs without violating the Jewish law. The pen had been built in such a way that the cages were raised a few inches off the ground so they weren't touching the holy land of

Israel. Liat heard where we were heading, and she resisted. "But won't you be crossing some family line?" I couldn't believe my best friend was doing this to me, and I was afraid Eren Shonsky would think I was some kind of religious fanatic and would never want to sleep with me. But before I could think of anything else to say, he asked me, with a smile, what kind of house I lived in.

I was hoping Liat would sense that my stomach was on the verge of collapsing the way it does when it hurts, or when I'm trying to hide my height, but she just forged ahead and said, "You're taking the rabbi's daughter to the pigpen, what could be more heretical than that?"

I thought I would die, but miraculously, as if an angel had flown over him and touched his head, Eren Shonsky didn't ask any questions. He just said, "Great, come on," and began walking towards the farm.

Liat knew that I hated it when people called me "the rabbi's daughter." Especially in front of people who didn't know me that well. At that moment, I was more concerned that Eren Shonsky would think I was a liar, because I had told him that Abba was a professor of film, and what worried me even more was that he'd think I was trying to fix him up with Liat. That must have been what made me say, stupidly, "I'm not even Jewish. I'm Buddhist."

Liat looked shocked, which made me add, "And my father's not really a rabbi, I mean, he's not a real rabbi, he even watches TV on Friday nights."

The two of them looked at me like I was speaking a different language; I couldn't believe what I had just said, either.

Eren Shonsky, who didn't grasp how dramatic this was getting, asked, "So you eat pork?"

"I never had the chance," I confessed, and quickly pointed to Liat. "She doesn't eat pork either. Lots of people don't."

"But would you mind eating it? I mean," he explained, "if you already don't feel Jewish…." I knew I could never eat pork, it was too revolting, so I said I was considering becoming a vegetarian, and in order to distract them from this conversation, I told them I had finally decided to do a year of service.

By that point, Liat didn't believe anything that was coming out of my mouth, but the whole confusing scenario came to an end anyway, because just then Eren Shonsky opened a big green iron door, and the whole area was filled with shrill screams.

Liat and I weren't a couple of city girls who had never seen animals in their natural habitats. In fact, in eleventh grade, we worked together in a sheep pen. We took the animals out to graze, nursed the new lambs, tagged their ears, and stepped in a lot of shit. Nonetheless, the sight of these pink animals, both large and small, pressed against each other in the light of the electric lamps, was like nothing we'd ever seen before. A pink pig of gigantic proportions, spotted with what might have been dirt or what might have been birthmarks, caught my eye. Gathered all around her were a slew of piglets, all nursing from her or fighting to latch on to an udder. Basically, all the animals were searching for the source, for direct contact with the mother. It's not surprising that Buddha, when he was growing up as a prince in a house that lacked for nothing, came up with his theory that all living creatures were our mothers. Freud, on the other hand, having grown up with a frugal, or perhaps even miserly, Jewish mother, had a different theory entirely.

It's hard to pinpoint what it was about the sight of the pigs that triggered such strong aversion in both of us. Maybe it was the fact that the huge and dirty pigs, which were practically crushing their own children, looked so human. That's what people say when they try to explain why pigs are considered the most forbidden animal; that there was something human about them. When I looked at them, what I saw was a bunch of huge, stupid faces that knew they were headed towards slaughter but were too lazy to even summon up any fear.

Eren Shonsky sat on a wooden crate and said, "I was reading about people who were starting to question their religious observance, and it said that eating pork was a turning point in their journey."

I finally looked away from the caged creatures; I respected my mother too much to imagine the pigs filling her shoes in another incarnation. To lift my spirits, I looked straight at Eren Shonsky's protruding lips, which were quite attractive. Liat, too, shifted her gaze when she heard what he was saying, but for an entirely different reason. She ran to the side and started puking her guts out.

Jane Austen wrote to her sister, "Run mad as often as you choose, but do not faint." Of course, her fictional heroines were always fainting, thus garnering the attention, and the physical touch, of a man. Liat was smarter than that, and she wasn't about to faint in the middle of all this muck. She chose a different approach to express her repugnance. The truth is, I understood her, and if I hadn't been worried that the vomit would stick to my hair, or that whatever came out of my mouth would smell awful, I would have done the same thing.

Eren Shonsky showed all his manliness when he approached her and tried to make a joke. "You ate in the kibbutz dining hall, huh?" He must have been referring to the chicken and rice mixture that constituted the repulsive mush spreading out beneath her, and I smiled with a spark of *schadenfreude* before asking, "Are you OK, sweetie?"

Liat stood up and blurted out, as if she were in a confessional, "I did eat pork, I only said I didn't, but I'm done with meat! From this day on, I'm a vegetarian." And she walked out of the pen like a lady.

Eren Shonsky said that he would clean up after her, and that it was ironic, because usually any creature entering the pen at that hour was there to consume food, not to donate it. I would have liked to stay there alone with him, in spite of the chubby animals and the oversize heating elements and every part of the backdrop that made the whole thing look like one giant sin, but instead I went to find Liat.

She was standing in the light, cleaning herself up with one of the tissues she always carried in her pocket along with her everlasting lip balm. I put my hand on her shoulder.

"I'm sorry I called you the rabbi's daughter," she said.

"It's OK," I said. "It's like getting a cold during the summer. it's the most aggravating and irritating thing, but it passes."

"What is it with you guys and repulsive things?" I liked it that she talked about me and Eren Shonsky as if we were one and the same. I liked it less when she said, "And you know that this business with your father isn't going to pass."

"That's true. Come on, let's go get you some water. Maybe if I eat pork, they'll kick me out of the house."

"I'd kick you out of your house. It's one of the most nauseating things I've ever seen. Let's wait for him, you're right, he really is sweet."

"My" sweet guy had just come out of the pen equipped with a polished sentence. "The pigs," he said, "are happy to get her share." Maybe when he saw the horror in our eyes, he thought she was going to vomit again, and immediately added that he was just kidding, he had mixed it in with the hay.

"I'm a vegetarian, too," he said, to our surprise. He touched Liat's shoulder, which made me jealous.

This time she got the message, and to prevent any misunderstanding, commented that she hoped she could stick to her decision, because her boyfriend lived on an Argentinian kibbutz, and whenever there was an excuse for a party, they would set up dozens of grills and cook steaks, and the whole kibbutz would smell like sacrifices to God. She said she would tell her boyfriend what kind of slaughterhouse operated behind the scenes so that he could get his plateful of steak.

Eren Shonsky suggested that we go make herbal tea in his room, and I felt like I had just won a million dollars. At least until Liat decided she wanted to go and see what was going on in the basketball field. Eren Shonsky said he'd had a really good time and maybe we'd see each other later. At first I tried to convince Liat to go back and dance some more, but with her pathetic condition going back to the pub wasn't really an option.

Usually, the drive home was quiet, because I would be thinking of all the clever things I could have said to Eren Shonsky and didn't, and Binyamin would be too drunk to talk. That night, Benny was pumped with adrenaline and smelled of sweat. I was surprised at how much I enjoyed breathing it in. He was singing along in full voice with R.E.M. and fiddling with the tape, rewinding and fast-forwarding it to get to his favorite songs. Towards the end of the ride, he said he wanted us to listen one more time to the fourth song on the cassette, a reassuring song called "Everybody Hurts."

"Listen," he said, "you can interpret it in two ways, because yes, everyone does get hurt sometimes, but everyone also hurts someone else."

Tonight, after the visit from the two friends who had once been such a big part of my life, the floodgates opened. I found myself unable to move. I sat down on the top step and realized that song was kind of a prophecy. Right there, at that very spot, in front of the door. The step where I saw Binyamin the evening after he'd called to tell me about Nirit's death, and I responded that it was impossible because I had visited her the day before, forcing him to insist, as if he were explaining the facts of life to me. I must have been naïve, or stupid, if I thought that a person could get better after having cancer for three years. If they've amputated her leg, if it's spread to her lungs, if she was sleeping with an oxygen mask and still choking every time she tried to speak - what was I thinking? I don't know what I was thinking. I was so innocent then.

The news of her death came on Saturday night. Over the phone. He said he had bad news and I should probably sit down, just like in the movies. After I hung up, I called Liat, but she was spending the weekend on the army base, so I called Binyamin back and asked him to come over. His parents said he was already on his way, and that was how I found myself sitting outside waiting for him, and it was there - that is, here - on this step that the two of us met, confused by our first encounter with death. We sat down immediately, as if that would make things easier. I remember he was wearing jeans and a black shirt, and he looked different. His army tan suited him. I asked him what had happened, exactly, and he said it had to happen at some point, since it was already in her lungs. It bothered me that he was talking like a doctor, and I didn't understand what that meant, "It had to happen."

"You never really wanted to hear about her treatment, about how she was doing - but it was obvious." I got angry again, and told him that Nirit didn't think it was so obvious.

Binyamin said he didn't think anyone was ever really ready to die, to accept that this was it, everything was over. The human instinct is to cling to life. He sensed my confusion, stopped lecturing, and apologized for telling me over the phone; he was afraid to tell me before Shabbat, he said, and afraid to tell me the news in person. He was so sweet, so shy, that I reached out and caressed him. I think he was blushing when he said, quickly, "It'll be OK." I looked at him skeptically, like someone seeking affirmation, and he nodded more confidently and put his hand on me like a protective father.

I don't remember which one of us suggested that we take a walk to get some air, but it was definitely him who suggested that we bring along a few of my father's beers. Each of us clutched two bottles, like babies holding onto their security blankets. We walked and talked and reminisced and laughed and made sure to avoid Nirit's house. We circled most of the town, we scurried up and down the playground equipment like when we were kids, until we finally reached our Scouts clubhouse. "Let's see if my master key still works," he said. And it did. Nobody was there. I felt like we were traveling back in time. Exhausted, we collapsed on the cushions in one of the rooms, and he looked at me with the same expression he had when he apologized for telling me about Nirit over the phone. A gaze that saw me. That needed me.

He touched me and I sat there silently. His half-closed eyes told me that the time was now, that I had reached an age when I had to face life in its entirety. Over our long walk, I had started to open up about my fears of this unknown moment.

Perhaps he concluded that this was a subconscious request from a friend in need.

. With confident hands, clothes were peeled off, the confusion gradually dissipated, and his eyes instructed me to cooperate. There must have been a kiss, a few kisses; those are the hardest for me to remember. All those years of friendship, and we'd never gotten anywhere close to the region of the mouth. I do know that I continued to function. I didn't stop, but I also didn't get swept away, mostly because I didn't know how. I felt like I was performing. I caressed when he caressed, I licked, maybe I even bit when I remembered that it was an option. When he took the condom out of his jeans pocket, I tried not to think about how it sparkled like candy; mostly I tried not to look at it, to seek out his half-closed eyes at the moment of entry. Still, it hurt. He tried to be gentle, and I think he wished he had a good CD to play in the background, but most of the time I was busy dealing with my blood, and how it would stain the cushion, and wondering if I was his first or if there had been some girl in the army whom he never told me about because we had grown apart.

My primary disappointment was that my first time was so casual, so uninspired. Even prosaic. As I passed a mirror on my way out of the clubhouse, I checked my reflection to see if my face had changed in any way; it hadn't. The following days were packed, between the funeral and the *shiva*. Binyamin and I, along with a few other people who had been close to Nirit during her illness, swarmed her parents' house in search of comfort.

I suspected that Binyamin was hoping to continue this unusual connection we had, but I didn't feel comfortable enough to ask if my suspicions were right. It was as if this intensity had taken us back to our childhood, when there was no room for outright sexuality. Not between us. Then he went off to the territories for nearly a month, and I carried on with my own life. There were moments when I was angry at him for ruining the mystique of the first time. I felt ashamed. Whenever I enumerated my "conquests" over the years, I always began with a lie. With number two. After all, it was Eren Shonsky I was brave enough to seduce after that episode with Binyamin. A one-time seduction, perhaps, but still. But when we got back the Friday night of Amy's visit, when the prospect of losing my virginity seemed about as plausible as winning the lottery, I was bothered by entirely different things. When I opened the door to my dark house, I thought, to my surprise, that I smelled cigarette smoke.

When I got to the upstairs hall, I saw that I hadn't been mistaken. In addition to a pile of books and a mess of clementine peels, Amy had also left a plate littered with cigarette stubs. It looked like we had been visited by a group of adolescents who were smoking for the first time. It was very strange, not just because it was Shabbat, but also because it seemed to come out of nowhere. Despite my fatigue, I decided to tidy up a little bit, to empty everything into a plastic bag and to stash it in the garbage outside so as not to raise Abba's suspicions the next day. Ever since Grandpa Ephraim died of lung cancer, Ima was very strict about not allowing any smoking in the house.

I opened the window overlooking the back yard to air out the hall. The cold May air made me shiver. I pushed aside the screen that kept the mosquitos and flies out; like many things in our house, it was frayed around the edges. I took a look at the hall, which seemed to be normal, as if nothing out of the ordinary was going on, and was saddened by the thought that despite the foul smell, it was unlikely that Abba had even noticed what was happening on the floor above him. He'd probably been sleeping while Amy was partying. A party of books, admittedly, but books can make you stoned, too. How can anyone with eyes to oversee his entire "flock" be so clueless about the people in his own house?

I waited for sleep, which for some reason wouldn't come. I turned out the light and tried to reconstruct Eren Shonsky's words and to transform his invitation to drink herbal tea into a lullaby.

Thinking about him only aroused me more. I felt the same soft feeling I would get when I read, with a trembling and abashed heart, romantic passages in books. Maybe it's pathetic, but I never had big fantasies. If I pictured myself in an intimate position, it always involved me sleeping on "my" side of the bed, and a faceless partner who climbed in next to me and woke me with gentle, fluttering kisses.

I knew what would calm me down, and I suddenly understood what it was about my encounter with the pigs, while standing so close to Eren Shonsky, that had frightened and aroused me so much. In my childhood, I had a book in which the heroes were a group of chubby, spotted little piglets; the book described what they did every hour of the day and night. The father pig - I think he drove a bulldozer - wore a shirt that was always bursting at the seams, secured by a single button. I don't know why this detail was etched into my memory, but I do know that because of that book (I have no idea what happened to it), I once took a pillow - it reminded me of the illustrated pig bellies - and put it between my legs. I bent over it, just like it appeared in the book, until I experienced a kind of redemption.

Despite my embarrassment, I've done it again since then, albeit rarely and without relying on the childish images of the book, which I'd nearly forgotten. Even though I'd read in *Teen magazine* about penetration with cucumbers and all kinds of other dangerous methods, I continued with my gentle ritual, never thinking of it as an extension of my vagina, which I was too scared to even look at. That night, I ended up falling asleep with the pillow between my thighs. And tonight, when I am finally able to get up from the top step, I am encouraged by the fact that although there is still a lot for me to learn about love, even after the dozens of young men I've slept with, at least I can now forgive the twenty-year old girl I once was. The one who didn't want to die a virgin and so pounced on whatever life had to offer.

Twelve

On the Shabbat morning after the incident with Amy and her cigarettes, I heard Abba calling my name from the other side of the door. I tried to pull myself away from my recurring hospital dream, in which I am lying next to a faceless man, and blood is flowing between us through transparent tubes, like in the Frida Kahlo painting. Abba's nearby voice prompted me to call out "I'm up!" as if I were heeding a battle cry instructing everyone to clear the area. When I didn't hear his heavy footsteps moving towards the stairs, I knew he was still standing right behind the door that I had once slammed so hard it fell off its hinges.

"Abba?" I spoke loudly but gently.

"Can I come in?" He was speaking gently, too. I said he could, and because I knew he wasn't going to turn on the light, I jumped out of bed and opened the blinds so the two of us wouldn't be in the pitch darkness that I liked to sleep in, much to everyone else's horror, especially my friends who slept over from time to time.

He sat down in the chair that doubled as a clothes rack. "Is everything OK?" I asked.

"Amy didn't come to shul. I thought maybe she was here. She hung a 'Please Do Not Disturb' sign on the outside of her door, just like your mother used to do."

"Because normal people like to sleep on Shabbat!" I don't know why I was trying to provoke him. Maybe because of the way he said "your mother." I toned down my voice and tried to respond in his language. "Don't the sages say that 'Shabbat sleep is a delight' or something like that? Don't worry, I'm getting up, and I'll make so much noise, she'll have to wake up."

Abba smiled, as if remembering me as a child, and, ignoring my comment about normal people, looked around the room. "Very neat," he proclaimed, and added, "comparatively! It's a good thing she hadn't promised to do the Torah reading."

My five minutes of glory came to an end with the three words he used to describe my room, because it was clear that he was looking for Amy and not me. I told him I had to use the bathroom. "Of course, of course," he said, waving me off with his hand. He continued to sit there in contemplation, as if he was waiting for me to bring him Amy on a silver platter.

I don't know if he snooped around like I used to do in his room. I was never worried that he or Ima would read my diaries; in fact, in some ways, I wished they would.

I didn't have to follow through with my plan to make a lot of noise. I could hear Amy's voice downstairs, telling Grandma that she was happy to see her, that she'd been in the backyard the whole time, enjoying her breakfast. Abba hadn't looked for her there because nobody ever sat outside in the mornings. In the past our garden used to be visible to our non-observant neighbors. They were the ones who could usually be found there, grilling their meat or mowing the lawn.

Abba quickened his pace; he was glad to find her awake. It was as if he were saying to me, yes, Shabbat sleep is a delight, but only up to a point. Whether out of chivalry or simply to avoid an argument, he didn't ask her why she hadn't come to services, although he did tell her how warmly his sermon was received. It's amazing how a person's opinion can fluctuate so quickly. At this time yesterday he thought Amy was a *dybbuk* whom he had to expel, and now he was treating her as if she were his mother, or his supportive wife.

I wondered if I should call Liat and find out how she was feeling, but then I remembered that for her, the evening wasn't centered on the minute right after she threw up, when Eren Shonsky and I were listening to the heavy breathing of the pigs. No, she finished the evening full of joy and energy; she even shot a few baskets. And anyway, normal people really did sleep in on Shabbat mornings.

I went into the kitchen, wondering why Abba wasn't demanding an explanation from Amy. Maybe he understood that she was on vacation, and that she wasn't so observant that she felt she had to go to shul. Personally, I was eager to hear her reasons for staying home, mostly because I remembered the pile of cigarette butts that I had cleared out the previous night. What could have caused such a strong craving for nicotine? Why did I automatically cover for her and defend her?

A good smell began to waft through the house, curling upwards like in the cartoons. Abba had surprised me. When I wasn't looking, he had made his famous lasagna, loaded with layers of sauce and different kinds of delicious cheese. In an act of Pavlovian conditioning, I opened the freezer door, and sure enough, Abba had not let us down and had bought ice cream for dessert.

The hot news coming from the oven made me interrupt the happy couple's animated discussion of *haggadot* and ask Abba when he'd found the time to make lasagna.

Pleased with the surprise he'd managed to pull off, he smiled and said that the atmosphere of Shavuot had inspired him. My guess is that he was just looking for an excuse to buy a real dessert - which is to say, a dairy dessert.

Amy let out a grunt that, to those in the know, attested to the fact that she had smoked an entire pack of cigarettes the night before. She hooked her arm around my waist, and, in a voice that struck me as slightly obsequious, said, "Shabbat Shalom, Eli. What were your adventures last night? Come sit with us, sweetie."

Nobody ever asked me what I did when I went out; it was as if the transgressive nature of my actions rendered them nonexistent. I had neither the desire nor the courage to tell them about my efforts to "find love," but still, there was something about her question that, at the very least, gave those efforts a kind of legitimacy.

Grandma, in her armchair, woke up. She, too, had sharp senses. She sniffed the air and declared that no man was permitted to leave this world without having tasted Jesse's divine lasagna.

"It's so delicious he even makes it on Pesach, with matzah."

Grandma, who ate matzah year-round and loved it for its resemblance to Hungarian bread, wasn't far off when she said that Abba's Pesach lasagna was a meal fit for a king.

I thought about all the things we don't say in front of other people; I especially thought about what Grandma had said about Ima's trip when I was a little over two. Because I couldn't get in touch with Ora and ask her to shed light upon the topic, I took some old photo albums off the shelf, ignoring Amy's efforts to draw me back to the table and to the discussion about Pesach.

As I had feared, in the green album, which mostly featured photos of Ora's children, was the proof I was hoping not to find. Between a picture of Ora's new kitchen (based on a kitchen she had seen in a Martha Stewart magazine) and a picture of a prayer shawl she had made was a snow-blurred photograph in which one could barely make out Ora's suburban house. What Grandma referred to as "one of the famous snowstorms" looked like a pastoral snowfall, and in the middle of it stood my mother. Wrapped in a stylish black winter coat and holding a giant snow shovel, she was apparently staging an attempt to dig out a car that was stuck deep in the snow. I removed the picture with a slightly trembling hand, as if the snow had come out of the picture and was buffeting me with frigid air. I flipped it over to find confirmation of what I had feared. Ora, ever organized, had made a copy of the photo for her sister and written on it, in pencil, February 1977.

I thought I could detect a kind of sadness hiding behind Ima's close-lipped smile and the glistening snow, the sadness of a woman who had drifted away from her unfaithful husband. No, that couldn't be my father; Grandma herself had said that it was a unique encounter. A good mother would have found comfort in her children, especially in a baby like me. Everyone always said what a delightful "extra" I was.

I stared at the photo some more, trying to unearth the story of my mother at that moment, to reconstruct her voice, as Amy had suggested I do, with the characters from the Bible. At that moment she was as distant as they were, and the only thing that emanated from her was a dispassionate gaze that masked a terrible rupture. I was used to hiding things from her, but it had never occurred to me that parents might conceal their own entanglements from their children. Suddenly I was able to tolerate the binary term "the rabbi's daughter," because it bequeathed both strength and weakness. For my mother, however, the rabbi's wife, who had the ability to renounce him, giving up the title could only work against her. Like Amy, who got divorced from her husband and found herself wooing us at our doorstep.

"Eli," Amy rescued me from my brooding. "Why are you sitting there on the rug, all alone? Come!" I closed the album and put it back, out of view, in case anyone tried to piece together the story I was trying to decipher.

Suddenly there was a quiet and unexpected knock on the door, and before we had a chance to say, "Come in," Liat entered, a shy smile on her delicate lips.

I stood up and greeted her warmly. I had learned enough from Abba to know not to ask what she was doing here on a Shabbat morning after having clearly spent the night on the kibbutz. Especially since her eyes were red and sore from holding back tears, and everyone sitting around the table had turned their chairs around to look at her.

Liat sat down in Avigail's seat, refusing Abba's offers of food. Grandma interrogated Liat about what she was going to do in the army, and complimented her on her fluent, if accented, English.

Amy said it looked like Lia had something on her mind, and she wanted to talk to her outside. Before anyone could react to her suggestion, and to Liat's new name, and before Liat could offer me even a kernel of an explanation as to why she was following Amy as if she were the Pied Piper of Hamelin, the two of them went out to the front yard. Abba restrained himself and didn't tell Amy to wait until they recited the Grace after Meals. Then, as if to console us on the unforeseen departure of our guest who was herself taking on the role of hostess, he joyfully announced that there was ice cream for dessert.

For Grandma, apparently, this didn't suffice. In a toxic tone, she asked me if I was worried that doing a year of service would distance me from Lia and that red-headed guy, the two friends with whom I spent all my time.

"Her name is Liat!" I raged against the new name Amy had attached to her, maybe because I was accustomed to getting angry at Ima who never remembered the names of my friends, or maybe because at that moment, Liat really did feel far away. I tried to come up with a good answer. Not just for Grandma, but for me. They would finish their army service before me, they'd travel, they'd enroll in university, all without waiting for me. And it wouldn't be anyone's fault.

What I really wanted was my mother's opinion. Ima's sadness, reflected in the picture, haunted me and made me think of her differently.

I knew that I shouldn't be leaving Liat helpless in Amy's hands, even though I was pleased that Liat also saw something protective, or perhaps nurturing about Amy, so I went to call them back in. Liat smiled a twisted smile, as if she were a robot obeying the instructions of its operator.

"Remember how I threw up yesterday from the pigs? I didn't stop throwing up all night. I'm afraid I might be pregnant."

I opened my eyes wide. I knew I opened them wide because Liat, who sometimes involuntarily mimicked the expression of whoever she was with, opened her own eyes so wide that I could see their blood vessels and the yellow residue that she hadn't completely washed off.

Before I had a chance to respond, Abba summoned us for dessert and Grace. Afterwards, while Grandma rocked in her armchair, Liat scrutinized the *bentcher, the* booklet for reciting Grace, that my father had given her. Abba announced that he would do the dishes later, and went off to his customary Shabbat afternoon nap. I was surprised that he didn't ask me to go with him so he could brief me on Amy's behavior, but I was too distracted by the interaction of Amy and Liat to suggest it myself.

Amy said that the three of us would go together to buy a pregnancy test. I hugged Liat and told her that this reminded me of the coming of age novel *The Preparatory Test* that we had loved when we were younger, but she looked at me severely and said that life wasn't a book. Her tone was once again so distant, so strange, as if a mountain of unfamiliar words had piled up between us and she was scaling it alone, with no expectation that I would follow. I wanted to ask her about the infamous pills she had so proudly started taking on the day of my seventeenth birthday, but I just kept stroking her hair and saying what I assumed she wanted to hear, that everything would be fine. She bit her lips, nodded, and waited for a sign from Amy, who was humming some tune with her eyes closed. Liat surrendered to my touch and she, too, closed her eyes, until Amy began to talk. "Come on, girls. Let's go."

As the four of us were leaving the house, Grandma spoke her mind about Amy's decision to desecrate Shabbat with her driving, and asked her if she wasn't afraid of *maris ayin.* I explained to Liat that this was the Jewish version of "What will the neighbors say." I, too, was struck by how easy it was for Amy, the former rabbi's wife, to break with Sabbath observances for Liat's sake. But Amy revealed nothing, keeping whatever misgivings she might have had to herself.

We dropped Grandma off near her cottage and she made her own way; but not before she squeezed out a promise from me to visit her in the afternoon. Amy came and sat next to me after I objected to sitting alone in the front seat, like a taxi driver.

When I stopped at Super-Pharm, the unspoken question that had been hovering in the air like an invisible passenger finally reared its head. Which one of us was going to purchase the test? Every one of us, like in the game Clue, had a reason not to get out of the car. We had to go easy on Liat. I was still a virgin and thought that it was inappropriate for me to carry out the mission, and that it made the most sense for Amy, an adult and a visitor, to buy the test. In the end she was the one who broke the silence, saying that driving on Shabbat was one thing, but carrying and using money on Shabbat was something else entirely.

"Please," Liat implored. I turned around; her brow was wrinkled, and she said "Please" again, holding out her wallet. Her plea pierced my heart because it testified to how much we'd grown apart over the last year. It was like something in our mutual language had changed. When she called out the window, "Buy two," I was relieved. At least her tone of voice was familiar.

Fortunately, the store was almost empty, and I quickly found what I was looking for, without having to ask for help. I added three challah-shaped pieces of marzipan, Liat's favorite sweet. When I proudly showed her the candy, Amy said it always amused her that in Mexico, the pharmacies sold not only medication and health products, but also candy and cigarettes. This was the second time I was reminded of how little I understood about her smoking. Like smoke rings disappearing in the air, I began to wonder if last night's event had actually happened at all.

Liat thanked me over and over again.

"You're such a good friend, Elish." She was speaking from her heart. She opened one of the slim boxes like a little boy who can't resist unwrapping a present.

She wanted to go back to my house to do the tests, which required drinking large quantities of water before urinating on the stick. When we got to the house we headed upstairs all aware of the excitement bubbling up inside us. Only when Amy made herself comfortable in the armchair in the hall did it occur to me that it was slightly odd that she, given her age and life experience, was behaving like one of the girls. I didn't say anything; I just went downstairs to get some cold water.

Because it was called a "home pregnancy test," I had envisioned the three of us squeezing into the bathroom and waiting for the colored strip to reveal her fate, but Liat locked herself in the bathroom with her kit, and Amy opened up the Bible. I debated whether or not this was a good time to ask her about the smoking issue that had come up the previous evening, in this very spot. As she tended to do, she beat me to the punch and led the conversation in a different direction.

"There's a wonderful phrase in the Book of Ruth: 'And God gave her a pregnancy and she had a son.' Giving someone pregnancy. Funny, right? Because the usual formula in the Bible for barren women is 'God remembered X', one of the commentaries asserts that God Himself had to intervene, because Boaz was too old. And as it turned out, it really was a special pregnancy, because it is from Boaz and Ruth's dynasty that David, the Messiah, was born."

Just as the word "Messiah" reached my ears, the bathroom door opened and Liat emerged, her face completely inexpressive, holding a small stick wrapped tightly in its plastic wrapper.

"I only used one. I'm pretty sure it's negative."

Just like when we had learned about the AIDS test in school, I did my best to remember if negative was good or not, and Liat's face - which looked disappointed - didn't help. With incomprehensible determination, she went to drink more water. She drank and drank while Amy and I pored over the medical instructions that promised an immediate answer along with other attractive promises that sounded nice but didn't necessarily have anything to do with raising children. We read that the test measured the level of Human Chorionic Gonadotropin, or HCG, in the urine. The purpose of measuring

HCG is to look for evidence of a living human being. Funny that you can find humanity in urine.

Despite the sense that I was watching a strange woman, and the strange feeling of defining my Liati as a woman, I knew that I was witnessing something primordial. If I were the future child of Liat, I would want to see the exact moment when she tried, like a tireless gardener, to bring her garden to life. Maybe I should investigate the circumstances of my own birth, and the births of everyone in my family.

It's terrifying to think about the moment you came into existence, or more accurately the moment your parents were informed of your existence, and it must be thrilling to see their first reaction. It's strange that the women's body "knows" something before the mind does.

Liat went back into the bathroom, then walked out a few minutes later. Her face was calmer, and paler. "I don't know why I thought I was pregnant. Maybe it's the pressure of the *bagruyot,* or my fear of the army. Or maybe it's just my fear of growing up?"

Her forthright question, in which I could hear the echoes of our childhood bubbles being burst, brought to mind the recent event that had touched our class. The discovery that Nirit's cancer had spread to her bones. Back then, we had no idea where that would lead and maybe this allowed Liat to believe, and perhaps unknowingly wish, that someone had "given her pregnancy."

Amy turned to Liat. "When the fruit is ripe, it has to leave the tree." It wasn't clear if she was referring to us, or to the baby whose time had not yet arrived. Liat only smiled with the weariness of a young mother. I thought to myself, it's a good thing it isn't going to happen, because never in a million years would her parents be supportive. My religious parents, despite my arduous attempts to portray them differently, wouldn't have been happy either, if I had made that kind of mistake.

Now over the course of this Shabbat, which was lovely and peaceful, if sad, we talked a lot about Grandma's life. As a child, her life had been very comfortable. She took piano and violin lessons, and studied French and German. She had a dressmaker who made her *haute couture* velvet dresses, and servants who carried her books to school on Shabbat. When you're little, you can't imagine what the rest of your life will look like. Take Evyatar, for example. Despite all the grief that surrounds him, he was having the time of his life, because we were all there with him. We played with him and spoiled him no end, as if the grief of children was something altogether different, an untarnished kingdom, a kind of quiet euphoria before the storm.

Avigail said she thought it was nice that even though Grandma's adult life was hard, especially towards the end when her legs and her heart were bothering her, she still liked to say that the most important thing was to enjoy youth, health and happiness. During all our conversations, I felt an invisible presence watching over the Pandora's box that in a short while - with the arrival of Ima and Ora - might well explode. It wasn't my place to tell them they had no idea of how much Grandma's childhood crisis in the aftermath of World War One, a crisis that was not just materialistic but also psychological, affected their lives and mine.

When Liat left after all the excitement, making sure to take some lasagna home with her, Amy and I stood at the top of the stairs and waved goodbye. We looked like a promotional film for the suburbs. Amy suggested we go for a walk; she wanted to see the hothouse in which I'd grown up.

After a long stroll in which I didn't dare to mention the cigarette's episode we returned to our street. Like a dog sniffing for new urine-marks, it took only a single glimpse to notice something dramatic. Right next to our Shabbat-observant cars was Steven's car. No wonder Abba had behaved like such a good little boy. He must have been waiting for me to go off to my Scouts meeting so Steven could come over and evaluate Amy.

The last of the sun's rays were still shining. Despite the hesitations and the buds of anger that were swelling up inside me, I knew exactly where I had to go, and how I had to market my plan. I told Amy that I thought Abba had guests and that I had the car keys, so if she wanted me to - and only if she wanted me to - we could drive over to Grandma's and come back later, when the coast was clear. It worked. Amy asked if I knew who was visiting. I didn't want to lie, so I told her the car looked like Emma's. I added that Abba was a big boy and could entertain the guest by himself. Amy responded that Grandma would appreciate our company more than Emma.

The changing colors of the sky reminded me of the paintball battles we used to have in the Scouts. If Abba opened fire on a peaceful front, he'd have to deal with the aftermath of the worry he so detested. I looked, again, at the area around my house, and suddenly felt that I had an obligation to do a pre-army year of service. To do it for myself. To choose. I decided to stop focusing on what everyone else had, but instead, to forge my own path, a path paved by what I *did* have. Like my brother Hanoch's five-year plans which he was brave enough to draft. For the first time, I felt a spark of love for my brother, as if his presence in my life was responsible for helping me get through this fork in the road.

I looked at Amy. I didn't want to leave her in the hands of the unqualified self-appointed judges. We got into the car and drove towards the setting sun. I decided that the three of us would go to the first screening after Shabbat, at seven-thirty, far from Abba's watchful eyes.

I looked at her again. Her eyes were ringed with dark spots of fatigue. Was this mark of exhaustion - the bleary eyes that made her look like a panda - the cost of her hunger for knowledge? As if the storms in her brain had burst and were bleeding beneath the skin, as if they were crying for help? And I had, indeed, helped her, just as she had helped Liat just by being there.

I'm glad I heeded my inner voice and took that year of service. It opened my eyes to a life that was very different from anything I had experienced in my first eighteen years. Then there was the post-army trip to the United States and Mexico. And, of course, film studies. Even though I sit in a chair during my studies, I feel like they take me all around the globe, if not the entire galaxy. Apparently, it's not just a question of age. You never know how your life can change in a single step, just like the way my hasty decision to drive with Amy - in defiance of Abba, who had invited the psychiatrist to expose the hidden pockets of Amy's mind - was my ticket to the inner world of none other than Ima.

Thirteen

As Amy and I walked, single-file, on the well-tended paths of the old age home, I felt bad. The woman who was walking in front of me had complete faith in me, with no hint of what I was plotting behind her back. It looked like I was on her side, the way I whisked her out of the house, but all it showed was that I knew there was a problem. Why else would I have been so afraid of the mental health assessment that Steven was supposed to conduct?

To keep Grandma from suspecting that my visit to her was a kind of "political asylum" for Amy, I decided that as soon as we entered her house, I would ask her about the circumstances of my birth. I wanted to know if I had been conceived with intent. And then, I would... what? Did it really matter if they had been dreaming of me, wishing for me? But that "And then" - the same "And then" that is always hoping for a better outcome - made me feel a need to clarify where, exactly, the sun and the moon of my life were positioned before they shed their light upon me.

The divining stone that I'd been planning to summon to my assistance was dozing in the armchair as "Swan Lake" played in the background. I gestured to Amy to sit quietly on the sofa, and I tried to make as little noise as possible so that Grandma would continue to stay where she was, saving her energy for the nocturnal excursion I had planned. Amy struck the same pose as Grandma, and closed her eyes.

Even though I knew it wasn't polite, I continued to stand by the front door, watching the two women sleeping peacefully.

Amy was opening and closing her mouth like a fish. Either she was talking to herself or she had some kind of tic.

Grandma woke up and was pleased to see us, while Amy slept on in silence. She explained that I was a "foam baby," but I shouldn't feel bad, because Ora's second son was one, too. In other words, both of our mothers were using the foam method of birth control, and the fact that we were born only attested to how eager we were to come into the world. Maybe, she added, it wasn't a coincidence that both of us were graced with boundless creativity. What she didn't say was that not only were we unplanned, but that steps had been taken to block our entrance into the world.

In order to spice up the story, and perhaps to comfort me, Grandma went on to say that Ima was always proud that I was conceived on New Year's Eve, 1975. The facts were somewhat insulting, but I actually liked the name. *Foam baby.* It seemed to denote a kind of glorious entrance into the world.

Grandma went into the kitchen to show us that the supermarket's assistant manager had accidentally included a box of pancake mix in the last delivery. Grandma thought it would be nice if she could treat us to pancakes redolent of the great Austro-Hungarian Empire. Despite the culinary temptation, I knew I had to refuse, to stick to my original escape plan. Soon, when Shabbat was over, Abba would come here looking for us. I told Grandma that we wanted to see the movie she had mentioned.

"And your father?" She was always looking out for her favorite son-in-law.

I had to lie and tell her he wasn't feeling well. Grandma raised an eyebrow. Illness was very unusual in our family. Ima used to joke that it was because of the poor hygiene she insisted upon.

"Something in that dairy meal upset his stomach," I explained. "But he really wants the three of us to go to the movie, though," I added, lying again.

Amy and Grandma looked up the show times, while I (who already knew that there was a showing right when Shabbat ended, and another one after that) decided to speed up matters by taking out Grandma's dusty Havdalah set. When I was a little girl, I used to think it was too bad that when we blew out the braided Havdalah candle, we didn't make a wish. Why could you make a wish on your birthday but not on Saturday night? If we could, our wishes had a much better chance of coming true.

Amy wanted to teach us a new Hasidic song, which required us to drape our arms around each other's shoulders. Up close, she looked even more unkempt. Maybe even dirty. It suddenly hit me that we didn't know her at all, and what if she wasn't who she said she was, and maybe Binyamin and Abba were right and she... I stopped myself. And she what? What could she possibly be or do? After all, Ima stayed with people all the time when she was out of the country, and I would never want anyone to suspect her of something like that.

Despite my concerns, the comfortable closeness we were sharing left us with a sense of cleanliness and renewal. It made me feel like we were betraying the rest of the household, like we were putting together a family of our own. Who was missing from this family? I couldn't say.

After the Havdalah ceremony - a symbolic dividing line marking a separation that didn't necessarily exist - it was hard for me to refuse the big hug that Amy proffered. Even if it wasn't what it seemed to be, it was exactly what I needed. I brought Grandma a sweater, and found myself wanting to give her a big hug, too. I reached out my arms; she laughed, looked at me with her narrow gypsy eyes that resembled mine, and acquiesced.

At the very moment she said, "Sweetie-pie, you miss your mother," I thought about how I couldn't remember ever getting a sincere hug, or even an insincere one, from Ima. I wasn't surprised that Grandma read me like an open book. She was the one, after all, who bequeathed me with the ability to connect feelings to books. The way she would sit me in her lap with a book, before I even knew how to read, transformed me anew every time. If I did have a dearth of parental attention, like Amy had indicated, every time Grandma and I sat down together and opened a book, a whole world of colors, characters and black print opened up before me, and my entire being was consumed by, and covered with, love. While I watched Grandma struggling with the buttons of her jacket, I wondered whether and when I would get that kind of love from a man.

Suddenly I was glad we were going out, taking a break from all this talk. Maybe in some cosmic way, it would influence Abba, too, and he would stop trying to understand what was wrong with Amy.

Grandma kept nodding off during the movie. On the way home, I had to explain to her that she wasn't getting dementia, that the whole premise of the movie was that time was standing still, and the man kept experiencing the same day, over and over again, only nobody else knew.

I myself was experiencing a surplus of awareness, and trying to decide, with growing anxiety, if it was late enough to go home. I didn't care about time standing still; it was just that I couldn't remember the last time I had defied Abba so blatantly.

As I slowly made my way home, I remembered Grandma's story about how I fought my way through the foam so I could make it into the world. Nobody presents your parents to you and asks you if you want to go into their world, where you are supposed to honor them forever, no matter how foolishly they behave. Clearly, there was something I wasn't seeing. A riddle I had to solve. I knew it wasn't anything straightforward, but I had no idea where to start my search.

Were there other things I didn't know about their past?

I couldn't come up with any excuses to put off our return home any longer. If we went to Grandma's, Abba would find us. Really, he would find us anywhere in town.

I wonder how Ima would have reacted to this whole bizarre story. The queen bee gives off special pheromones that tell the worker bees when to get their food. If she ever gets lost, all the bees feel her absence, or, more accurately, the absence of the pheromone. That was precisely what I was missing: a special sense that would guide me wisely. A maternal instinct, perhaps.

By the time we dropped off Grandma, it was after ten. Once it gets dark, acts of defiant courage, like walking through a desert without a compass, start to seem stupid. I could feel the pressure building up inside me.

I decided that the smartest thing to do would be for me to cultivate in myself a classic maternal kind of love for Abba, a love without boundaries. He was still my father, regardless of the circumstances of our encounter, or of how likely he was to get angry. We went inside. Amy went to settle in her usual spot, and Abba was sitting at the table with a bowl of popcorn. His feigned serenity was simmering like a pot of boiling water as he asked if we had a good time.

Amy said we enjoyed the film and Abba said that the Jewish filmmaker had borrowed the idea of putting an entire community to sleep while the hero went out into the world from Jewish sources. During Saul's crazed pursuit of David, David had the perfect opportunity to kill Saul, but he didn't want to smite "the Messiah of God," so he just took Saul's spear and water flask as proof that he could have injured him had he wanted to. The only reason this theft was possible was that God had put the entire camp to sleep.

Amy said that if I wanted to study some more for the test, she'd be happy to help me, and that in her opinion the best way to learn was through translation. I couldn't believe that that's what I was doing in the middle of the night before my English test - looking for Biblical books in Ima's bookcases. But anything I could do that would keep me occupied, that had the appearance of being constructive, was like a lifeline for me.

While I searched, Amy insisted on reciting the verses in English, which sounded like something out of a children's book and not out of the weighty Bible.

So David took the spear and water jug near Saul's head, and they left. No one saw or knew about it, nor did anyone wake up. They were all sleeping, because the Lord had put them into a deep sleep.

I didn't say that the filmmaker could just as well have been inspired by Sleeping Beauty, because I was afraid that at any moment Abba would shoot his arrow at either one of us and, in his rage, put us to sleep.

Surprisingly, after a short period of reading Bible stories in English, Amy commented on how tired she was, and stood up. It's true, Shabbat had been incredibly busy. It was hard to believe it had only been one day. It felt endless. Amy leaned wearily on the banister and said to both me and Abba (who had stubbornly refused to study with us), "Good night. Thanks, Elisheva."

I felt like we were playing parts in a play, and she was intentionally stumbling over her lines. I followed her up the stairs and asked her, in a pleading tone, "Don't you want to see the material that will be on the test?"

She shook her head no and responded, "You really wiped me out, my girl. Tomorrow." Then, just like Ima, she blew me a dismissive kiss.

"And what about your meeting? What time is that?"

This time, she didn't even turn around. She just tossed out, Scarlet-O'Hara-style, "Tomorrow."

I remained stuck on the stairs, feeling like a sacrificial animal headed for slaughter. Above me, the sun refused to shine, and underneath its shadow I could just make out the foggy image of the moon, shaped like a monster's jaw. When I heard Amy's door close firmly, I caught a glimpse, between the slats of the blinds, of Abba's body standing up. He had never hit me, not once, but I could sense that it was about to happen.

I went down the steps first. "Don't be angry, Abba," I said quietly.

"Don't be angry! Where were you?" He wasn't the kind of person to count to ten to cool down, so he ushered me into his bedroom so Amy wouldn't hear him repeating himself, his rage barely restrained. "Don't be angry! You don't understand, Elisheva. You have no idea what you're getting yourself into. This isn't some Scouts activity that you go to on Saturday mornings when you're supposed to be in synagogue. This is serious."

I ignored the derogatory comment and responded that bad-mouthing a guest was equally serious, as was kicking her out of the house on account of a messy room.

"Why can't you just talk to her openly? What's the hurry? She's a decent person, you saw how she helped me study. She's turned into a friend, hasn't she? Why can't you just ask her what's going on, or tell her what Ronit saw? I don't know, something."

"This has nothing to do with her. I asked you to stay home. I was worried about you; I told you, she might be sick."

Suddenly he stopped talking. Maybe because we were standing so close to each other; or maybe he understood, as I did, that there was no real reason to worry, she was just an unusual woman. I wanted to ask him when it had become acceptable to make medical diagnoses based on messiness, like reading coffee grounds, but he kept sputtering.

"Steven and I saw the room. He wasn't optimistic. You know what, fine, I'll talk to her, but you have to cooperate, no matter what happens."

"Oh, come on, Abba, what could happen?"

"Don't be fooled by her wiliness."

"What happened to 'innocent until proven guilty'? 'Favorable bias,' that's what you call it?"

And then it came, just like in the movies, a hand darting out unexpectedly, a hand that, I could see, was trying to return to its launching pad but, like a falling star, ended up landing right on your face. On my face. It's silly, but my first reaction, along with the insult and the pain that erupted like fireworks, was to wonder if I had a hand-shaped mark on my cheek, like in the films.

My instinct was to cry. His was to grip my shoulders firmly, as though if he held me tight enough the pain would diminish, or maybe I would understand, in my heart, that this slap, the first I had ever gotten in my life, was deserved. I touched my cheek to comfort myself, and Abba didn't know what to do with himself other than apologize. He took his hand off my shoulders and held my other hand, the one that was dangling down; he sat down on the bed, stood up in confusion, and sat back down.

After a moment I sat next to him, as though it was my job to console him.

"There are certain things, Elisheva, that... that you don't understand. And it's good that you don't understand them. You've grown up in a protected environment; you can't even imagine what people have going on inside them. People come to me, members of my congregation. You have no idea how lonely some of them are. They're wounded; they're ill... mentally ill. You can't see it when you look at them; they can hardly see it themselves. They don't know where to go for help. And me, well... there's a limit to what I can do. Remember how I wasn't accepted into the psychology program?"

And only then did he let go of my hand and smile, returning to his usual self. "Are your hands always this cold?" Then he continued in a sort of confession. "I don't know if you ever met Shofman, you were just a little girl at the time. He came to see me, and I thought I helped him. He thought so, too. But about six months later, he committed suicide. I was new at my job, and I was so sure of myself. You didn't learn about these things in rabbinical school. He was the last man you would have expected to take his own life. He had a good life, he had a family. Something can happen out of the blue, and there's no way for us to know what's going on in people's minds. Do you understand? You have to think of people as packages. What's it called, that game you liked to put together for birthday parties? 'Pass the Parcel?' Layers of history, of secrets. It's very hard to get to the core. So you understand why I'm worried about you. And about her."

I nodded. I don't know if I understood what he wanted me to understand, but I understood some things. When you focus on someone else's pain, your own pain begins to dissipate. I understood how much I didn't know about what it meant to be the rabbi of a congregation.

"You really remember I made those parcels?"

"How could I forget? You used to get so angry at us for not having newspapers like everyone else did. You'd sit in the living room with your markers and scotch tape, lost in concentration. You wrote wonderful challenges."

I smiled, and so did Abba. It made me happy that for all these years, he'd been carrying this memory in his heart.

Abba looked at the clock on his shelf and said he'd come with me to lock up the house, to put it to sleep. He got up, reached out his hand, and apologized, this time in Hebrew. I just nodded, because I thought if I said "I forgive you," it would sound silly. When we left the room, I felt like I was taking leave of an important moment. I considered asking him if he thought Amy's life was at risk, but I didn't want to put her between us once again. The front door was locked. When we got to the steps, Abba asked me if I needed to get up by a certain time the next morning.

I was already on the first step, and I turned around to say that I was going to get up at a very particular time, the last possible minute, eight-thirty; I had a ten-thirty test. Even though it was understood, Abba told me to get an extra-good night's sleep, and reminded me how he used to encourage me to sleep the day of the Seder so I could stay up until the search for the *Afikoman.*

Because of the step, we were the same height, and even he could see that blowing me a kiss wasn't the right thing to do. He dropped his arms and pulled me towards him. It was a rare and poignant moment that allowed us to forget the circumstances that had led up to it.

Influenced by my new mentor, apparently, I went to sleep without brushing my teeth for the first time in a long time. When I rested my head on the pillow, I thought I could smell the last vestiges of the night before last; they smelled cloyingly sweet. It embarrassed me to think about my most private fluids as sweet. I stopped thinking about submitting to myself once again, and focused instead on the impetuous slap Abba had given me. I didn't know why I wouldn't let him apologize fully, explain himself or at least clarify what it was that made him so eager to evict Amy from the house as if she had some kind of plague.

I remembered, again, the cold, despondent photograph of Ima piling up snow outside Ora's house in 1977. That picture, I thought sadly, in which Ima was trying to project the illusion of happiness, was so typical of our family. We always tried to pass ourselves off as a liberal, Conservative family, and only I, like the boy in "The Emperor's New Clothes," pointed out the blemishes, the gusts of frigid air that blew all around us. Unpleasant thoughts began to surface, thoughts that originated in Amy, who had, in a way, exposed the foundations of our home, foundations that wanted to remain hidden. Still, I fell asleep feeling optimistic, glossing over anything troubling just like the rest of my family always did. I fell asleep with the sense that my ability to see, or more precisely my ability to love, had somehow improved.

Fourteen

As much as I like the idea of thanking God for restoring our spirit after taking it from us overnight, so to speak, I've never said *Modeh Ani,* the Morning Prayer that does just that. This morning, the morning of the first Sunday of my life without Grandma, I spontaneously and sincerely thanked God for having two eyes that could see. In my dream, I woke up in Liat's house and my left eye was so crusted over I could barely open it. I was waiting for it to pass, and instead of treating it with medication, Liat and I climbed into her parents' bed. The bits of crust were spreading all around my eye, to the point that it felt completely sealed, like a very tight knot. Liat assured me that it was only temporary, and told me we were going to the pool. On the way, the only thing that troubled me was whether or not people could see the repulsive fibers crisscrossing my skin like melted cheese on top of a lasagna. As we walked, I kept thinking that the seal had broken, and I tried to open my eye, but it was useless.

The dream reflected how much I still live in the past, in the "what will people say" mindset of the town where I grew up, and how a part of me is still jealous of Liat.

I went downstairs. Nobody was in the living room, but a sense of chaos still prevailed. After tidying up a little, I decided to get started on my day before everyone woke up to the first week without grandma. I offered to pick up Ima, Ora, and Sam, Ora's husband, from the airport. My enchanted year of film studies was almost over. Next year, if I get accepted into the screenwriting program, everything will be different. Maybe, now that Grandma has died, I'll start taking myself seriously.

I'll waitress; I'll experience the hardships of life; I'll earn money from something productive. And with all the social interaction that takes place in a café, I'm sure to meet young men. I was surprised by my own optimism; it was as if I was getting stronger in anticipation of my encounter with Ima. As if something good could come from Grandma's death. Maybe I'll have a different perspective on her legendary words about what one wants. Until now, I had approached her motto with a kind of resignation: whatever it is that you want, you're not going to get it. But maybe there's another way to look at it. Since I don't know what I want anyway, why not let life surprise me every now and then.

The feeling of escaping the sleeping house - even though this time I was doing it from a place of strength - reminded me of the morning after my pathetic escape with Amy. An escape that I believed would rescue both her and me, and even strengthen the bond between me and Abba. As if he would finally see that I could stand on my own two feet.

On that Sunday morning, like this one, I came downstairs to an empty house, to the scent of the runners that still lingered in the air. I found a note from Abba in the kitchen, telling me I had a message on the machine from the previous day. At the end of the note he had drawn a smiley-face and written "Good luck on the test."

It was Liat's voice I heard on the answering machine, saying she didn't know where we had disappeared to. She also wanted to thank Amy - "you know why" - and to figure out how she was getting to the *bagrut.* After her message, I heard Ima's voice: she was looking for us. I pressed the replay button so I could hear her distant voice asking Abba to get back to her as soon as possible. The timing of the message showed that she'd been up in the middle of the night or in the early morning, as if she had caught Amy's insomnia - the same Amy who was, metaphorically, and only metaphorically, sleeping in her bed.

I thought this pair of messages was odd, because according to my calculations, Abba had been home when Shabbat ended. Then I realized that he'd gone out to look for me; that was why he was so angry when I came home. I stroked my cheek, suddenly feeling like I was in some kind of danger.

And indeed, outside the front door, I could hear a conversation. I recognized Amy's voice, pontificating in English. If I had the nerve, I would have taken advantage of her absence to run upstairs and take a look at the notorious mess in her room, but I didn't have the courage. I must have used it all up.

I peered through the peephole and ran out at the sound of Amy's laugh, hoping she hadn't said anything inappropriate. She was sitting in the front yard talking to Steven, who was wearing running clothes. The way he was dressed was proof of the intensity of my father's determination. Abba would do whatever it took, even if that meant tricking me and embroiling Steven in a lie by trying to pass him off as another one of the runners. His decisiveness made it clear that this was no time for games. Even I played my part in the conspiracy, and didn't divulge the truth about Steven. I told Steven that clearly, our terrific guest had enticed him to give up his morning run. I silently wondered if he'd been able to make a diagnosis yet, and what he would have done if Amy hadn't been an early riser.

Steven acknowledged that everyone else was out running. "As I was just saying to Amy," he explained, "I'm always intrigued by psychologists who go into hospitals to observe how we humble physicians try to heal the ailing body. The minute I heard about her job offer at my hospital, I knew I had to give up the run."

When I heard these few sentences, I understood that he was hiding his real profession. Given his appearance, that wasn't hard. He looked like someone who lived in the jungle, not like the Chief of a psychiatric hospital. Even presenting himself as an ordinary physician might have raised some eyebrows. His thin lips sought shelter inside the black, bushy beard that always made him look so disheveled. It was only when he opened his mouth to speak, and a British accent came out, that you realized that this was a person of status and culture. Abba used to joke that the beard allowed him to go in and out of the psychiatric hospital without anyone guessing what he did there.

Steven stood up, stretched, and said that it would be best if he could get out of there before the runners came back, so he wouldn't have to feel guilty about his dry shirt. Everything felt awkward. I wondered what was going to happen when they realized that Amy was perfectly fine, when she moved to our town and became an integral part of the community. Steven said that if it wasn't too much trouble, I could help him maintain his record of laziness and give him a ride home.

I knew he wanted to share his findings with me, and I eagerly agreed. I wanted to put an end to all the suspicions that were whirling inside me like clean clothes in a sudsy washing machine.

I told Amy she should get ready for her meeting, and I would bring us back something good to eat. She winked at Steven and asked him if he knew what she meant when she said she'd found the ideal family.

I felt like she was intentionally plucking on my tautest strings. Steven nodded and shook her hand, thanking her for a pleasant morning and telling her he'd like to follow the progress of her research, particularly if it pertained to the work she was doing when she took on the personae of different Biblical characters.

I knew this meant that she had recited Tamar's monologue to him. Maybe the words she put into the mouth of that ancient character shielded her from the world. I hoped Steven had taken this into account.

Aside from instructing me to drive to the synagogue, Steven didn't open his mouth during the entire ride. When we parked at the synagogue, in an attempt to get a better idea of what was going on, I asked, wasn't Abba out running? Steven looked at me, surprised, as if I had kidnapped him and deposited him in this strange reality, as if it had been me and not him - the doctor - who had brought us here.

"I don't even remember what we decided," he admitted, putting on his absent-minded-professor cap. "You changed everything yesterday, and your father was furious. I just don't remember."

And again, he looked at me with troubled eyes, as if I was the key to a secret code. I summoned up my most rational thinking, and even though I knew that between his trembling lips he was holding information that was potentially life-changing, I said what he wanted to hear, I would go inside and see if Abba was in, and if he wasn't, we'd go back home and wait for them on the sidewalk.

On weekdays, the synagogue didn't seem so ominous, and as I expected, Abba wasn't in his office. Really, it didn't suit him to be so manipulative that he would actually stage a run. I drove Steven to the corner of our street, and we waited for Abba as if we were planning an ambush.

Before I had a chance to ask, Steven said he was sorry to tell me this, but the news wasn't good. Just as Abba suspected, she had "tested positive," and he was afraid she was suffering from schizophrenia. As far as he could tell, she'd been sick for a few years already.

"She talked about it very openly; she thinks that it was a single episode and that now it's behind her."

"What does that mean, 'positive'?" I don't know why I was fixated on that particular word. Then I added, with disbelief, "Schizophrenia?"

"There's no need to panic. Do you know what schizophrenia is? You don't have to be scared, it's not a split personality like in the movies. That's very rare, and some people think it doesn't even exist. Schizophrenia is a real disease, a neurological disturbance in the brain that afflicts almost one percent of the population."

"So what does she have?" I felt an uncontrollable fear surging through my body. Given the involuntary closeness between me and this certified psychiatrist, surely he could sense the turmoil rushing through my mind. The illness wasn't dangerous, he explained, but yes, he thought she should leave.

"Schizophrenia manifests itself in a variety of ways, and quite honestly, we can't always pinpoint a single diagnosis. It's a broad illness, and it includes a wide spectrum of psychiatric and neurological diagnoses. Basically, it's an illness characterized by an impaired understanding of reality and by delusional thoughts or fantasies, severe enough to make normal functioning impossible. And that's what Amy has. She doesn't have a persecution complex, but she does have delusions and ambivalence...."

"Since when is ambivalence a bad thing?"

"It's more than just ambivalence, it's contradictory feelings that affect her state of mind, that prevent her from understanding her own feelings, which is why her responses are so often inappropriate. Right now, Amy isn't entirely 'governed' by her illness because she is taking medication, even if only sporadically. But overall, the schizophrenia doesn't allow her to think clearly, to connect with other people...."

"But the way she connected to me was great! Better than great!"

"Maybe. It's entirely possible. Some of the time, she can distinguish between imagination and reality, but on the whole it's hard for her. Besides, she might imagine that she has been sent to save you, or...."

"To save me from whom?"

"I don't know, it's only hypothetical. Here comes your father. I suggest you go inside and act normal. The patient's environment is a significant factor, in terms of both the onset of the illness and its aftermath. Once a psychotic break occurs, denial sets in immediately." Even though Steven didn't have a chance to finish - he jumped out of the car to greet Abba and the rest of the runners - I understood that we were in the aftermath stage. The five of them stood there whispering to each other, and I, with clinical ambivalence, went into the house, occasionally glancing behind me to see if by some miracle they had changed their minds. I had no idea how to rescue Amy, who had shown me only kindness.

Amy was engrossed in her activities and didn't notice how long it had taken for me to get back. When I started up the stairs to get ready, she asked what happened to the food I was supposed to bring back. I wondered what Steven would say about his patient's remarkable cognitive abilities, and what excuse he would have conjured up for me, the so-called normal one.

"Oh, shoot," I said, getting into character, "I totally forgot, because when I dropped off Steven, his son ran out and asked if I could take him to the entrance to the town so he could hitch a ride. On the way, we started talking, and it completely slipped my mind. Maybe there's something left over from yesterday."

I went into the kitchen to look for some food; all that morning's chaotic activity had made me hungry. Amy came in on my heels and didn't even give me a chance to get near the refrigerator. On the one hand, she looked like a clean, well-kempt person, but on the other hand, her piercing gaze accentuated the dark circles under her eyes, which seemed to be getting deeper. Her hawkish eyes scared me, and I wondered if schizophrenia was contagious. Clearly, I myself was becoming paranoid as I waited for the moment when Abba would walk in. I thought about how Amy's daughter, Debbie, was studying to be a psychiatrist; she must have been trying to find a cure for her mother's illness.

A big smile on her face, Amy asked when we'd be leaving, and, as casually as I could, told her we'd be going right away. It wasn't time yet, but something inside me, or really outside me - her close proximity - was pressing me to leave the house.

I asked her what time the meeting was, and she said it didn't matter, she'd like to be able to walk around the hospital for a while, to familiarize herself with the department. I told her we'd leave right after I called Liat to offer her a ride. I considered taking a spare set of clothes in case Amy and I decided to run away to some faraway place. Regardless of the verdict, I could go with her, to whatever destination she chose; I could be like Ruth the Moabite who insisted on accompanying

Naomi until the very end, even if it meant believing in a different god.

When Amy and I met at the top of the staircase and started heading down, she asked me if I knew about the *mitzvah,* the Jewish commandment, of *shiluah haken* – the dispatching of the mother bird. This sounded like a military operation to me, and I was glad that my rebellious mind had spared me from learning about these seemingly esoteric commandments and their meanings.

A smile of contentment flickered across Amy's face. It surprised me that she had no idea what was going on around her, and to keep it that way, I pretended to be interested in the *mitzvah.*

"So what is *shiluah haken?* It sounds like an anti-pigeon spray."

"Anti, yes, you could say that the way Judaism relates to motherhood is anti. Although, there is something a little bit cruel about motherhood that can't be ignored."

At that very moment, Abba walked in. The expression on his face was one I hadn't seen before: warm-hearted and mistrustful at the same time. One thing was for sure: he and the three runners who followed him inside weren't the ones who were going to provide Amy with "the last-minute rescue" – the cinematic term for the plot twist that leads to a happy ending.

The quartet pretended to be winded. Who knows, maybe they really did sprint another lap. Instead of staying for coffee, Jerry, Avraham and Moshe hurried out, each with his own excuse.

It is to Abba's credit that he tried to be nice, or, more accurately, to maintain the façade of thoughtfulness and generosity that he had erected. He announced that he was going to take a shower, after which he'd make us a delicious breakfast.

I reminded him that we were both hurrying off, I to the *bagrut* and Amy to her interview, and he made a face, like a little boy who wasn't getting his way. His offer, which didn't seem appropriate for a regular weekday, put me on guard, but his measured stride gave me hope that maybe things would return to normal after all. I wanted time to freeze, to stand still, like in the movie, so we'd never have to reach the unforeseeable ending. In fact, I would have been happy to freeze the entire week that had just passed, reliving it day by day, but then I remembered my encounter with Eren Shonsky. I knew I wouldn't want to have to spend the rest of my life lugging around my frustration over not visiting his room. It seems that's what prevents people from moving forward or changing direction, the hope that something will get better. Suddenly Ruth the Moabite's devotion to her mother-in-law no longer seemed as extraordinary, as trusting, as people like to think. It was just that she had nothing to lose. Maybe that's also what brought Amy to us.

Like a merchant haggling with a customer, Abba said he would just make us something small. Also, he wanted to show me something before I left. Once we were in the kitchen, he tried to talk like a fish, meaning he silently distorted his lips and hoped that I would understand him. In the end, defeated, he walked right up to me and whispered that Steven had said that the three of us had to stay together all the time.

"Together?" I felt the literalism of the word getting caught in my throat. "You're not exaggerating?"

"Unfortunately not." Again, he had a calm demeanor, as if he'd had experience with this. "She might say that we tried to hurt her, that I in particular tried to hurt her, you know, as a man."

Here was yet another thing that Amy's presence had shown me. Another stage of maturation that I had to master. To see Abba not only as my father but also as a man out there in the world. What exactly did he want me to do with this information? I couldn't supervise his marriage, spy on Amy, and worry about my education at the same time.

Abba took out fish roe salad, imported peanut butter, fancy goat cheese and placed them on the counter, and I could feel my appetite screaming inside me. Our conversation about birds had made me think that perhaps I should become a vegetarian; after all, there were plenty of delicious foods besides meat. Plus, I would have one more thing in common with Eren Shonsky.

Abba went to shower, and while Amy and I were making our sandwiches, I asked her to tell me more about sending the mother bird away. Amy explained that if a person comes across a nest, he is not allowed to take the eggs or the chicks unless he chases away the mother, who is guarding over them, first.

"So she won't get depressed?" I tried to understand the reasoning behind this commandment.

"Don't try to figure out why this *mitzvah* exists. In fact, people use this commandment to prove that the main reason for keeping *mitzvot* is that God commanded us to do so. If you still feel like you need an explanation, most commentaries agree that the main purpose of the *mitzvah* is to foster the virtue of compassion in human beings. Not taking the goslings in front of their mother."

"But you said something about the element of cruelty in motherhood, where's that?" I asked impatiently.

She let me finish up with the sandwiches while she went to get a Bible from Ima's library, a library in which she'd already made herself at home.

"It says in Deuteronomy…here it is: 'If you happen to find a bird's nest in a tree or on the ground, and there are young ones or eggs in it with the mother sitting in the nest, do not take the mother with the young. You shall let the mother go, but the young you may take for yourself, that it may go well with you, and that you may live long.' Do you see? The reason for doing the *mitzvah* is that it will be good for you, and the promise is that it will give you a long life."

"And where's the compassion here? And compassion towards whom? The person who wants to nab a meal?" Amy looked at me as if I had gone crazy, then burst out laughing. And so did I.

After we composed ourselves, Amy said that it may have been a limited interpretation, but it was still a call for compassion. It's true that after the flood, God allowed us to eat meat. But this interpretation tells us not to take it too far, not to abuse animals beyond this initial allowance.

I still didn't understand what could be worse than being allowed to eat them. Amy smiled and said that unfortunately, there can always be something worse. Maybe I was right and this was just a kind of rationalization for humans, or for God, being kind to the animals that you are planning to eat. Still, she thought that this ruling was based on the insight that children and parents lead separate lives, and that it was nice that the Torah was trying to cultivate the idea that "As a man measures others, so shall he be measured."

"You mean, measuring the difficulty of getting a meal," I said, and we both laughed again.

Abba appeared, washed and dressed. His gaze bounced back and forth, like he was trying to understand why the two of us were smiling like we had some kind of secret. When he saw the Bible, he asked, "What did you two stumble upon?"

"*Shiluah HaKen,*" I answered knowingly, hoping it would signal to him that so far, I hadn't disobeyed him. I continued: "It's a *mitzvah* that asks people to be merciful and moral, but actually points them to take care for themselves. What do you think about this strange *mitzvah?*"

"It's not surprising that she objects to the *mitzvah,* right?" Abba winked at Amy, and I was glad that he was finally breaking down the wall that had been separating them. Then, as if attempting to gloss over the possible connection between the topic of discussion and reality, he veered off and said, "According to the Jerusalem Talmud, this *mitzvah* is one of the reasons the heretic Elisha Ben Abuya decided to leave the world of Torah. It tells us that once, Elisha saw someone climb to the top of a palm tree, remove the mother bird from her bustling nest, and climb down safely. The next day he saw someone climb another palm tree, shoo away the mother, and gather up the chicks. On his way down, he was bitten by a snake and died. Ben Abuya asked, where's the justice?"

"Where indeed?" I asked. No reaction came from Amy. She hadn't spoken since Abba had entered the room. Abba was defensive. "Justice is a complicated thing. Sometimes it happens only over time."

"But the man died!" I argued. "There was no more time!"

Now Abba, too, noticed Amy's silence, and her distant gaze. He muttered something about justice taking place in the world to come, while trying to tell me, by making the kinds of faces you make when you're arm-wrestling, to let it go.

Amy nodded. Maybe she also felt like the mother bird, who didn't really care whether or not the person climbing the tree was going to do the *mitzvah;* the ending was pre-determined, and the thought that someone might do this bad deed in a better way was no consolation. Abba went into his apprehensive mode, which valued a united front above everything else, and reminded me again to return home after the *bagrut.* He didn't forget to wish Amy good luck in her interview, but I couldn't help feeling that we were both being sent out of the nest.

Now, here I was, back on the road again. Heading north this time, and with no reason to hurry. I thought again about the different screenplays I could write. I had already written the scene in which I'm getting ready for my first date - that is to say, my character Amalia is getting ready for her date. She comes out of the shower with a towel wrapped around her hair, and is checking her underarms to make sure she shaved them well, when the phone rings. It's her heartthrob, Yoav Shimoni, suggesting that they go to a concert instead of a movie. Over the course of their animated conversation, in which she gives him directions to the town and instructs him to honk when he gets there, she hears the beep of call-waiting. When she finally hangs up and, blissfully, answers the other line, the voice of her childhood friend asks if she's sitting down, then tells her that Nirit, their long-time mutual friend, has died. I got stuck there. Next he's standing on her front stairs, and he tells her the news in person. Still stuck. I'm planning to add that more and more friends gather at Amalia's house, and she forgets to tell Yoav Shimoni, who's been honking repeatedly to no avail, until she finally remembers her date and goes out, with bare feet and uncombed hair, and doesn't know what to do with herself, and with him. This not knowing still feels very fresh to me. I don't know if this would draw an audience, which makes me think that it would be much more interesting if she slept with him, it would be more convincing and more cheerful than what happened in real life, which is that she slept with her childhood friend who took advantage of the opportunity and the mayhem.

Somewhere between Gedera and Ashdod, I realize I need a script advisor. And it wouldn't hurt if I went for some counseling myself. Maybe therapy could bridge the gap between the parcels of family history that I received when Amy was here six years ago - parcels that have been waiting for someone to open them - and my love life, which remains locked away somewhere, with no key in sight.

Fifteen

I love airports. When I was in the army, serving as the liaison for an American volunteer program, I had many opportunities to visit Ben Gurion Airport. An airport is a neutral area, unusual in that it is open to every kind of person, to all the citizens of the world, without distinctions, without discrimination. The big airports in the United States are even open to travelers from hostile countries; nobody is ever turned away at the door. You can be tired and stretched out on a bench, or even throwing up, and you'd still be accepted.

And now I'm here, waiting for Ima. A whirlpool of memories and expectations.

According to the arrival board, their flight was delayed, so I went to get a drink and eavesdrop on other people's conversations. "A mother is not a hanger where you can hang all your troubles," I heard one woman say to her friend. I quickly jotted it down in the new notebook I'd bought at the university, determined to apply, at least once before the end of the semester, what my film teacher suggested at the very first class. I was disheartened by the cruelty of the word "hanger" so close to the word "mother." "Hanger" sounds a lot like "hunger."

When we drove to our English *bagrut* exam, I was troubled by the fact that I hadn't really picked up on Amy's clinical pathology. Was I not sensitive enough to nuances?

After a few minutes of silence, during which our minds strayed to wherever they were meant to stray, Amy told Liat about the movie we had seen, and about the brilliance of both Abba and the Biblical sages. And again she sounded like Ima, when she said that every artistic creation, particularly verbal ones, were footnotes to the Bible and *midrash.* According to Amy, the movie used the motif of sleep to demonstrate the fragility of man and to comment on the contrast between the nature of man and the nature of the God who created him. When God created Adam, the angels helping Him, thought Adam was holy, and worshiped him as if he were a god. That's why God put him to sleep - so the angels would see his mortality, the transience of his breath.

We reached the hospital, a useless place for gods and angels. After exchanging estimated times, we decided that we would just meet at home, as we had done after the previous exam. We wished each other luck, and Liat, who had climbed out of the car so she could join me in the front seat, was granted a hug from Amy.

Something about the image of that embrace pierced me in some invisible spot, and made me feel like I'd been looking for this image for many years, since the day I came into the world. I was suddenly afraid that I would never see Amy again. I opened the door, called her name, and got out of the car. I told her with conviction that I would pick her up at 1:30 and she should wait for me right there. She smiled a peculiar, compliant smile and said that was fine. I got back into the car, not thinking about the fact that I, too, could have gotten the hug that I wanted.

When we returned after the exam Amy was standing - sitting, really - on the sidewalk where we had dropped her off. She asked if she could sit in the back seat and take a nap, and she didn't want to answer any of our questions about her interview. Liat and I chatted about the remaining *bagruyot,* even as I kept stealing glimpses of Amy, who was sitting in the back staring out the window. I could feel how she was turning into some sort of plaything in my hands. I feared that this was further proof of her peculiarity, and the way she was sitting so passively in the back seat accentuated it even more.

After we dropped off Liat, I felt like I needed some more time away from Abba's injunctions. Amy agreed to move up to the front seat, but still wouldn't talk about the interview. There was something strange in the air. I decided I needed a real escape, and there was only one option. I suggested to Amy that we drive over to see the *andarta*, the Monument to the Negev Brigade. She gave me a big smile - a little too big, and somewhat threatening.

We drove. The car inched up the road, and the monument, which looked like a space station, was exposed in all its concrete heft. Two cars and a stray dog stood in the parking lot.

Amy looked up, and said she didn't have the energy to climb up the dirt road. I told her the view was spectacular, that you could see the entire town from the other side, as well as Tel Beersheba, but it didn't change her mind. Her tone reminded me of Ima's constant refrain - "I don't have the energy, Elisheva, do what you want" - and I started up the road.

I had never visited alone. Halfway up, I realized something: I was finally running away from home. Officially. And it wasn't because of Hanoch or Ima, whom I had always blamed for making me do things I didn't want to do, but because of Abba. Abba was always convincing the rest of the family to follow his lead, but because of his disarming personality and his infectious, childlike enthusiasm, nobody noticed his powers of persuasion. Was it him I was running from?

Recently, in my university class on movie adaptations of plays, I saw "The Tempest," starring John Cassavetes and his wife, Gena Rowlands. In that film, too, the daughter prefers her father. Or perhaps the father is so dominant and self-centered that there's no other option but to trail behind him. The movie also dealt with the entrance of a third character into the family, and with the price children pay for the fulfillment of their parents' wishes.

After walking around the monument and reading all the explanations of its symbolic components, there was nowhere else to go. I realized it was a little too late and a little too silly to run away. Anyway, it wouldn't really have been my escape. I returned to the car desperately wanting Amy to enchant me with some story or *midrash,* but like the desert surrounding us, her words had dried out and I drove us back home with a slight fear hovering me.

If I'd been hoping that Abba would give up on us and take his usual nap, I was very wrong. For the first time in his life, he had made us lunch on a weekday. Pots of rice, vegetables and chicken were sitting there, as if our house was an advertisement for domestic happiness. He didn't say a word about our tardiness, he just told Amy to sit at the table and me to join him in the kitchen. It was there that I finally grasped that Amy was leaving that same day and, after some more effort, that he had spoken to her brother in Netanya. He said they would meet in Jerusalem. Abba was so distressed that he couldn't even speak; instead, he scribbled some notes in his chicken-scratch Hebrew.

When he was done, he said something out loud about how he still had to cook the chicken, and passed me the note describing everything Ima had discovered across the ocean. To me it looked like an old-fashioned telegram.

"She was in a psychiatric hospital for two years, two years ago. She did correspond with Soroka Hospital. A month ago she disappeared. Her daughter and ex-husband didn't know where she had gone. They were mad with worry. She was released from the hospital because of some glitch in the system. We can't be responsible for her. She's leaving today!"

I looked back and forth between him and the page. I felt like a colorblind person trying to put together a multicolored puzzle, or someone trying to identify a gift by its wrapping paper. I searched for a peephole that would reveal something beyond the words themselves, that would shed a different light on the person who wrote them. The person standing right across from me. The person I had to honor because that's what God commanded me to do. I listened to him blabbering on, trying to defend himself while I read his testimony.

"Elisheva," Abba said softly, as if making sure I hadn't drowned inside the sheet of paper. And indeed, my hands that continued to grasp the paper did feel numb, like they were trying to erase what was written there. I tightened them into fists, shoved the note in my pocket and looked him straight in the eye, a desperate look that accepted his authority and was now awaiting his verdict. He smiled his broadest smile, trying to offer me some solace. I spread my arms to the sides: *now what?* And I waited for the salvation that was supposed to follow the exclamation point he had inserted after "she's leaving today." Abba said I should trust him, but I wasn't sure I could. I figured that if everyone else practiced repression so skillfully, so could I, and I walked away.

Amy didn't heed Abba's orders either, and went back to Ima's chair. The Bible was open on her lap, and she was looking at the pictures hanging across from her. She gave me a look that struck me as profound and said, "The hospital made me change my whole interpretation of the Book of Ruth. I had no idea there were so many Bedouins, especially in the maternity ward. Here in your town, you don't see them at all."

Now it was easy for me to detect, and even, perhaps, to admit, her odd associative manner, a manner that had impressed me so much by the way it mingled the sacred with the profane, by the way it ignored time, context, everything around us.

I giggled nervously, unsure if this was a criticism or just an innocent observation, and I worked up the nerve to ask her what the connection was between her meeting and the Bedouins. I thought I was throwing her a life raft that would give her some direction, that would help her arrange her thoughts in some kind of order. But she ignored my question and called for Abba to come out of the kitchen; she wanted to say something. The way she introduced it, "I want to say something," was another one of her habits, one that heightened the sense of drama.

Abba worked up the courage to leave the kitchen, and arrived at the table with his own bait, an incredible plate of food. He stood by the chair and talked to Amy, but to me he looked like a servant tendering a peace offering to his goddess.

As she flipped through the pages of the Bible, Amy told him that every now and then, one of these stories surfaces to remind us that we ourselves are strangers. Strangers to ourselves, sometimes. And with his permission, that's what she would like to use for her Bibliodrama presentation.

Abba nodded silently; he wasn't prepared for that. That in the midst of all his eagerness to assign her a particular illness, she would remind him of how he needed her, of his enthusiastic invitation a few days earlier to take part in the all-night study session on Shavuot.

With difficulty, Abba extricated himself from his confusion. His face tormented by his unspoken lie, said it sounded like a compelling and unusual idea, and we should probably eat before the food got cold. I hoped that the Shavuot session would make him alter his plan, but I couldn't see any trace of change in his eyes.

Suddenly I realized who could save us: Grandma. She was so fond of Amy; surely she would be distressed and want to help. Even if she agreed with Abba, at least I could use her house as a base from which I could get in touch with Avigail to arrange a visit to Jerusalem. Most importantly, she could lend me money for the trip.

I said that I might go get Grandma, and behind Amy's back, I pointed upwards, hinting at the difficulties we were likely to encounter when we asked our guest to pack up her belongings.

"That's a great idea," Abba pronounced, and I could hear the relief in his voice. "But let's do that later. The food's going to get cold, and besides, Grandma doesn't like to eat in the afternoon. Let's sit down."

Amy stood up, and I could tell that Abba no longer trusted me to go by myself. While Amy ambled over to the table, I tried to delete the information about her past that had been laid before me. I especially wanted to erase the picture of her as a long-term resident of a psychiatric hospital, wearing pajamas and conducting her roommate to the sounds of Madame Butterfly. I tried with all my might to savor the pleasure of my taste buds, to imagine, for a moment, that everything was forgotten, had gone back to the way it was. Though I wasn't successful, the food gave me strength and gave me back the feeling that Amy's visit hadn't been in vain. Despite Abba's not entirely understandable pressure, I wouldn't abandon her.

Abba decided to bring us back to the story of *Shiluah HaKen.* He told us that the original *mitzvah* appeared in the Torah portion *"Ki Tetze"* – "When You Go Out." *"Ki Tetze"* follows *"Ki Tavo"* – "When You Arrive." He said he loved the names of the

Torah portions; it was as if the names were telling us that any time a person leaves, he can still come back.

I felt like Abba was trying to console himself for what he was about to initiate, and I noticed Amy opening the Bible, then closing it immediately, as if she'd just been bitten by a snake. I didn't think Abba noticed her gesture. He preferred to learn from our sages rather than emulate them. I stood up and began clearing the table. When I was in the kitchen, I casually called out, "I'm going to get Grandma, OK?" Within seconds Abba appeared, and in a voice louder than was necessary, he asked me if I could take him to synagogue first, so he could pick up the Bibles he needed for the Shavuot study he was leading at Grandma's residence. I knew he wasn't lying, but still, it was sad to see the fear in his eyes replace the joy that had gripped him only a moment earlier, when he was sitting on the other side of the wall. Amy was still sitting at the table, stone-still, with the Bible on her lap tightly closed. She budged only when Abba told her that we'd be right back; she looked towards the door and smiled in agreement.

At the end of the film "The Tempest," they sail away from the Greek island in a cramped, colorful boat that reflected the joy of returning to regular life. Now, in contrast, Ima, Ora, and Sam were wheeling their luggage in a state of exhaustion, with nothing flowery or festive among their wares. The only thing that stood out, really, was a box containing a small car, a gift for Evyatar, my mother's first, and so far, only, grandson. It's funny to think of her as someone's grandmother. Like me, he's also more attached to my father--his grandfather--who buys him little trinkets and plays with him. When the right day comes, I will explain to Evyatar that she's just waiting for him to grow up; just like she waited for me. Then he'll enjoy her company.

Sixteen

On the way home from the airport, Ima kept saying how lucky it was that she had a chance to talk to Grandma on the phone, and how unfortunate it was that Grandma's doctor was so convinced she'd once again pull through, that he told Ima not to take the next flight to Israel. If he hadn't said that, she might have been able to say goodbye. Someone recently taught me the difference between regret and guilt. Guilt, he said, is a useless emotion; it's like a giant swamp. It jabs you in the gut but it doesn't change anything, whether it's your own guilt or the guilt you're trying to incite in someone else. Regret, on the other hand, is healthy. It is both natural and vital, allowing you to learn from your experience, so you can approach things differently next time, so history doesn't repeat itself. I didn't think this was the best time to enlighten my passengers on the difference between these two concepts, which are as fundamental to the Jewish soul as a floor is to a dancer.

Even though I was playing the part of the responsible, savvy driver, I felt confused. Just like I did back then, when Abba and I bade a somewhat peculiar farewell to Amy. I couldn't understand how Abba could be so distressed by her presence, and at the same time so unconcerned about leaving her alone in our house with all our precious belongings, and with herself. He himself had said there was no way to know what a disturbed person could do. On the other hand, the escape demonstrated just how horrified he was by the thought of staying alone with her, as if she might infect him or blame him for harassing her. Maybe it was his own sense of guilt that made him run away.

When we loaded the Bibles into the car, Abba elaborated on what he didn't say in his hurried note, on the words that weren't written. "Like Steven explained, the current treatment of schizophrenia is based on tranquilizers. They don't cure the illness, exactly, but they control the symptoms. The problem is that once someone starts taking medication, she thinks she's getting better, even though it's not a real improvement. It is more of a cognitive or emotional anesthetization. The patient deludes herself into thinking she no longer needs the medication, and stops taking it. Then she suffers a relapse. She goes back to the hospital and is given the medication once again, but by then both the body and the mind have undergone some kind of change, and even if she does get better eventually, all the attacks have a cumulative effect. The attacks can be triggered by different things, and we can't be responsible for someone in her situation. It's only a matter of time until something even more serious occurs."

"But Steven said she's aware of her illness."

"He's assuming she's aware, but it doesn't matter. You saw how clever she is. In the last year, she's been going to some kind of outpatient clinic that helps her cope with her thoughts, but truly managing this illness requires self-discipline and the avoidance of anything jarring, anything that isn't part of one's routine."

"But…."

"No buts, Elisheva. A lot of people with schizophrenia are very bright. Above average, even. And yet, more than fifty percent of them attempt suicide. I can't be held responsible for that." There was no point in asking how he explained the fact that she had been corresponding with Soroka hospital, so instead I asked for an extension - even though I knew the answer would be no. Just until after the holiday, I said, so she could help me study for my literature exam.

"Absolutely not," he replied, and repeated that we couldn't be responsible for this kind of situation, not even for one more day. I asked him what his plan consisted of, exactly, and he said it was very simple. He'd already spoken to her brother, who was surprised to hear that she was in Israel. Abba had the sense that the siblings hadn't really been in touch in recent years. The brother was waiting to find out how she reacted to the news, and he would pick her up wherever we told him to. He suggested that if she resisted, we send her by car service, and if she didn't resist, we put her on a bus and he'd wait for her at the station. Amy's daughter was already on her way to Israel; she would take care of the rest.

"But what are you going to tell her?" I asked as we put the carton of books on the seat next to me. "I don't get it."

"That's the hard part," he admitted, and said that that was why we needed to bring in Grandma. "Maybe I'll tell her that Ima's coming back early," he said in a voice that sounded like he was a defense attorney about to give a closing statement. "Or maybe I'll just tell her the truth. I'll think about it while you're gone. Let's hope for the best; I checked the schedule, and there's a non-stop express bus every hour."

It was a little strange that her brother wasn't coming to pick her up, especially since she was sick. After all, this was Israel, not America, where you had to get on an airplane to visit another state. Even Ima used to pick me up from the Beersheba bus station whenever I asked her to. Either the siblings had a very strained relationship, or Abba was desperate for her to leave as soon as possible.

Just like in the story of Little Red Riding Hood, Abba warned me not to get into any mischief, and told me to go straight to

Grandma's without stopping on the way. In twenty minutes, he said, he expected to meet us back at the house. Attempting a serene smile, he watched me start the car. He stood there, as if to be sure that I was not only leaving, but also coming back.

What a strange business, I thought to myself. I couldn't imagine us serving her an eviction notice, nor could I imagine her going crazy. I couldn't imagine how it felt to be mentally ill. Where do you draw the line between sickness and health, between delusional thoughts and rational thoughts, between pathological ambivalence and healthy self-reflection? Abba always said that wisdom is based on asking questions; that's what makes us grow.

As soon as Grandma opened the door, I could see in her face that she already knew; Ima must have called to update her. It was funny that Amy's visit, which for me made Ima's absence that much keener, was bringing Ima and Grandma closer. Grandma was always complaining about her younger daughter's neglect of her. I was a little disappointed that she already knew about the chain of events because I wanted to hear her reaction, to feel that I wasn't the only one who was tormented by the situation. And of course I wanted to manipulate her thinking, so she would help me help Amy.

Grandma was so excited when she showed me all the information she'd gathered about the illness from her magazines that I wondered if perhaps I should invite myself over to Avigail's and spend Shavuot in Jerusalem with them. I cut off Grandma's rushing stream of words to tell her that Abba wanted her to come over and help him speak to Amy. She was pleased for she truly empathized with the complex situation.

After she said "Poor thing" for the thousandth time, I was brave enough to voice my opposition to the plan and to ask two things of her. First, to give me money and second, to convince Abba to let me take the bus with Amy.

Grandma's emphatic response shocked me. "Over my dead body." I told her that such a strong phrase warranted an explanation, but since Abba was waiting, maybe she should explain herself to me in the car.

"Don't you feel sorry for her?" I asked bluntly.

"Feeling sorry for people is judgmental." Grandma was a smart woman, and I knew she wasn't getting distracted by anything trivial. The fact that she had used such strong language to voice her objections was significant.

"You know what I'm trying to say. We can't just throw her to the dogs." I tried to reason with her by using an expression she liked, but her mind was made up.

She took a deep breath. "You don't understand that mental illness isn't something inconsequential. It's so sensitive, so dangerous, that only close family members can and must assume responsibility."

"But her family's not here, and she chose us, she chose me. You saw how nice she is."

She took another deep breath, deeper than I'd hoped for, and said she was going to tell me something that might shock me. Something she wanted me to put behind me immediately, because it had nothing to do with me, and her telling me was like a doctor breaking his oath. I nodded in consent. Her tone surprised me, but I figured she was going to tell me something about one of her many uncles and aunts. I almost said that I remembered something about some uncle who had gone crazy, but when I saw her staring at her palms, I stayed silent, remembering with anguish the story she had shared with me earlier, the one about Abba and Rebecca Klein.

Grandma said she was making it brief so we could hurry up and get the "poor thing" out of our house as soon as possible. "I don't know if you know this, but your mother was brilliant for her age."

Amy's visit had made me think about my mother a lot, but hearing her mentioned by her own mother, in the context of her childhood, was unexpected. I didn't say a word, and she continued.

"When she was in first grade, they wanted her to skip a grade. They thought that maybe her behavioral problems were caused by a lack of interest in her schoolwork. In other words, that she was too smart, and she needed to be surrounded by children at her own level. But even after she moved up a grade, she still made everyone crazy. They couldn't pinpoint any specific disorder. Because I had never received a real education, it was clear to me that this move was the best thing I could do for her. But then, out of the blue, things started to deteriorate. Emotionally. She was suddenly blinking her eyes all the time, and she became rebellious, making a scene about every little thing, like going to shul or cleaning her room. One day the school called and told me she'd had a breakdown. Her legs were paralyzed, and she refused to speak."

I couldn't imagine my mother refusing to speak. The expression on Grandma's face didn't help. There was something exposed about it, and at the same time, something concealed "We had no choice. We took her to Mount Sinai Hospital, where they wrapped her legs in warm sheets, and, very gently, encouraged her to speak. In order to comfort her, and to help her pass the time, we rented the hottest commodity around: a television. It cost us a small fortune. She stayed there for six months. What I'm trying to tell you is that not everyone can understand mental illness. The fact is, nobody ever figured out what brought on the paralysis or what made it go away. Clearly it was something psychological, some kids are weaker than others, but nobody could ever tell us exactly what it was. They insisted that it had nothing to do with moving her to another grade, or with the fact that she was born the day the bomb fell on Hiroshima. It was just one of those psychological episodes that couldn't be explained. And as you can see, it never happened again. For a while her soul was weakened and impaired. Fortunately, we were able to get her the medical care she needed right away."

"And that's it?" What else could I say after hearing this bizarre story?

"That's it. She had to go for physical therapy to learn to walk properly, and then all the symptoms disappeared without a trace. Oh, and we had to buy a TV, because once your mother discovered the addictive power of the magic box, we had no choice."

Grandma took another deep breath. "Now do you understand, sweetie? Do you understand why you can't get in the middle of this?"

I said I understood, even though I didn't understand a thing. I especially didn't understand why I had never heard this story, which had been hidden away in the closet like a skeleton. It wasn't nice, or maybe it was just natural, but all of a sudden I no longer cared about Amy's future. I cared only about my mother's past. I felt like my whole body was sprinkled with question marks.

Grandma, who wanted to bring me back to the present, started showing off her new mastery of schizophrenia. In her expert opinion, Amy's illness was triggered by her daughter's Bat Mitzvah. She had read that all the changes and separations that come with the realization that you're aging, changing, and eventually dying, cause intolerable stress in people who are predisposed towards the illness. I was surprised by Grandma's analytic tone, by her ability to repress or distance herself from everything she had just told me. Some people may say that repression is healthy, but up close it sure didn't look that way. I remembered Steven saying that a person's family, or the miscommunication within that family, were not necessarily what brought on schizophrenia. But I found myself thinking that if schizophrenia meant having a hard time understanding the complexities of family life, and of life in general, then maybe we should all check ourselves into a hospital. At that moment, with my grandmother standing next to me, I was getting all kinds of mixed messages. It was as if my ability to process and understand the world had been stolen from me, and I suddenly realized that there was a part of me that wanted Amy to leave.

This pronounced desire, which was accompanied by a sense of suffocation, had become unbearable by the time Grandma and I got home and saw Abba waiting for us outside. The fact that I never told anyone about this suffocation for six years attests to how overwhelming those emotions were.

Abba and I slowly followed Grandma upstairs, as if the house we were entering wasn't our own. Amy was still sitting at the table, paging through the Bible, utterly unaware that the three bears who had just walked in weren't going to greet her affectionately the way they did in the fairy tale. Abba and Grandma headed left, towards Amy, and I, scared of the stand-off, went into the kitchen to get Grandma some water. I tried to focus on how it felt to be a cog in a wheel, and I tried not to listen to their conversation.

Only after I put the glass on the table and sat down did Abba stop talking about Eritrea, which had declared its independence and broken off from Ethiopia that very day. He turned to Amy, trying to maintain the tone of a newscaster reading the headlines. She looked at him expectantly as he repeated her name, as if to confirm that she was his primary audience.

"Something unexpected has come up, and we have to ask you to leave."

"I understand." I couldn't believe she wasn't asking him what the unexpected event was. Abba must have been surprised, too, because he said, as if explaining the punchline of a misfired joke, that he meant she had to leave today. "What happened?"

In a measured tone, as if she had just asked him his name, he answered, "Our future in-laws are coming from Jerusalem to celebrate Shavuot with us, and they just told me that they're planning to arrive today so they'll have some time to travel around the south." Grandma, as if on cue, explained that that was why she had come, to help with the cooking.

"When you got here," Abba continued, "you mentioned that you had plans in Jerusalem, so I figured it wouldn't be such a big deal for you to go there. Of course, you're welcome to use our phone to make all the arrangements."

"And after the holiday, I can come back?" Never had anyone ever sounded so eager at the prospect of "after the holiday," but Abba didn't let her childlike request throw him off course.

"That's just when Ruth will be coming back from a long trip. I suggest that you pack up and take everything with you, and at some later point we can be in touch and, God-willing, you can come back." I was shocked when Abba said "God-willing." If Amy had really been a part of this household, she could have helped me catch him in the act, but apparently she wasn't interested in catching anyone. She just put her hand on her mouth and played with her lips as if they were piano keys. She tilted her head toward me and looked at me. All I could do was give her my crooked smile. I knew I was abandoning her and my demeanor was cold, but I had nothing else to offer. I was busy pondering the future. I had no intention of remaining indifferent, of forgetting what Grandma had revealed to me. Not even if she made up the whole story just to stop me from going.

Grandma announced that she was going into the kitchen to get started on the cooking, and asked Abba to help take down some of the pots and pans from the shelves. Abba got up and pressed a comforting hand on my shoulder. Amy, taking the hint, trudged upstairs. I didn't want to analyze, or even think about, why she was being so compliant. I couldn't follow her with my gaze, much less offer to help her pack. Once, after repeated rebukes from my parents, I went upstairs to clean my room, and was surprised when, after just a few minutes, Hanoch appeared at the door, his face radiating good will. He sat on my bed and told me he'd be the angel sitting on my shoulder, telling me what to pick up from the floor and where to put it. It was a true moment of kindness. As pleased as I was at the time, I couldn't cultivate a similar measure of altruism towards the woman whose soul was entwined with mine.

The aroma of sautéed onions swirled through the air. Grandma always started her cooking with tears – a preemptive strike.

I started to calculate the time difference between Israel and the United States, and decided that after Amy left, I would call Aunt Ora. She was the most reliable source for the research I had to do, and not only because she was a psychologist. Aside from this resolution, I didn't have the strength to move, and I flipped through the Bible that Amy had left on the table. In similar situations, when I had occasion to page through the Bible as if it were a women's magazine at a beauty salon, I would usually turn to the Book of Genesis, but this time I found myself turning to the Biblical portions "Ki Tetze and "Ki Tavo" - "When You Arrive" and "When you Leave" - that Abba and Amy had been studying earlier.

Even without focusing on a particular verse, I could feel the negativity of the words. A whole slew of prohibitions erupted in my face. "And God shall strike you with madness and blindness and confusion of mind."

If Amy had read what I just read, she wouldn't have had to be schizophrenic in order to think that the verse about madness was directed at her, at the reader, and that is showed no mercy. With some difficulty, I managed to stand up and walk away from the Bible.

Grandma was pleased to see me, and allowed me to taste the cabbage balushka, the Hungarian dish she was cooking, one of my favorites: wilted cabbage with noodles, onions and lots of paprika. She pointed to her next project, the peppers that Abba scooped out, and asked me if I could make her a cup of coffee. She thanked me profusely. I thought she, too, deserved a little rest. I didn't understand how Abba could go to sleep under these circumstances. Maybe he should be checked for some kind of apathy disease.

"Elisheva?" I heard Abba's voice emerging from his room.

He was sitting on the edge of his bed. Only yesterday we'd sat here just like this. It felt like a lifetime. He massaged his temples, looked at the clock, and asked if Amy had come downstairs.

"Not yet. When are you going to tell her that her brother will be waiting at the bus station?"

"Not until the last possible minute." His voice was soft but firm.

He opened the drawer and took out some Advil. "Or maybe I won't tell her at all. So far everything's gone smoothly; I don't want her to raise hell on the bus. I'll just tell her brother what time she's due in, and he'll go meet her."

Both of us stared at his tight fist holding the simple pill, as straightforward as the casual scenario he'd just described. He might have been thinking about the meeting between the siblings, but I was wondering how much he knew about the woman who slept next to him every night, between the crisp sheets. At that moment, nothing seemed simple to me.

Abba got up, and I understood that it was time for us to leave the room and contend with what was about to happen. I peeked in on Grandma, who was napping in her chair, and went to boil water for the coffee she had requested. I wondered if she had more secrets stashed away.

The noise of Amy's suitcase bumping down the stairs almost drowned out the whistling of the kettle. Grandma, who had woken up, gestured to me to stop standing there staring into space and to turn off the flame.

Abba hurried to help her, then went upstairs, picked up Amy's second suitcase, and asked if everything had worked out in Jerusalem.

"Of course it worked out. Everything always works out in the end. I just don't understand why I'm so tired."

And then, as if possessed by a demon, Abba asked her if she wanted a cup of coffee before heading out. To everyone's relief, she declined, and I helped Abba carry the suitcases to the car. Grandma, who turned out to be the best actress of all of us, apologized to Amy for not being able to accompany her to the bus station, and thanked her for the opportunity to meet a woman as unique as she was. She didn't forget to hug her, and to tell her that soon she'd be able to meet her daughter Ruth.

I wondered why Amy wasn't saying anything about the whole production that had been staged in her honor. Perhaps she didn't detect the cracks in our behavior that threatened to bring the whole house down. Maybe it was my mistake. Maybe I thought they'd have to carry her out of the house in a straightjacket, lying on a stretcher. No, the departure was seamless.

On the way to the bus station, I didn't even glance at the side of the road to see if anyone I knew was looking for a ride, nor did I listen to Abba and Amy's chatter. The two of them no longer reminded me of the sun and the moon, but of regular people who concealed their thoughts and were capable of hurting each other deeply at any moment.

The Beersheba bus station was no different than usual, except that to me everyone there looked like they might have had some kind of mental illness.

At the information desk, we were told that the bus was leaving in twenty minutes and we should probably wait at the platform because the express buses tended to fill up quickly. Abba, eager to complete another stage in the process, hurried off to buy a ticket. We dragged the suitcases to the grimy platforms. My heart ached for Amy, who might have thought of the two of us as her guardian angels. It also ached a little for myself, and for all the so-called healthy people, who didn't really see the people around them, who didn't really see at all. Only very rarely do we dare to get close to someone, to really understand what's going on with the people next to us, to intimately familiarize ourselves with the demons and fears and loneliness that haunt them, or that haunt us all.

We stood in line, and I offered to go buy Amy some snacks for the road, even though she said she didn't need anything. I had no words of farewell, and I thought that if I bought her white-chocolate-covered pecans, a bag of "grill-flavored" Bissli, and a bottle of apple juice, she would understand that I was on her side, that she mattered to me. Smiling weakly, I went into the air-conditioned store. At the sight of all the fancy candies and the chocolate rabbits, I almost cried. In the glass display case, I could see my anxious reflection. As if the fact that I hadn't thoroughly washed my face that morning was an indication of just how imperfect I was. Nobody is perfect, but I always thought there was something particularly pleasing and benevolent about me. I believed that I lacked the ability to hurt other people, and that in every situation I could be gracious, I could put my own egoistic desires aside.

In the polished glass I could see, how far I was from perfect. With immeasurable shame, I remembered the arguments I used to have with Binyamin, who claimed that was my problem, that I wanted to be perfect, and I had to understand, for my own good, that perfection was unattainable.

Even the well-groomed saleswoman could see the crack that had erupted inside me. She smiled as she weighed the pecans, then threw in an extra piece of candy. I trudged back to the line, and was happy to see that the bus had just pulled in.

I offered Amy the snacks, and in exchange she took my chin in her hands and forced me to look into her eyes. There was no judgement in her gaze, no anger over the fact that I had exposed myself in all my imperfection just when she needed me most.

She hugged me tight. "Eli, my Eli," she said. "Never stand quietly when there is a scream stuck in your throat." We both felt my body softening and the first tears falling on her shirt, which, as always, smelled moldy. My grip tightened, and she added, "Be your own mother."

Her comment moved me, but more than that, it raised a huge question mark, which allowed me to break away from her and stifle my tears. In the meantime, Abba put the suitcases in the belly of the bus, and the driver opened the passenger door. Despite her exciting words, I had no desire to slip away from my life and accompany her to Jerusalem. Abba managed to squeeze through and get to us just as it was her turn to get on. He, too, hugged her tightly, then said goodbye.

After she waved through the window, we furtively looked on from the side, waiting to see what would happen to her, the way Moses' sister Miriam looked on as her baby brother was sent down the Nile. Nothing happened, and we waited patiently until the bus, with our emissary, started on its way. Abba took out a piece of paper and wrote down the bus number.

The drive home was silent, aside from the voices on the radio. They were talking about the case of John Demjanjuk, and of his chances for indictment or acquittal. As far as liberating the scream that Amy had mentioned, I had no idea what that scream was, or how to set it free.

When we got back home, each of us engrossed in our own thoughts, it was already late. For a moment we panicked when we saw that the door was unlocked: we'd forgotten about the cook whom we'd left to her own devices. I suggested we sit down and devour all the delicious dishes that Grandma had prepared. Abba consented willingly, with the added admonition not to eat all the food, since we really were having guests of a sort. Avigail had been so surprised when he asked her to spend the holiday with us, that not only did she accept, she decided to come early. Hanoch was arriving the following day, and he would help Abba with the *tikkun*, the all-night learning.

Abba went to call Yaakov, Amy's brother, to give him instructions, and I set the table, which was still covered with the food. Amy had said I should be my own mother, and something inside me shook as if I had suddenly turned responsible. I was now privy to Ima's secrets from long before she'd ever dreamt about becoming a mother.

While we ate Grandma's freshly cooked food, like mourners at a ritual meal, Abba filled us with the details, some of them unimportant, like the fact that the famous Coen brothers were members of the same synagogue as Amy's husband. Facts that may have been less important, but were certainly more interesting.

Abba continued to deliver Ima's findings. In women, he said, the illness usually peaks between age twenty-five and age thirty-five. Amy was about thirty-seven when the illness struck, right around the time of her daughter Debbie's Bat Mitzvah. Ima had spoken to Debbie, too, and had reported that she was a wonderful and intelligent young woman.

The trigger for her illness, apparently, was a boy under her care whom she was unable to rescue from the jaws of his parents. The family had decided to leave Minneapolis, and Amy had to say goodbye to him. By her son's Bar Mitzvah, Amy was already gone; she was in her first inpatient hospitalization. It took nearly half a year for the doctors to figure out what was wrong, half a year in which she barely slept, neglected herself and her house, experienced both depression and religious ecstasy, and was obsessively jealous of her children and her husband.

The daughter vehemently defended her father. She said her parents remained married until two years ago, when Amy was again released from a long hospitalization. At first, it actually seemed like things were improving, but then Amy asked for a divorce. When Debbie started college, the situation seemed more or less stable, thanks to the pills and the fact that the symptoms came and went. Amy had never demonstrated extreme paranoia - she didn't believe that people were chasing her or that aliens were communicating with her - but she definitely experienced other extreme symptoms, mostly because of her faulty metaphoric thinking, and she seemed to be constantly testing the truth of the phrase "Life and death are in the power of the tongue."

Abba sighed, and completed his monologue with the words of Amy's brother, who claimed that there was no bitterness or conflict between the two of them. He sounded like a reasonable man. Abba said the situation was complicated because the symptoms of schizophrenia were so varied, and to a large extent the illness was a kind of psychiatric "garbage can" into which a wide range of behaviors were tossed.

"Thank you, Sylvia. You really saved us." Grandma replied that cooking wasn't like swimming, but if, despite your age, you jumped into the water, into the pots, you didn't feel the difficulty or the fatigue.

Abba smiled and added that Amy's daughter seemed to be interested in our family, as if she were retroactively scrutinizing the conditions of our hospitality. She said it didn't surprise her that her mother had chosen a warm family with a bookshelf full of Judaica, because that made her obsession less blatant. With a sad chuckle, Debbie told Ima about her mother's undiagnosed delusions of grandeur: she considered herself one of the great sages of Israel. Debbie then added that if that was a sign of illness, many more Jews ought to be hospitalized.

I wondered if all the information about, and close encounters with, Amy's mental illness caused Ima to think about her own past? I hoped so. Abba said he would take Grandma home, since he had to give a class on Shavuot where she lived anyway. We got up from the table full and satisfied, as if we hadn't just experienced a collective trauma that shed light on our own life choices, too. Amazing how one short visit could change a person's life.

Now Ora and my mother started discussing which verse of *Eshet Hayil*, the song from Proverbs in praise of women, was the most appropriate one for Grandma's epitaph. "Strength and splendor are her clothing, and smilingly she awaits her last day" emerged at the top of the list. It suited Grandma, who made sure, at least in her mind, to always remain dignified and magnanimous. Like any death, Grandma's death made everyone want to express only the positive aspects of her life story, but I couldn't shut out everything that had been swept under the carpet, and I waited for someone to shout, like in the movie "The Tempest," "Show me the magic!" and make the house of cards come tumbling down.

A few minutes before we got home, Ora asked how I was doing, and whether I had enjoyed my first year as a student. I had a lot to say, but I summed it up as awesome. My uncle asked if I was planning to continue on the practical track or the theory track, and with surprising confidence, I replied that I really hoped to get into the screenwriting program.

When we got to our town and saw the first death announcement posted in the entrance on a wall, Ora told me that if Ima hadn't been in the United States with her, she herself might not have made it to the funeral; after all, it had been only three weeks since she had been here and said her goodbyes. But, I asked her, wouldn't she regret it for the rest of her life if she didn't perform this particular act of kindness, the kindness you do for someone who isn't even aware of it? She said I was right, and chances are she would have come anyway.

I remembered our dramatic phone conversation, the one I'd been planning during Amy's departure, when she said that in our culture, it's understood that a mother's job is to love her daughter. It's not even a job, it's a given. But this raises the question: does it necessarily follow that the daughter will love her mother?

Ora told us that on Friday, when she was tidying up her office, she caught a glimpse of a picture Grandma drew, and immediately started to cry. She took it down from the wall and saw the label of Grandma and Grandpa's framing shop, Fraime'le. Underneath the picture were the words, "To Ora with love, February 1940." Grandma had painted the picture when she was in the sanatorium with tuberculosis, when Ora was three. It made her burst into tears again, thinking of all that Grandma had done for her that would now exist only in her memory and could never show itself in the world. And suddenly I could understand that in order for Ima to survive – to overcome her vulnerability and to protect her own children – she had to lock something away inside her. No wonder she didn't remember anything that had happened before the age of ten. I, too, tried to forget the moments of weakness that were my lot in life, preferring to imagine myself as someone running free in a field of wildflowers, like in the opening segment of "Little House on the Prairie." When we got out of the car, I offered to carry in the luggage. I watched as Ima wearily climbed the stairs, reminding me of Grandma in her last days. How hard it must be to grow up when your mother stands in your way, a physical barrier to freedom.

Seventeen

The house crammed with people, and the endless chatter, reminded me of that day years ago, when Abba and Grandma left. I remember enjoying the silence and the solitude, then going to call Aunt Ora. When I identified myself, she was thrown off by the sound of my voice, and, uncharacteristically, raised her soft voice to ask me if something had happened to the woman who was staying with us. I assured her that everything was fine and she had just left. Ora said, impudently, what none of us had dared to say: "Thank goodness."

I was surprised that she asked if something had happened to Amy and not to one of us, but first I wanted to know if Ima was around. She said no, she was spending the holiday in Boston, and if she hadn't been invited to teach in a *tikkun* study session there, she would have gone back to Israel earlier than planned because she was so anxious about everything that was going on with "that Amy".

I got straight to the point. "Grandma told me something, and it's bothering me. It's not that I don't believe her, but I just wanted to confirm it with you. Is it possible that Ima was paralyzed when she was young, and had to be hospitalized for mental health evaluations?"

"Is that what she told you?"

"Yes."

"And did she tell you why?"

"No, she just said the doctors never figured it out. She was only telling me, she said, so I would understand that a person's mental and emotional state is often beyond our comprehension."

"That's true."

"So it's true that Ima had mental problems that necessitated hospitalization."

"Yes."

I don't know if there was a bad connection between the two continents, or maybe I was just imagining it, but I was positive that she wanted to add the word "but" after her hasty "yes." I said the "but" in her place, and asked, wasn't it odd that I had never heard this story before, and wasn't it unusual not to come to any conclusions after half a year of hospitalization.

Despite her soft voice, my aunt was also blessed with the gift of rhetoric and the ability to talk endlessly, especially when it came to family history. In light of this, her prolonged silence was particularly concerning. And, as if I were the therapist and not her, I asked, "Is there anything else that comes to mind in this context? Something I should know or understand?"

Resuming her role as a protective caretaker, she finally responded, "It's not something I want to tell you over the phone."

"But we're not going to see each other any time soon," I grumbled.

"I understand, sweetheart, but it's something that belongs to the distant past."

"But it's become part of my present. I have to know!"

"Yes, Elisheva." Still speaking in her sympathetic, professional-therapist tone, which was starting to irk me, she said she had to go to work.

I felt like a detective, or, more accurately, like a drowning person trying to grab hold of a rope; I had to know, desperately, what she was hiding. I told her that. It was interesting that I could always talk straight with Ora. I don't know if it was because of her mellow personality or simply because she was my aunt. Being someone's aunt or uncle automatically makes that person as close to a parent as possible. It's a closeness that provides an extra measure of security, like a second anchor or a spare parachute.

"OK, I'll tell you," she said, after I reminded her that she'd see me at Avigail's wedding, where she could see for herself what impact her news had on me.

"But I'm asking you not to do anything with this information."

I gave her my word, but again, she stressed the importance of keeping it to myself, not even telling my siblings. "You're sure you can do that?" I didn't know if she was asking me or just trying to convince herself that she was doing the right thing.

"Yes," I said, and before I could ask the reason for all this secrecy, she explained that she was the only one who remembered the facts. That there was never any reason to talk about them, because they could only cause pain.

"Grandma must have told you that your mother was a genius as a child, but she had no discipline whatsoever."

As if I were afraid to hear the rest, I cut her off and told her I already knew that her outbursts were caused by the fact that she had skipped a grade and wasn't adjusting well.

"The problems between them started many years earlier. Your mother's crisis was a physical reaction to emotional strain; it had nothing to do with a difficult adjustment."

"What?" I didn't know what she meant by "the problems between them." I had issues with my mother, too.

The rest of her sentence was spoken in a cold, professional tone and was hard to absorb.

"What Grandma didn't tell you, and what your mother recoils from, is that until the crisis, Grandma used to beat her."

"Beat her?" For a moment I thought perhaps I had misunderstood the meaning of the English word. I hoped I had.

"I'm sorry, sweetheart, but Grandma used to beat her. With a belt, with her hands. True, it was more acceptable back then, but still, their relationship was a violent one."

"But wasn't Grandma using it as educational tool, and Ima was just too sensitive and she broke down?"

"There's no such thing as too sensitive. Grandma wouldn't abuse her, but beatings were definitely a part of their relationship. Sometimes she'd get so angry she'd use the stick from the American flag hanging in her doorway."

"That sure sounds like abuse to me."

Ora didn't answer.

She went on. "But after Ruth was released from the hospital, Grandma never hit her again. Never. Once they bought her a television, things really did improve. And as soon as your mother learned to walk again, she erased the whole thing from her memory. Maybe this was their unspoken bargain. I'll never know for sure."

"How can you erase something like that?"

"You just can. Don't forget, she was ten years old, and unusually intelligent."

Now I was the one who didn't speak. I wanted to erase, on Ima's behalf, the injustice that was done to her, and to ask Ora a question that might seem ungrateful. Why didn't Grandma hit Ora? Instead I asked, "And what about Grandpa Ephraim?"

"Your grandmother was a very strong woman. You know that expression, you can take the Jew out of the shtetl, but you can't take the shtetl out of the Jew? That's how my father was. He believed that the mother was in charge of the children's education. He tried to pamper Ruth as much as he could, which of course made Grandma even angrier."

"But," I repeated, "How can someone forget?"

"It's a defense mechanism. A few years ago, when your mother began her research on battered women, I said something about how interesting it was that she had chosen this particular topic. She asked me, in all sincerity, what I meant. When I answered, 'because of your past, as a child who was beaten,' she opened her eyes wide and listened to my memories in complete disbelief."

"She didn't deny it?"

"No, all she said was that she didn't remember it. Her memories of the hospital are hazy, too. She thought she was hospitalized because of some physical illness. All she remembers is that after her stay in the hospital, we got a TV."

"So the TV is the only evidence that something in the world had changed?"

"That, and me. I was sixteen, and they made all of us meet with a social worker. I loved those meetings, and to some degree, they were the reason I chose this career."

"But how did Grandma forget?"

"I'm not sure she did forget. She was devastated by the breakdown, absolutely devastated. The fact is, she's right, there's no way to know exactly what triggered the paralysis. Clearly your mother was experiencing some kind of distress that she couldn't tolerate or describe. The fits of rage that Grandma couldn't control in the past were replaced by constant worry. That's why she was always helping her out financially - to reduce your mother's anxiety so she wouldn't have another breakdown."

I could have asked about Ora herself, but by then the answer was clear. Quite simply, Ora was a good, self-disciplined girl, like Avigail. When Ora realized that I wasn't letting go of the question about denial, she said that subconsciously, they both knew that my father - six foot three and full of good humor - was her ticket out of their mother's clutches. Even though Ima was only seventeen.

"Wow," I said.

"Indeed," she responded, using one of her favorite words.

I had so many more questions, about the past but also about the present. How would I respond to Grandma's loving caresses? How would I keep all this from my own sister?

Ora said she wanted to read something to me, about schizophrenia. Something that would help someone sensitive like me understand this psychological enigma. She told me to wait a minute; I knew it wouldn't be long, because Ora was the most organized person I'd ever met, including Liat. All her articles were filed according to some impeccable system, and I could picture her easily extracting this document from its folder.

"'Sometimes schizophrenics believe that they can change the entire world. At other times they feel that they can't even control their own thoughts and their own bodies. One of the paradoxes is that they can actually experience both these feelings at the same time.'"

Ora said she liked to tell her patients about the two notes that Martin Buber used to carry around in his pockets. One said, "The world was created for me," and the other said, "From dust you have come, and to dust you will return."

I hadn't heard that story about Martin Buber, but I was very familiar with the feeling. Because every time I was on the way to the pub in Eren Shonsky's kibbutz, I charged myself with self-confidence, resolved that that night I would conquer his young heart. But then, when I looked at him, his eyes reflected the ugly duckling I actually was, and I knew that my campaign was doomed to fail.

"This is the anguish your mother experienced. Luckily she was released from it."

I said nothing. I looked at the stack of dishes I had to wash, and the overflowing pots Grandma had left for us. It was no wonder that Ima liked to freeze everything, as if she had unwittingly learned to freeze her heart and use it judiciously.

"Sweetie? I have to go to work. Are you OK?"

Instead of saying a simple "yes," I said, as if I were five years old, "I want my mother."

"I know, darling, but don't forget, you're the one who's going through this. For your mother it's a distant, non-existent memory."

I understood that with these words, she was telling me that Ima would still be the same absent, imperfect mother she always was, the mother I was almost ready to replace with Amy.

"So it has nothing to do with me?"

"Yes and no. Let time do its work."

"But I won't forget it," I said dramatically.

"Everyone in this family has a role. And if that's your role, you'll remember."

"But I remember so much," I said, as if complaining about an excessive amount of homework.

"Yes." I heard the smile in her voice so clearly. "Yes, from the time you were born there was something free about you, something loving. You talked endlessly, you danced, you sang, as if you were freedom itself. Apparently, something about that was intolerable for her. Just for her. Now I really do have to get out of the house. Call me again whenever you need to."

"Thank you, Auntie." She loved when I called her that; it reminded her of Jane Austen novels. "I'll be fine," I added. She said she knew that.

I hung up and went to lie down on Ima and Abba's bed. I tried to feel Ima's presence. Maybe this was why childhood existed: it's a time to make mistakes, to indulge in youthful mischief. Later, there would be time to pull yourself together, and anyone who wanted to could forget. But what about the people who remember? Do they end up going insane?

The words I spoke to Ora burst forth with a familiar kind of pain, as if they were from an ancient tune that had been playing in my mind from the day I was born - "I want my mother." Along with the words was a deeply buried feeling that she was always gone. Or maybe I was the absent one?

On the card he gave me on my Bat Mitzvah, Uncle Harry quoted from a letter my mother had sent him when I was six. "Elisheva continues to be an independent five-year old, though she still comes home for comfort and food." He wrote that despite the adolescent challenges that awaited me, he hoped I would always have the intelligence and the privilege to return home when I needed comfort.

If this were the ending of an American movie, I thought, Ima would, despite her obligations in Boston, return sooner than planned, tiptoe into the room, and peek under the blankets to surprise me. I spent a few minutes waiting for this to happen. I implanted my head in Ima's pillow and sniffed it, like a dog looking for the familiar scent of home. I smelled Abba's pillow, too, which had a different smell. I lifted my head like a turtle and tried to imagine their faces right before sleep. I looked for tear stains on Ima's pillow. Her pillow smelled nice, despite the tinge of chlorine from the pool. This was one of the few things my siblings and I all agreed upon, and we objected vehemently when Ima would try to convince us to shower in the pool's locker rooms rather than at home. It was strange that it was us, the kids, who had to explain to the parents about the feeling of home. I wonder if the television that arrived at their house after Ima's hospitalization satisfied this need.

I buried my face into her pillow, burrowing in as deeply as I could, to reach some kind of root, to hear, as if I were putting my ear to a conch shell, Ima's private whispers, Ima's dreams. And then, like that moment when you're swimming and you suddenly realize that the world is going on without you, I understood that there was a whole world that had nothing to do with me, a world she had chosen to put behind her, and there was no point in exposing it, and I couldn't expose it even if I wanted to.

And there, submerged into Ima and Abba's bed, the same bed on which they had made me, unintentionally but without any ill will or desire to hurt me, I suddenly realized how lucky I was. Ima's experiences could have played themselves out in a more harmful way, like an illness such as Amy's, or a painful estrangement from Grandma. Amy's suggested, be your own mother. When a person goes out to seek the reason for his existence, and for his model of self-mothering, it can be an endless journey, laden with contradictions and setbacks. If that was the case, I thought, I would also have to be my own rabbi. If, somewhere along the way, Ima had made peace with her life story, then the only option I had, was to come to terms with my own autobiography, because nothing else would do any good. Again, I was filled with appreciation for the freedom she gave me over the years. From a place of choice and competence, I went into the kitchen to make Ima's famous cheesecake so we could all miss her properly.

I practiced repression starting that holiday of Shavuot. I let Abba tell my siblings the story of Amy from his perspective, and didn't share the more intimate moments. I didn't know if he was taking stock of his own actions. My siblings were interested, but like me, they didn't dare ask why we had to throw her out of the house, what was so bad he couldn't cope with it. Over that holiday, I felt like I was participating in a farewell ceremony for my childhood.

I saw how much stock we put into my father, how he was the "rabbi of the house," how little room he left for Ima, or for us, to separate from him. It didn't make me sad, because I knew that he had given me so much along the way, including allowing Amy entry into our house. Just like when you cross the equator, he had ceased to be my point of reference, and as sad as that was, it was also very liberating.

Ima came back the day of my graduation and everything returned to normal, meaning I came and went at my leisure. And, as always, they interfered as little as possible and helped me when I asked. I didn't tell them that in the middle of that summer, on August 6, 1993, fifty years after the atom bomb that was called "Little Boy" fell on Hiroshima, a week after John Demjanjuk was acquitted in Jerusalem, I got a letter in the mail.

"Dear Elisheva, 'How well you direct your course to seek love (Jeremiah 2:33).'The rest of the verse doesn't matter. The good things you encounter - those are what count. Words are weapons. Silence, too, and doors. When you see a butterfly, know that it's a good sign. Don't be alarmed. You have strength, like Elisheva the wife of Aaron the Priest, the sister of Nahshon son of Aminadav. Like my Devorah, whom Barak served. There's a cure for everything. 'He heals the broken-hearted and binds up their wounds (Psalms 147).'

P.S. Hi Elisheva, this is Debbie, Amy's daughter. I wanted to send a written thank-you to you and your father for opening your home to my mother. Writing to you was her idea, and she speaks of you with tremendous affection. We have returned to the United States, and she is doing well. She is undergoing a new treatment in which she is getting shots twice a week. We'd love for you to come visit after your army service. Yours, Debbie and Amy Solomon."

I read the letter three times, and thought about what a lovely opening sentence that was, 'How well you direct your course to seek love.' I wrote myself a note on the back of the letter, reminding me that if I ever published a book, whatever kind of book it was, I would end it with this verse. I thought I was off to a good start, knowing how something would end. I also thought it would be nice to finish with this verse out of humility, out of respect for the words of prophecy, out of the memory of the visit which, while short, changed my life.

After the army I lived in the United States and Mexico; I traveled all over, and not once did I think of visiting Amy. When I thought about her, mostly what I felt was fear. I also had some unpleasant conversations with Ora, mostly when she diagnosed me with some of the hallmarks of an abused child: fear of rejection, a sense of profound loneliness, identification with the abuser. She tried to explain to me that on the one hand, I was lucky that even if I had the symptoms of an abused child, I had never actually been abused, but on the other hand, she admitted, Ima's absence, which stemmed from her adjustment difficulties, made it possible for my brother to tyrannize me, and even to beat me up. She encouraged me to talk about these issues with Ima, but she understood my reluctance and difficulty. She kept saying she trusted me, and that I should let time do its work.

On the morning of Grandma's funeral, the crying started before we even left the house, because Evyatar was left with a babysitter and was sad that we were going. Ima reminded all of us not to dress up too much and to put on sunscreen, and reminded Ora that they were going to make a small rip in her shirt as a sign of mourning, so she should wear something old and tattered. I suddenly grasped that my ability to pay attention to detail, to find my way around, to remember, and to be in control of whatever life threw my way - all these I received from her. They aren't necessarily positive qualities, because they stem from a lack of faith in the world, or more precisely in the people who populate it. For a moment I knew how it felt to have a heavy cloud always hovering over you, and why it was important for her to have a second, thick skin, like a gecko's tail. As if you had to go through life with armor, always trying to minimize the opportunities for someone to penetrate, to harm you.

The funeral was very hard to take in and to process. I was sad, grieving my grandmother who no longer existed, who was lying in a coffin not far from Nirit, whose grave looked like a tropical garden because her parents were constantly tending to it. Avigail, Ora, and Grandma's doctor all spoke beautifully, and Ima, too, of course, who began her remarks by saying how sad she was that she wasn't here for her mother at the very end. She had thought Grandma would hold out and that they would be able to experience closure. Her words surprised me; I never thought Ima was interested in that kind of thing.

I was also surprised by the childhood memory that she shared with the large gathering of people who'd come to pay their final respects. She described how, when she was a little girl, Grandma would sing her to sleep with lullabies, and how she'd thought her mother had a beautiful voice, which of course she didn't. In addition, these songs inspired her as a child and encouraged her to sing herself. For me, hearing about Ima's love for her own mother added a new element to the story.

At night, after a long day of *shiva,* I went downstairs to tell Ima that her eulogy was wonderful. She got choked up, and showed me some of her earlier drafts. She said maybe I should write something for our visit to the grave at the end of *shiva,* because I was so creative.

I asked to see the eulogy again. I had missed something important.

She wrote, "I also vaguely remember how you survived that terrible year when I was nine or ten years old. Your father was dying in our house and you were taking care of him, I was in the hospital, and Ora, who had tuberculosis, was home. How could you be that strong? How did you deal with all of these things happening at the same time? You remind me of the verse from Proverbs, 'She rises also while it is still night, and gives food to her household and portions to her maidens.' Your strength was always reserved for us."

So there you have it: somewhere deep inside, she remembers. I wondered what else I didn't know about this woman, whom I call Ima, whom I wasted many years blaming. I wanted to tell her that I knew about her past, and that in terms of how it affected me, I forgave her. I no longer needed her to chase me in the park or to teach me how to ride a bicycle or do my hair. Mostly I wanted to tell her that I still needed her, as a mother, an affectionate mother who could hug me easily, who could say, "Of course I love you, my dear Elisheva, and whoever is lucky enough to marry you will be very happy."

I looked at Ima, sitting there surrounded by papers, trying to derive comfort from them, and I saw how much I resembled her. I understood that I didn't have to write a screenplay, I only had to tell her, here and now, that I loved her unconditionally. I felt all this, but the words wouldn't come out of my mouth. Instead, I said that even though the song "A Woman of Valor" describes a strong woman, it is a woman who functions in the world only for others, not for herself. I reminded her that she never liked this song, and it wouldn't be right to eternalize her mother's memory with it. I suggested instead - and this made her tear up again - that we engrave Grandma's stone with the verse from Jeremiah, "How well you direct your course to seek love."

Acknowledgements

There many people I want to thank who supported me in this long process of editing and translating my debut novel into English. First, to all my teachers in the M.A. Creative Writing Program at Ben Gurion University of the Negev, who honed my skills as a writer and gave me the courage to write a full length novel, especially the noted author Haim Be'er. Then I am indebted to my amazing translator Shira Atik and to the people who supported my project on *Jewcer*.

My brother, Rabbi Tzvi Graetz, once said he was amazed I was able to write a novel about our "boring life" and I thank him for his support and encouragement. My sister, Rabbi Ariella Graetz Bartuv, made me lists of 'must read' books which, like her, have enriched my world every day.

I greatly regret that my uncle, Dr. Aubey Rotenberg, did not live to read my book and that so many members of the wonderful community of Omer, my home town, have passed away. I single out my friend Dr. Lora Warshawsky-Livne who read my novel in Hebrew and hoped that it would be translated so that her parents could read it. Lora passed away a week before my daughter was born and I carry this reminder of this proximity of life and death wherever I go.

Buddha said that even if you carry your parents on your shoulders your whole life, it still wouldn't repay the generosity they showed you by giving life to you and caring for you. He said that a way to repay their goodness was by allowing their influence to spread beyond the small circle of the family into the world at large.

My parents, Naomi and Rabbi Michael Graetz are a huge fountain of creativity, goodness and wit and it is my privilege to be their daughter. I am so grateful for all their deeds in supporting me and this book. And a particular thanks to my mom for doing the final editing.

My partner, love of my life, Eitan Herman teaches me kindness and patience every day, allowing me to be who I am as I am. I look forward to the day when our daughter Shira Esther Salaam reads this novel in whatever language she chooses and writes her own book.

May all beings be happy, healthy and free!